# KILLING
# PACE

# KILLING PACE

DOUGLAS SCHOFIELD

Minotaur Books New York

KILLING PACE. Copyright © 2017 by Douglas Schofield. All rights reserved. Printed in the United States of America. For information, address St. Martin's Press, 175 Fifth Avenue, New York, N.Y. 10010.

www.minotaurbooks.com

Designed by Devan Norman

Library of Congress Cataloging-in-Publication Data

Names: Schofield, Douglas, author.
Title: Killing pace : a mystery / Douglas Schofield.
Description: First edition. | New York : Minotaur Books, [2017]
Identifiers: LCCN 2017024854 | ISBN 9781250120557 (hardcover) |
    ISBN 9781250120564 (ebook)
Subjects: LCSH: Traffic accident victims—Fiction. | Amnesia—Fiction. |
    GSAFD: Suspense fiction. | Mystery fiction.
Classification: LCC PR9275.C393 S365 2017 | DDC 813'.6—dc23
LC record available at https://lccn.loc.gov/2017024854

Our books may be purchased in bulk for promotional, educational, or business use. Please contact your local bookseller or the Macmillan Corporate and Premium Sales Department at 1-800-221-7945, extension 5442, or by email at MacmillanSpecialMarkets@macmillan.com.

First Edition: November 2017

10  9  8  7  6  5  4  3  2  1

For Krystyna Skarbek, and Eileen Nearne, and Iris Origo . . .
and all the courageous women the world forgot

# ACKNOWLEDGMENTS

I've said it before, and it bears repeating: Random ideas kicking around in an author's head don't become published novels without the contribution of many willing hands. So I'm very grateful to St. Martin's Press for allowing me a page to express my appreciation to all the people who helped me with research for this novel, and supported me with their loyalty and encouragement.

In New Jersey: A big thank-you, once again and always, to my old friend Sgt. David Conte of the Bayonne Police Department.

In Everglades City, Florida: My thanks go out to Steve Markley and his sidekick Otis McMillen, of Captain Steve's Swamp Buggy and Airboat Adventures; to Petra Gegenbach, owner of Right Choice Supermarket; and to "Chris," a National Parks Service officer at the Big Cypress Welcome Center. None of you had any prior warning before I showed up in your lives, but you all gave freely of your time and shared your depths of knowledge about Everglades City and Big Cypress National Preserve. For that I am truly grateful. If I got anything wrong in the novel that follows these comments, that's my mistake, not yours.

In Clewiston, Florida: Thank you, Harry Patel, owner/manager of the Executive Royal Inn, for allowing me to roam your property, take photographs, and interview you about your business.

(Here I should mention that I was not able to access each and every pertinent location during my research trips to Florida. Consequently, my descriptions of, for example, the interior facilities at the Collier County Sheriff's substation at Everglades City, and the U.S. Customs Service's offices in Miami, are the product of my imagination. But that's the whole point of fiction, right?)

Elsewhere in North America, at an undisclosed location: Let me express, once again, my admiration and my deepest gratitude to J.S., former federal undercover agent, whose true identity must remain "in the wind." Thank you again, my friend. One day your story will be told.

In Caltanissetta, Sicily: Once again, *amore e rispetto* to Silvia Sillitti, Bruno Fantauzza, and Professor Enrico Curcuruto, a trio of indomitable, fascinating, and endlessly generous Sicilians who have taken my wife, Melody, and me into their hearts. Every day we spend away from Sicily, and away from you, is a day we regret. And a very special thank-you to Enrico, who took us on a memorable geological tour—deep underground in the Realmonte salt mine.

I also thank my agent, Kim Witherspoon at InkWell Management, and, of course, my editor, Daniela Rapp, a veritable font of wisdom, who long ago earned my profound respect.

Finally, and this will come as no surprise to anyone who knows us, my deepest admiration and devotion are reserved for my dear wife, Melody. As one of our friends once said, in a tone of profound wonder: "Amazing! Between the two of you, you actually make a whole person."

How do I argue with that?

*One thorn of experience is worth a whole wilderness of warning.*
—James Russell Lowell

# KILLING PACE

The woman awoke in pain.

She was lying on her side.

Her head was pounding, and something hard and sharp was pressing remorselessly against her back.

She raised her head. Her cheek felt sticky wet.

Half-conscious, she felt behind her. Her torso was jammed against buckled, deformed metal.

Her eyelids were sealed shut. She rubbed at them until one finally opened, then the other. Even then, as the woman struggled to free herself, her eyes could barely make out a blurred image of her surroundings. It was only by the light of a dying sun that she was able to detect the gap in the van's buckled rear doors.

Half-blind, she crawled out of the wreck.

In a fog of disorientation, blood streaming from a laceration in her scalp, she rose unsteadily to her feet.

*Where am I?*

As the woman's confused brain processed that seminal question, the growing recognition that she didn't know the answer imparted a terrifying sense of isolation. Even more frightening, the question felt like the first thought she had ever had.

As if she had just been born.

*That can't be right! How would I know about the concept of birth?*

Abruptly, the source of light shifted. The fading sunset paled against a more intense intrusion. It came, bright with danger, from somewhere behind her tottering form. Distracted from her panicked speculations, she shuffled around in time to feel a sudden blast of heat. Flames leaped upward from the wrecked vehicle. No . . . now she saw there were *two* vehicles. A WWII-era jeep was crushed against the front of the van. A man's twisted body lay across the jeep's hood.

She stumbled backward, almost fell, regained her balance, and fled.

Behind her, the wreckage exploded in a ball of flame.

After several seconds, she stopped, aware of fresh pain. She looked down. Her feet were torn and bleeding. She'd been running barefoot on crushed rock.

*Where are my shoes?*

She sat and studied her bleeding feet.

Puzzled, she plucked at the shreds of pale adhesive that clung to the cuffs of her slacks. She pulled at her shirt.

*Why don't I recognize these clothes?*

Her exploring fingers touched something protruding from her left forearm. She felt a jolt of pain. She slid the object out of her flesh.

*A needle?*

A sulfurous swamp-like smell assailed her nostrils. She looked around, studying the tangle of cypress and myrtle that crowded in on each side of the narrow, graveled track.

*Where am I?*

She strained to remember.

*WHO AM I?*

The whoosh of leaping flames drew her attention back to the scene behind her.

She stared, confused.

*What's burning?*

Then she heard a noise . . . a sliding, crunching sound, approaching fast.

Seconds later, her rapidly improving eyes were blinded by the heartless glare of headlights.

# 1

Lisa awoke with a ripple of anticipation.

She'd been waiting for this day ever since Roland had finally agreed to let her join him on his bimonthly supply run into town.

She'd been increasing the pressure for the last two weeks, and he'd finally relented.

"Okaaay! Okay! But we'll have to do it on a Sunday morning."

"Why Sunday?"

He'd explained that most of Everglades City's townsfolk would either be at home, or in church, or out fishing. "Not so many people around to upset you."

Ever since early February, when Lisa had wandered away from their homestead in the Big Cypress backcountry—ever since he'd finally found her, sick and bleeding on a remote stretch of back road, with no memory of where she was, or who she was—Roland Lewis had been completely obsessed about never letting her out of his sight. And obsessed, as well, about keeping the outside world where it belonged:

*Outside.*

No visitors, no TV, no internet, no newspapers—nothing could be allowed into their lives that might unsettle Lisa in her delicate state. And, just to keep her safe, and to protect her from any lapses, he had locked her in a secure room whenever he went to town. He called it their "safe room." It had a cot, and a chair, a rusting pole lamp, a pee bucket . . . and no windows.

Yeah, it was a bit like a cell, but for a good purpose.

After this last incident—after her injuries had started to heal and she'd calmed down enough to listen—Roland had explained the purpose of the room. They had designed it together, he said, after an earlier episode when she'd wandered away in a disoriented state. A "foog state," he'd called it. He claimed he'd looked up the word, but she didn't know where because the only book in the cabin was a workshop manual for his pickup. After a while, it came to her that he must have meant "fugue state." She'd forgotten her name and everything she'd ever done, but for some reason she'd retained her vocabulary, and it seemed to be better than his.

That earlier time when she'd wandered off, he said, he'd found her sloshing around in an alligator-infested strand two miles from their compound. "After ya recovered, you were really scared it would happen again. That safe room was your idea."

Somehow Lisa couldn't imagine herself asking to be locked up. But then, she didn't really remember what kind of a person "herself" was.

And probably the safe room had been a good idea because, before they'd finished building it, "that crazy foog thing," as Roland called it, *had* happened again. He said that was in early February and now it was late March, so it had been almost two months and her memory still hadn't returned.

It did seem like everything Roland did was for her own protection, and she knew she should be grateful. But lately she'd had the persistent feeling that something didn't quite mesh. It wasn't just her missing memory.

It was something bigger than that.

He'd told her they'd been together for three years, that they'd planned to get married before everything went to hell. A little over a year ago, he said, she'd had her first spell. She lost her memory, didn't know her own name, didn't remember him. Then her memory came back. Then it happened again, and it lasted a little longer. "Ya'd lose your memory," he said, "and then it'd come back, then go again. Really crazy. The docs said you was mental, wanted to put ya in the nuthouse. Couldn't let 'em do that, so I brought ya out here."

Lisa didn't know what to make of it. Whenever she stared at her image in the black-streaked mirror above the sink in the cabin's grimy bathroom, she'd get a prickly feeling that a stranger was staring back.

Someone she couldn't quite bring into focus.

And then there was the other thing.

As Roland led her to the truck, grumbling because he wouldn't be able to stop for a beer at Joanie's diner, his iron grip on her hand reminded her of that other thing.

Reminded her that sometimes sex with him could get a bit rough. He would zone out . . . almost like, in his mind, he was just getting a quick screw from a hooker, not making love to the fiancée he had saved from an asylum.

And then there was that last time, two weeks ago.

They were on the cot in the safe room. He was on top of her, pounding away, when something snapped in her head and she'd started fighting back and he'd smacked her. Hard.

It had only happened that one time.

But it had happened.

He'd smacked her and something inside her head had commanded her to fight back, to make him pay for that humiliating blow. But self-preservation told her she simply owed him too much, that she'd be completely lost without him, so she'd suppressed the urge.

He'd apologized later, saying he thought she was drifting again and he'd only hit her in the hope it would bring her back to her senses. In the hope, as he said, that it would stop her from "fooging" so he wouldn't have to teach her who she was all over again.

He'd played that card too many times.

Lisa's inchoate thoughts and sensations had been nudging her toward a single conclusion:

*I'm his prisoner.*

After that incident, she had carefully adopted the role of the submissive sweetheart, all the while manipulating Roland into letting her join him on today's excursion. She'd already decided that—amnesia or not—if he didn't agree to take her, she was going to make a run for it. The problem with that plan was that she had no idea where she was, and no idea of which direction to run.

At least this way she'd have a guide.

# 2

Roland opened the passenger door of his old F-150 pickup and made a show of helping her in. As far as she could remember, this was only the second time she'd ridden in the truck. The first time was when he had found her sitting on a gravel back road, bleeding and confused.

He climbed in, started the engine, jammed it into gear, and wheeled across the patchy lawn, making a wide circle around the faded clapboard cabin they called home. The building's tar-papered roof had been extended on one side to provide rain cover for a rough plank deck that sat on pilings next to a narrow channel of algae-choked swamp. Roland had told her, with no trace of irony, that their little waterway was called Clearwater Strand. There was an old canoe lying upside down on the deck, but Lisa had never known him to use it.

A few hundred yards of rutted driveway brought them to a chained metal gate. Roland got out, unlocked the padlock, released the chain, and swung the gate wide. After driving through, he got out and reversed the process, double-wrapping the chain and snapping the lock in place. Craning to look out the rear window as they drove away, Lisa could just make out a handwritten warning sign wired to the gate.

PRIVATE PROPERTY

NO TREPASING

NO DUMPING FISHING HUNTING

She thought she should at least recognize that misspelled sign from the night Roland brought her home, but she had no memory of it.

*I must have been really out of it.*

Idly, she asked, "How much property do we have?"

"Twenty acres." Roland swung the truck onto a gravel road.

"What's this road called?"

"Parks guys call it Loop Road."

"We live in a park?"

"Yeah. When the feds made it a park, part 'a the deal was they hadta leave us Gladesmen alone."

"How far is it to town?"

"Thirty miles." His pale eyes cut across to her. "Too many questions, girl! Just concentrate on staying calm. And when we get to the market, stay close to me and don't talk to no one."

Lisa covered her prickling suspicions by asking mildly, "Why?"

"I already told ya! If someone figures out who you are, the word could get back to those quacks who want you locked up in the bughouse."

Lisa managed a compliant nod.

The drive was uneventful. The graveled surface of the Loop Road eventually turned into pavement, and after a few more miles, it intersected a main highway. Roland made a left, heading west. Lisa sat in silence, taking in the passing scenery as if for the first time. She knew she must have seen it all before, must have driven these roads before, but nothing looked familiar. They passed signs: MONUMENT LAKE CAMPGROUND . . . BURNS LAKE CAMPGROUND . . . BIG CYPRESS SWAMP WELCOME CENTER . . .

She remembered none of them.

Finally, after another left, they rolled past a multicolored mural that proclaimed:

WELCOME TO EVERGLADES CITY
ESTABLISHED 1923

They crossed a bridge, with waterways and float houses on both sides. There were motels and cafes and gas stations, interspersed with gaudy signs advertising airboat rides and alligator shows. To Lisa, these everyday scenes all carried an air of unreality, as if she had plunged headlong into someone else's life, with no memory of her own.

After a few more turns and jogs, they arrived in front of a yellow building adorned with red lettering: RIGHT CHOICE SUPERMARKET.

Entering the store through its automatic double doors, Lisa stopped short. What had been an unprepossessing block building on the outside, signaling, at best, a dingy minimart within, turned out to be anything but. Spotless and well-lit, the market featured up-to-date cashier checkouts, polished inlaid flooring, and broad aisles leading to an impressive meat department that spanned the entire rear section of the store. And everywhere—above the meats, over the frozen food coolers, wherever wall space permitted—were enormous, wildly colorful photographs of dark watercourses, mystical stands of mangrove, and dramatic examples of exotic Everglades wildlife.

As Lisa's protector had hoped, the store was almost empty. In fact, the sole customer in sight was a woman paying for her groceries at the only staffed checkout. Roland grabbed a shopping cart and headed for the meat section, with Lisa trailing behind. As he bent over the cooler, digging through packages of ground beef—his usual cheap and easy standby, as Lisa had learned—she devoted herself to looking around, drinking in the scene, hoping against hope that something might seem familiar.

Her eyes were drawn to a certain product at the end of the aisle behind them.

*Nutella.*

She had a sudden compelling feeling that she'd eaten Nutella as a child—a deep memory, just out of reach. A memory that carried with it the sensation of an older woman.

"Roland! Look!"

"What?"

She grabbed his sleeve and tugged him toward the display. "Nutella! I think I used to like this when I was a kid! I must have told you that, right?"

He eyed her carefully. "Yeah. Maybe you did."

His vagueness unsettled her.

They rolled up and down the deserted aisles, filling the cart. Roland seemed to be working from a list in his head. Or, Lisa thought as she watched him make selections, maybe no list at all. Maybe he just bought the same things every time out of habit.

Not once did he ask Lisa for her input.

As they rounded the end of an aisle near the single working cashier, the front doors slid open and a man in his late thirties entered. He was accompanied by a girl of about ten. Roland pulled Lisa closer. "Here, you push the cart," he whispered. He led her down the next aisle.

After a few more minutes of hurried shopping, he told her to take the cart to the checkout. "Start unloading. I'll be right there." He headed for the beer cooler.

*This is your chance! Run! Out the door!*

A small television was playing on the wall behind the cashier. It was tuned to CNN.

*No! Tell the cashier to call the police!*

As Lisa wrestled with competing impulses, the news anchor was reporting on a plane crash in the French Alps. A sudden chill washed over her. For some reason beyond morbid curiosity, the story seized her attention.

*"We're learning chilling new details about the last moments of German- wings Flight 9525, as well as about the copilot who intentionally crashed the jet, carrying 150 passengers and crew, into the French Alps. CNN's senior in- ternational correspondent Frederik Pleitgen is in Cologne, Germany. Frederik, a German newspaper has just . . ."*

A vision of twisted wreckage suddenly assaulted her mind. A huge chunk of fuselage lying in a field . . . a foreign policeman wearing high- visibility gear . . . painted words that read CLIPPER MAID OF THE SEAS . . .

"103," she muttered. She turned to the cashier. "It was 103! It was 103 that killed him!"

"Killed who, dear?"

"103 . . . 103 . . ."

She stood there, almost in a trance, repeating the number.

Roland arrived with a brace of six-packs.

The cashier said, "Mister, I think there's something wrong with your wife!"

Roland set down the beer.

"103!" Lisa's eyes were wide and faraway. "103, Roland!"

"*Shit!*" Roland grabbed Lisa by the arm and pulled her toward the door.

"103!" Lisa cried. "It's something important, Roland!"

He ignored her. As the doors slid open, he half-pulled, half-dragged her across the sidewalk and into the space between his pickup and a late-model car parked next to it.

In that instant, Lisa's last vestiges of restraint gave way to boiling anger.

"*LET ME GO!*" she shouted. "*I need to find out!*" With a strength that took her captor by surprise, she yanked her arm free and ran back to the store. Impatient with the timed delay of the sliding doors, she forced them open with her fingers. She rushed over to the alarmed cashier and stood, transfixed, staring at the television.

Almost instantly she was struck by a blinding flash of memory . . .

*It was late at night and a woman was moaning. The sound had woken her. She left her bed and ran crying to the woman.*

*Crying because she was afraid.*

*The woman wrapped her in her arms, but it took many long seconds before she could speak. Finally, the woman wiped her eyes.*

*"I want you to be strong," she said, looking deep into the child's eyes.*

*"I am strong!" the child sobbed. "You teached me! I want to grow up like you! I want to be just like you!"*

*"And you will, my little angel. It's just you and me now." The woman clenched her teeth, suppressing a sob. "Just you and me."*

*It had taken two more days for her to understand.*

*Two more days to understand that her father, her wonderful, beautiful, loving Papa, would never be coming home.*

*He had died on Pan Am 103—blown out of the sky over Lockerbie, Scotland.*

As the horror of that memory crystalized in Lisa's shocked consciousness, other memories began rushing in. But even through this flood of distractions, another part of her brain had switched onto high alert.

That other part of her brain registered a sudden change in the cashier's facial expression.

And it simultaneously registered movement coming from her right.

She spun in time to see Roland closing fast. He reached for her, his face contorted with rage. Guided by some inexplicable instinct, Lisa's body swung into action. Her assailant's fingers came up empty as she neatly sidestepped his lumbering form, and in the same movement lashed out with a lightning kick.

There was an audible crack as the blow shattered his left knee. He crashed into a newspaper stand, toppled a greeting card display, and landed in a writhing heap. As he struggled to rise, Lisa knocked him cold with a single, well-timed punch.

She kneeled beside his unconscious form. She pushed back an eyelid and then checked his throat for a pulse. Satisfied, she was about to rise when she noticed the front page of one of the newspapers that had been scattered by his fall. It carried the story of the air crash in the French Alps. She scooped up the paper, rose to her feet, and faced the ashen-faced cashier. By now, the woman had a cell phone pressed to her ear.

"Sorry about the mess," Lisa said, with eerie calmness.

She started for the door.

The male customer who had entered after them had witnessed the commotion from a few dozen feet away. In contrast to his own shocked expression, the preteen girl at his side wore a look of unreserved awe.

"Lady!" the man called, hurrying to block her exit. "Wait for the police."

Lisa fixed him with a stare that stopped him in his tracks.

She stepped out into the sunlight and slowly walked away.

Crossing the street, her step faltered. Fragmented memories flashed through her mind. She couldn't remember exactly who she was, but she was now positive she'd had another life. Another past. Not the past Roland's fabric of lies had woven for her.

Not that life. Not that life at all.

Disturbing mental images welled up from nowhere. Heedless of her surroundings, she wandered into an empty lot, almost tripping over a faded realty sign that leaned at a crazy angle. She found herself standing beside a dilapidated boat trailer that was parked among tall weeds near the back of the property. She sat down hard on the trailer's corroded yoke.

As she stared at the front page of the newspaper, a torrent of revelations flooded through her consciousness.

First came tears of joy at a life miraculously rediscovered.

Followed by sobs of horror at what those memories revealed.

They kept coming . . . and coming . . . and coming . . . threatening to overwhelm her.

When the sheriff's deputy found her, she was retching up her breakfast.

He stood back respectfully, waiting until she'd finished.

"Miss, my name is Deputy Newman. We had a call from the market. Do you need a doctor?"

Lisa looked up, taking in the uniform, the young male face, the look of concern. She wiped her mouth on her sleeve and stood up. Instead of the embarrassment or nervousness the deputy had expected, he found himself looking into a pair of dark eyes that were cold with unyielding intent.

"I want to report a missing person," Lisa said.

"Who's that, ma'am?"

"Me."

# SARAH

# 3

The offices of the Consolato Stati Uniti D'America in Sicily were located in an eight-story building in Palermo, at 1 Via Giovan Battista Vaccarini. The consulate shared space in the building with the local offices of Istat, the Italian National Institute of Statistics. To the east, the shabbier, graffiti-covered neighboring buildings housed the offices of Agenzia del Territoria, the territorial tax agency, and the Sicilian Regional Council.

Customs and Border Protection Officer Sarah Lockhart was sitting in front of a gigantic desk. The desk was so offensively ultramodern, so surgically clean-lined, so spotlessly melamine, that it told her all she needed to know about the man sitting behind it.

United States consul Anthony Nicosia examined the contents of a thin file that lay before him. He was a short, thickset man with bushy eyebrows and the drooping features of a bloodhound. He looked unhappy, and Sarah—who'd had her share of encounters with prickly low-level bureaucrats—was pretty sure she knew why. Until twenty-four hours ago, Consul Nicosia had been completely unaware of her presence in Sicily, mainly because the powers in Washington had pointedly not bothered to advise him of her posting. Encouraged by her bosses' attitude, Sarah had spent the last two weeks setting herself up in a loft apartment on Via Reitano, near the port in Catania, before bothering to make contact. During that period, she'd liaised with her counterparts in the Guardia di Finanza, Italy's police responsible for financial crime and smuggling. Then, with the Guardia's assistance, she'd established her credentials with Agenzia delle Dogane, the Italian Customs Agency. Only when everything was in place had she set off on the three-hour drive to Palermo to belatedly introduce herself to the consul.

As the file she had brought with her was now revealing to the testy diplomat, Sarah had been posted to Sicily as an overseas CBP officer. Although there were already a half dozen CBP-staffed ports on the Italian mainland, and one in Sardinia, Sarah was the first officer to be posted full-time to Sicily. Based in Catania, a port on the island's eastern shore, her remit was to institute CBP Container Security Initiative protocols at that city's container facility, and also to keep tabs on the influx of migrants and refugees at the several smaller ports on the island's western and southern coasts and, when required, at Palermo.

In recent decades, the economies of scale had revolutionized international maritime trade, leading to the construction of ever larger container ships. Only major seaports could handle these Panamax and Triple E class vessels. The Port of Catania's modest size and shallow depth restricted entry to small and midsize general cargo vessels, but in the past two years several ships owned by Ikaria Marine Group, a Greek shipping company, had been making regular direct sailings from Catania to Miami, Florida. Although Ikaria's fleet contributed only a tiny fraction to the transatlantic tonnage arriving annually at the Port of Miami, the security of those shipments, together with the worrisome influx of undocumented refugees reaching Sicily from North Africa and Syria, had led Sarah's supervisors to authorize a permanent Homeland Security presence on the island.

Sarah had been chosen for the posting because she had proven herself to be a shrewd and resourceful officer during an earlier high-profile investigation . . . and because she spoke Italian.

And she'd been happy to come. Relieved, in fact. In the wake of her earlier experiences, much of it in undercover operations, her recent stint in uniform at Miami had felt far too predictable. Too scripted. Too boring. This new posting suited her much better.

Especially because she was not in Sicily solely for the reasons outlined in the file.

She was also there on a separate mission—one that she had no intention of sharing with this junior State Department functionary. Customs had come under severe pressure from U.S. multinationals to interdict traffic in counterfeit commercial goods. Fake brand-name merchandise—electronics, drugs, watches, designer handbags, and all the rest—had become a trillion-dollar business worldwide, and U.S. companies were losing billions. Customs had received credible intelligence that a counterfeit goods ring with stateside Mafia connections was operating in Catania.

"Sar-ah Lock-hart . . ." The consul's tone was faintly supercilious as he rolled the syllables off his tongue. "How's your Italian?" he asked in English.

"È passabile," she responded.

In fact, Sarah's Italian was more than passable. She had learned the language at the knee of her grandmother, and she spoke it fluently.

But she wasn't about to tell Nicosia that. Nor was she going to tell him that Sarah Jane Lockhart was not her name. There was always a chance that one or more U.S. Customs officers might be complicit in the fake goods racket—and Sarah's real name was notorious in the service. For that reason, she had dyed her hair—naturally cocoa brown, now copper blond—and assumed the identity of a nonexistent CBP officer. Should anyone decide to check, they would find a carefully assembled personnel file for the fictitious Sarah Lockhart in the Homeland Security database. But if that person decided to look deeper, he or she would have a hard time identifying anyone in the department who had actually met and worked with her. Not that the hypothetical snoop would get a chance to expand those inquiries. Within minutes of anyone searching her name, an alarm would go off in a remote computer, a telephone would ring, and the inquisitor would receive an unwelcome visit from cold-eyed men in suits.

The consul grunted. "Why Catania? Palermo is twice the size, and it's the busiest port in Sicily."

"Since last year, there have been regular sailings directly from Catania to the U.S. Here in Palermo, you have a lot of regional ferry traffic, but not a single container leaves this port that doesn't pass through one of our other stations on the mainland before leaving for the States."

"That can't be right."

"It is right, and it concerns us. Certain cargo vessels are regularly clearing CBP-staffed ports on the Italian mainland and then stopping at Catania to take on wine and agri products. These are shipments that could easily be consolidated through the Medcenter container terminal over in Calabria. Instead, they're being picked up here and taken straight to the States."

"You're talking about ships coming here after inspection on the mainland, picking up a few more containers to top off, and then leaving for the Atlantic?"

"That's right."

"How often?"

"One or two a month."

"And you're in Catania because of that? Sounds to me like a complete waste of manpower. Your department could have arranged for Italian Customs to check those extra containers."

"I'm not here just for that. There are ports in Sicily that are currently receiving refugees from North Africa and the Middle East. Since we don't have any ICE officers posted to Sicily right now, I'll be helping the Guardia and local Immigration with their screening."

Nicosia remained skeptical. "Still . . ."

Sarah wasn't interested in debating with this man. It wasn't as if he had any say in the matter. She stood up. "I reported to you as a courtesy, Mr. Nicosia. If you have other questions, call the CBP officer at the embassy in Rome."

"I already did, when you called to make your appointment. He claimed he didn't know you."

"I'm glad to hear that. It means we're in agreement."

"What do you mean?"

"He and I both agree that this operation is above your pay grade."

She left the man narrow-eyed and glaring. As the automatic door swung shut behind her, he muttered "Fuckin' bitch!" and picked up his phone. He didn't know she'd heard him. Sarah Lockhart had inherited a number of her grandmother's skills—one of which was to listen carefully at the shrinking gap of a closing door after retiring from any tension-fraught encounter.

She had heard exactly what Nicosia said, and she'd heard him pick up his phone.

She allowed herself a tight smile as she ambled to the elevator.


"The worst part of the job is the migrants."

Her companion's pronunciation of the word—"*mee-grunts*"—though correct in Italian, sounded faintly like some repugnant form of insect life when he included it in an English sentence. But Sarah already knew that Major Marco Sinatra, the fifteen-year Guardia veteran who had been assigned as her on-site liaison and guide at the Porta di Catania, was as good-hearted as he was astute. She sensed from his tone that the plight of the migrants caused him deep pain.

Major Sinatra was a great bear of a man who stood six inches taller than Sarah and outweighed her, she judged, by a good sixty pounds. In full uniform, shoulder boards and all, he cut an imposing figure—except when he strode quickly, because he tended to swing his arms across his body rather than at his sides, a gait that was odd to see. Despite that, his face had a pleasing openness, and he'd revealed his genial nature from the moment they were first introduced. As Sarah's eyes widened and she opened her mouth to ask the obvious question, he'd cut her off with, "No relation, signorina, and I can't sing worth a damn."

"A lot of people say he couldn't either," she'd replied with a laugh.

A grin. *"Bene allora!"*

Today, the mood wasn't quite as insouciant as they threaded their way between two rows of containers on Sporgente Centrale, one of the port's main piers.

"You've been involved? I thought the refugees were being landed at Porto Empedocle and Trapani."

*"È vero.* But three times this year, the navy has brought survivors of sinkings to us. Little children screaming for their drowned parents; fathers and mothers wailing for lost *bambini.* In *la Repubblica* and all the other papers, these people are just numbers—one hundred drowned here, two hundred there. But in person, walking among them, the living and the dead, it is terrible to see."

"I suppose I need to prepare myself."

"Nothing will prepare you for the misery you will see, Sarah. Compared to that, the rest of our work is as nothing."

Contrary to Marco's comment, the rest of their work was decidedly not "as nothing."

But it was definitely tedious.

Sarah spent much of her time isolating and inspecting shipments that arrived by road from all over Sicily—olive oil, organic farm products of every description, wine in specially designed climate-controlled containers—all consigned to U.S. importers. Her days on the docks, inhaling exotic dusts and smells, followed by desk-bound nights in her cubicle at the back of the customs office, might have kept her focused on the job, but they were hardly invigorating.

That lack of stimulation, however, stood in marked contrast to life away from work. The open-air fish market was a visual delight—stall after stall of tuna and swordfish and squid and sardines, some so fresh they were still twitching and flapping. The vegetable and fruit and cheese stalls that lined many alleyways were a hubbub of activity and color. And unlike the cloak of sharp indifference she was accustomed to on American sidewalks, in

Catania, approaching strangers often met her gaze with a simple smile or nod.

That not-unwelcome feeling of connection with fellow pedestrians rendered all the more bewildering her encounters with Sicilians behind the wheel. All signs of order and respect disappeared when locals took to the road. City traffic was really just a form of ordered chaos that never quite sank into complete anarchy, but often came dangerously close. Outside the city, on the autostradas, driving was a bit more manageable for someone who had cut her teeth on the interstate highways of America, but the incessant tailgating and the white-knuckle speeds at which her fellow road users blasted by were sometimes unnerving.

Her host country's liaison officers included not only Marco Sinatra, but also two younger officers from the Italian Customs Agency, Elias Terenzi and Filippo Morelli. The pair, both unmarried, made no secret of their extracurricular interest in this American agent with the glint of steel behind her dark eyes. Not that it was going to get them anywhere. The idea of dating while on a mission—much less dating a coworker—was something Sarah viewed with a jaundiced eye.

Equally intriguing to Sarah's fellow officers was her spoken Italian, delivered not with an English speaker's accent, but with a regional one that reminded Elias, he said, of cousins who lived up north, near Bologna. When he mentioned that, she made a vague comment about learning the language from her grandmother, who was born somewhere near there. She kept her expression carefully blank when she delivered this information.

She had a very good reason for being closemouthed. She knew that nothing in Italy was a matter of indifference. The last thing she needed was to be drawn into a long discussion about the Fascisti and the Nazis and the Resistance—a topic that even now, two generations on, could arouse strong emotions.

*"Read this book," her grandmother had ordered. "You are old enough. You will be strong for me, and you will read every word. When you are finished, I will tell you the rest of the story."*

*It was an old book. Published in the 1960s, it was twice as old as the fifteen-year-old girl who lay on her bed that night and opened its battered cover.*

*Inside, she found a list.*

*A list that went on for nineteen pages. Before the preface. Before the first chapter.*

*A list of the dead.*

*She stopped counting them after one thousand names.*

*There was also a list of survivors.*

*Just sixty-two names.*

*The author explained that the list of the dead was incomplete, that no one knew the exact number.*

*Every name was Italian.*

*She read each of the sixty-two names, her eyes ticking down the columns, tracking across the pages. She imagined faces, ages, clothing . . .*

*One name riveted her attention.*

*Her grandmother's.*

*The author told the story of seven days of mass murder on the slopes of Monte Sole, in Romagna, in 1944. He documented a succession of massacres of civilians, perpetrated by Waffen-SS troops, assisted by Italian fascists. Back-to-back massacres that ended the lives of over eighteen hundred Italian civilians.*

*Grandmother Silvana—"Nonna," as she had always called her—had been born in a village near Monte Sole in 1928. She was twelve years old when Italy entered the war, and had just turned seventeen in September 1944, when she and her mother were gang raped by a squad of SS soldiers who had accused them—wrongly—of supporting a local band of partisans. Her mother was so severely beaten during the attack that she died three days later. In years to come, Nonna would discover that the attack had left her permanently damaged and unable to bear children.*

*Two weeks after the rapes, the SS arrived in force.*

*"My father was dead," she told her granddaughter. "I had nowhere to stay, so I moved in with my aunt Clarissa, my father's sister, and her three children. They had a small house in Casaglia. It was a village on the mountain. It is not there anymore. Clarissa's husband was away. My mother had told me he had joined the partisans, but my aunt never admitted that to me. Then, a few days after I moved in, three men came to the house. They were GNR—Fascisti police. They said the German army was making an antipartisan sweep through our area and for our safety we should join the rest of the civilians at the church. So we went. When we arrived, villagers told us the Germans and the Fascisti were burning down all the farms because they believed the farmers were providing food to the partisans. Then they came to*

*the church—German soldiers and those same fascist police who had come to our door. They came and they said we had been supporting the partisans, that we had been hiding their weapons. They herded us to the cemetery. There were nearly two hundred people—villagers, peasants, women, and children. Lots of babies and old people."* Nonna stopped speaking and fixed her with haunted eyes. *"You know what happened next."*

"The graveyard . . . it was surrounded by a wall," she had replied, still deeply upset by the account she had read. "The only way out was through the gate. The Germans set up a big machine gun. They threw grenades. They fired into the crowd. They mowed the people down."

*"I only remember the explosions and the screams and the raging of the gun. Then I was unconscious. I don't know for how long. When I woke up, I was lying under bodies. There was blood everywhere, but I had no pain. No bullet had touched me. I was soaked in the blood of other people, and with urine, and . . . worse. I stayed there. I didn't move until I was sure the soldiers had left. Then I worked my way out. It was very hard. I was weak, like rubber, almost helpless from the horror I had witnessed, and the bodies above me were heavy. My auntie and my cousins were all dead. I found a place where I could climb over the wall. I got away through the brambles. I slept in the forest. When I woke up, I knew what I had to do."*

*Her grandmother had awoken to a single realization. Her father had died four years earlier, during Mussolini's failed invasion of Egypt. And now, in less than a month, she had lost her mother, her aunt, her cousins—and uncountable friends—to the unspeakable brutality of fascism.*

*Her grandmother's conversion from weeping teenager to partisan fighter was complete.*

During her first month on the job, Sarah came to enjoy Marco's company, and he hers, and she dined twice with him and his wife, Marta, at their home. Marta's initially wary reaction when her husband showed up at their home with a fetching young woman at his side soon evaporated, and the couple's warmth and generosity provided Sarah with a welcome respite from long hours spent on the docks. Marta even offered to give her a few lessons in Sicilianu.

"Sicilianu?" she had asked, a bit openmouthed.

"Our dialect. An ancient language, older than Italian. Your grandmother never told you?" Marta answered her own question. "Of course. She wouldn't! Northerners always looked down on us. After Risorgimento, they were running the country. They didn't understand our speech, so they forced us to learn Italian. In Sicily today, Sicilianu is not even taught in the schools."

Sarah heard the deep, long-held resentment in Marta's voice, and she thanked her stars she had a way out. She smiled and said, "My Nonna left Italy when she was very young. She probably had no idea Sicilianu even existed. But I'm here, and I would like to learn."

And so, with a grunt of forgiveness, the lessons began.

She'd tried to return the Sinatras' hospitality by taking them out to dinner at Catania's top-rated restaurant—top-rated, at least, by a prominent travelers' website. Marco and Marta both admitted to her that they had never been there. The meal was terrific, but Marco and Sarah had no trouble ruling that Marta's cooking was superior. They agreed that all future get-togethers would be back at the house, with Sarah supplying the wine.

The morning after that dinner out, and their two-person straw vote, Marco told her that Marta's face had shone with delight all the way home from the restaurant.

Other than those occasional social moments, and when she wasn't dealing with flirting Customs officers, Sarah spent some of her off-shift hours masquerading as a tourist. Decked out in T-shirt, tight jeans, and a short jacket, a messy ponytail swinging, she would drift in and out of waterfront restaurants and bars, pretending she spoke no Italian, hoping to pick up any snatches of conversation that might provide a lead in her counterfeit trademarks investigation. The disguise was designed so that no one would take her seriously, but it came with a downside—fending off passing pickup artists. Even the nerdy stage-prop glasses she'd bought before she left the States (saucily marketed as "Bookworm Chic") didn't always dampen her would-be suitors' ardor.

But fend them off she did. After her last investigation, after all that turbulence and betrayal and media madness over her role in the arrest of a United States senator, the last thing Sarah wanted right now was a man in her life.

# 4

"There's a man out here to see you," the receptionist informed her.

Sarah was working her way through a pile of paperwork in her cubicle. She'd been forced to slide a stack of files aside just to reach the telephone receiver. The local head of Customs had promised to find her better accommodations as soon as he was given clearance from Rome. Based on what she'd been hearing about the Italian civil service, that might take weeks.

"What man?"

"He sounds American."

"Did he give you a name?"

She heard a muffled exchange, followed by, "He says he is Signor Nelthorp. He says you do not know him."

As Sarah marched toward reception, she wondered darkly if her visitor had been sent by Consul Nicosia to snoop into her activities.

There were only two chairs in the small reception area, and the man in question wasn't occupying either of them. He was hovering near the receptionist's desk, his eyes fixed on the door leading to the operations area. As soon as Sarah opened that door, he broke into a smile.

It was a late-thirties, carefully groomed, square-jawed, perfect-teeth smile.

*Oh, great.*

"Agent Lockhart?" He held out a hand. "I'm Conrad Nelthorp." His warm, firm grip, and his mellifluous baritone, prompted an inward groan.

"Sarah Lockhart. What can I do for you, Mr. Nelthorp?"

"Is there somewhere we can talk?"

"Maybe. But first, how did you know I was here, and how did you know my name?"

"Elias Terenzi is a friend. He mentioned you'd been stationed here."

*So, Terenzi's not only a flirt, he's a loose lip.*

She filed that away for later discussion with Marco.

"Okay. And?"

Her bluntness seemed to catch him off guard. "And, uh . . . I'm in the private security business. For the last two years, I've been working for Durasteel Aftermarket. They're a U.S. auto parts manufacturer. Maybe you've heard of them."

"I have."

"My job is to track and intercept shipments of counterfeit merchandise bearing the company's trademark. It's become a real problem."

Sarah's eyes narrowed. "I see."

A few feet away, the receptionist was shuffling papers and rummaging in her purse. It was obvious she was getting ready to leave for the day.

Trying for a quick recovery, Nelthorp glanced at his watch. "Look, I understand your reticence. Obviously, you need to be careful." He plucked a business card from his shirt pocket. "Here's my card. Why don't you check me out with Durasteel, and with your people at Homeland? After that, if you're comfortable, give me a call on that direct dial number. It's a landline in Trieste, but it forwards to my cell."

"All right. And assuming you 'check out,' what are you proposing?"

"Lunch tomorrow. I believe we can help each other."

"I'd have to think about that. And I'd need clearance."

"Thanks. That's all I can ask."

They shook hands again, and he left.

At the man's mention of counterfeit merchandise, Sarah's suspicions had been raised. Her investigation into that illicit trade was the sole aspect of her mission that wasn't documented. So, was there a leak in the department, and someone had alerted Nelthorp? Or had he approached her only because he'd heard she was in Catania and that she worked for U.S. Customs?

"Never trust a coincidence," her grandmother had always lectured. "Look behind it."

It was coming up to noon on the U.S. East Coast, so she sent an encrypted heads-up to Phyllis Corbin, the CBP's Miami area port director. Corbin had been her supervisor when she was working the docks there, and she was her designated line manager on this operation. She attached a scanned copy of Nelthorp's business card to her message. She knew her boss usually ate lunch at her desk, so she waited a few minutes and then tried a call.

Corbin answered on the second ring. She'd already read Sarah's message.

"Why do you want to know about this guy?"

"He's courting me."

"You mean . . . ?" The bated note of lubricious curiosity in her boss's voice caught Sarah by surprise. Corbin was in her early forties and had never married. She was what snide Hollywood critics would refer to as a "fading beauty"—one who, in this case, might have retained some of her youthful allure had she favored a less severe hairstyle. But Corbin was a woman in command of a hundred-plus, mainly male, Customs agents. It wasn't difficult to understand why she'd decided that short hair and a hard-bitten manner would make her more effective.

Whatever was going on behind the woman's exterior, Corbin had always been careful to keep her private affairs determinedly private, so it struck Sarah as mildly amusing that the word "courting" had sent her imagination straight to *amore*.

"I mean courting *us*. The department. He's looking for cooperation."

Instantly, Corbin was all business. "Okay, I'm on it. Watch your emails."

When Sarah checked her inbox the next morning, a message from Corbin was waiting.

*He looks okay. Hear him out. Report back.*

Sarah shook her head. Phyllis Corbin's emails were as curt as her conversation.


"Why Trieste?"

Sarah and Conrad Nelthorp were sitting in a back corner of Osteria Antica, a restaurant tucked into a small square near Catania University. The waiter had taken their orders and they were getting acquainted over a couple of cold Peroni's.

Nelthorp was doing his charming best to break the ice.

"My cases take me all over Eastern Europe, so I set up my base there. Trieste is part of Italy, but it's almost completely surrounded by Slovenia.

It's only connected to the country by a narrow strip of coastline. It's a great gig, Sarah—it's a city with a fascinating history, mainly as a haven for exiles and misfits. I get the feeling that's what some of my stateside friends think of me." There was that commercial smile again, and Sarah couldn't help wondering if the surreal gleam of his teeth was a shade of white actually known to nature.

"Seems a bit remote," she observed, keeping her tone carefully neutral. They'd met on the street less than ten minutes earlier, but already the man was busy radiating warmth and camaraderie. Sarah wasn't quite ready to bask in it.

"That's the perception, and it works for me. It's not crowded with thousands of tourists like Venice, and I can easily get to anywhere in the old Eastern Bloc from there. It's also nice and handy to Geneva." He took a pull on his beer. "As you probably know, most knockoffs originate in China—designer clothes, Rolexes, and a lot of the deadly stuff, like pharmaceuticals—but Durasteel's core business is auto parts, and most of the fakes flooding our market are coming out of Russia and Eastern Europe."

"Do you speak any of the languages? From the Eastern Bloc?"

"Nope. English is all I've ever needed over here."

"From what my Guardia friends tell me"—Sarah left the reference to Marco ambiguously plural—"counterfeit designer stuff doesn't just come from the Far East."

"That's right. Back in the eighties, a lot of fake Italian labels came out of Romania. Most of it was smuggled across the Adriatic from Montenegro. That route was disrupted during the Kosovo war, but it's coming back."

"What about the mafiosi?"

"You mean the Cosa Nostra?"

"Since I'm posted in Sicily, they come to mind. Anything you can tell me?"

"They were in deep at one time." He took another pull on his beer. "Not now."

"I'm listening."

He set down his bottle. "They were pretty powerful during the Cold War, and that's the period most people remember. They had strong ties to the Christian Democratic Party, which was Italy's strongest political party after '45. The politicians figured they could help keep communists and union agitators in line, so they formed an informal alliance with them. For years, whenever some cop or prosecutor got too enthusiastic about an investigation, some padrone would call a politician and the case would go away. But that only worked until the Soviet Union collapsed. After 1990, the CDP was scrambling to hold on to power and they lost interest in protecting their criminal friends. When the Sicilians realized they were on their own, they made the mistake of assassinating a couple of well-known prosecutors. They also thought the Church had betrayed their traditional hands-off policy, so they bombed a couple of Catholic churches in Rome. It all backfired. The media and the public started calling for action, and the cops and the courts got the backing they needed. A lot of Mafia guys ended up in prison, along with some of their old politician friends. So—bottom line—these days there's not much Mafia involvement in the fake goods trade."

"Sounds like you've made a study of all this."

Nelthorp flushed. "Yeah. Sorry for the lecture. That was lifted from one of my boardroom talks."

Despite herself, Sarah chuckled.

"I figured I'd better learn the history," Nelthorp added. "Helps with the investigations."

"And with the marketing?"

"That too."

"What's in Geneva?"

"Hmm?"

"You said Trieste is handy to Geneva. Are the Swiss involved in this business?"

"No. I just like going there. Ever been?"

"No."

"Worth a visit. The streets are spotless, hardly any crime, the food's great, and the desserts are unbelievable. There's this one place that brews the most amazing white chocolate coffee. It's called 'Precision.' Perfect name."

"So, you're a man with a sweet tooth."

"I'm having lunch with you, aren't I?"

Sarah couldn't help smiling. "Nice comeback. Did you tell me all that just so you could use that line?"

He grinned.

Their meals arrived.

"Why Customs?"

"Sorry?"

"You're obviously an intelligent woman. I'm guessing you've probably been to university and picked up a degree."

Sarah nodded.

"In what?"

"Criminal justice."

"They give degrees in that?"

"Some colleges do."

"So . . . why Customs? Why not the FBI?"

*"They said they were from the Lockerbie investigation," Nonna had told her, years after the disaster that had taken her father's life. "Somehow they found out I'd been a member of the Resistance. And that my brigata was called Stella Rossa. 'Red Star.' They came to our house. They asked me to come with them. I told them I was alone, and I needed to pick you up from school. I told them I wouldn't go anywhere with them unless they were there to arrest me, which I doubted. They were angry. They questioned me about my year in the Resistance. They said I must have had communist sympathies. They said that they suspected that I had poisoned your father against America. I couldn't believe what they were saying. They were saying I might be some kind of communist infiltrator, and my Angelo, your dear father, might have been the one who blew up that plane. They sounded just like those Fascisti bullies who destroyed our lives."*

*Scorched by her personal history, her grandmother had managed to control her rage long enough to ask one question of her own:*

*"Did I not read somewhere that all FBI agents are required to have a college education?"*

*"Most of us have law degrees," came the supercilious reply.*

*"Then you should have spent more time studying history."*

*"What's that supposed to mean?"*

*"Any fool who took the time to study history would know that our band was nonpolitical. Our leader, Lupo, adopted the name Stella Rossa because it sounded good. He copied it from another group operating against the Germans in the Balkans. He didn't even know that the other group were Stalinists. Our job was to help the Allies—your government!—by killing Germans and Italian fascists, and that's what we did. We also saved many escaped American prisoners of war. And if you are so well-educated, why don't you know that communist fanatics have never been in the business of blowing themselves up along with their victims?" She stood up and shouted at them. "Leave my house! Instead of harassing an old woman for saving American lives, get out there and find the people who killed my son!"*

///

Sarah wasn't about to explain to a virtual stranger why she hadn't joined the FBI, so she replied, "I preferred the job offer I got from Homeland." After maneuvering past a few more questions that were plainly aimed at establishing a warmer bond between them, she decided she'd had enough.

It was time to find out what this man really wanted.

"This has been nice, Conrad. But you haven't told me the reason you asked for this meeting."

Nelthorp set down his fork. "It's simple. I want to be in a position for you and I to work together if either of us turns up anything that can help shut these bastards down."

"By 'these bastards,' I assume you mean the people shipping fake Durasteel parts."

"That's right."

"Okay. I have your card. If I come across any fake Durasteel parts, you'll be the first to know."

"That's it?"

"You had something more in mind?"

"I have sources. I come across information. It's not always directly related to my client's business, but it could be useful to you."

"You mean, useful to U.S. Customs."

"Yes."

"So now we come to it . . . you're looking for a deal."

"You're Homeland, Sarah! You get intelligence reports. Updates. Briefings."

"I wouldn't be able to share those with you."

"Not even intel on counterfeit auto parts? Even stuff that doesn't relate to Durasteel might lead back . . . might help identify plants, warehouses, locations."

"You mean . . . help identify possible new corporate clients for you."

"Okay, yeah. That too."

"This is the best I can do: If I come across something that bears directly on your work—and on your client, Durasteel—I'll give you a summary. If it bears on some other aspect of the fake auto parts trade, but I think it might help you, I'll ask for clearance to share it. If I get that clearance, I'll call you."

"So, I'm relying on your judgment."

"Yes, you are."

He thought about that. "Guess I can't ask for more. Deal."

A few more minutes passed as they ate in silence.

"You aren't here just to screen containers, are you?"

It was Sarah's turn to set down her fork. "What are you after?"

"Just guessing. You're not ICE, but you *are* Homeland. This island is getting a lot of migrants. Syrians looking for asylum. Africans looking for a better life. Some of them might have another agenda."

"Your point being?"

"I hear things."

"Does terrorism concern you?"

"Of course it does."

"Then if you hear something, you'll call me."

"You have my word." A pause. "What are you doing tonight?"

Sarah studied his face. More gleaming teeth. Behind the surface expression of expectation, was that . . . complacency? Entitlement?

"Spending it alone."

"Sarah, I was only thinking of dinner."

*Sure you were . . .*

"How often do you come to Sicily?"

"Once a month. Sometimes twice."

"Call me next time you're in town."

"I will. But I'm here now. So what is it? Need more time to background me?"

"Something like that."

"Thought you'd done that already."

"Never hurts to recheck your work."

"You're a very careful woman."

"Blame my grandmother."

She didn't bother to explain.

# 5

A week after her lunch with Nelthorp, Sarah drove to Porto Empedocle, just west of Agrigento on Sicily's south coast. A group of refugees had managed to make it from North Africa, but not before their two boats had sunk in the Mediterranean. The sixty-odd survivors were about to be landed at the port by the Guardia Costiera, the Italian Coast Guard.

Accompanying the survivors were over a hundred recovered bodies.

Sarah's route cut across the southeastern interior of the island. Despite the grim realities awaiting her at Porto Empedocle, the trip offered a genuine chance to spend a day playing tourist. She stopped at Caltagirone and spent a few hours wandering through its famous ceramics shops. After lunch, she continued on through the rolling vastness of the Sicilian interior, deliberately choosing secondary roads, winding through orchards and vineyards and fertile hillocks rippled by the wind. Reaching the Mediterranean at Gela, she swung west. Towns sparkled in the lowering sunlight as she worked her way along the coastal plain. She had an ominous feeling about the task that awaited her in Porto Empedocle, so it was a relief just to empty her mind, enjoy each new vista, and bathe her senses in the ethereal clarity of Sicilian sunlight.

It was nearly dark when she reached her hotel. She had booked a room at the Carlo V, a small hostelry located directly across the street from the port facility. She grabbed a quick supper and turned in early.

*/ / /*

*"Nothing will prepare you for the misery you will see, Sarah."*

Marco's earlier warning, and Sarah's lurking misgivings, had been fully justified.

The first day was the worst. A coast guard officer escorted her to the makeshift morgue the police had established in a collection of empty shipping containers on the docks.

"There were two wooden fishing boats—leaky old derelicts, both of them," the officer told her. "One had no engine, and it was being towed by the other one. The survivors say the second boat started leaking right from the start. Everyone kept bailing—men, women, even the older children, but as time passed, and more and more of the passengers became exhausted, the incoming sea got ahead of them. When it finally began to sink, the smuggler in charge of the first boat cut the towline. It didn't help. His own boat sank a little while later."

The sheer numbers of the corpses were horrific. When Sarah stepped into the first makeshift morgue, the faint odor of putrescence had just begun to taint the thick, still air. She felt her stomach react, but not because of the smell. What churned her insides was the sight of a long row of drowned children. Sarah Lockhart had witnessed her share of mayhem during her short life, but the sight of all those dead children, their little faces still shining as if they would awaken at any moment, was almost more than she could bear.

That gut-churning tour was followed by three and a half days of intense interviews, listening to stories of deaths at sea and pitiless smugglers, many of whom had imprisoned, starved, and raped the migrants who fell into their hands before cramming them into leaking boats. There were even rumors, unproven but certainly credible, that some migrants who couldn't pay for their passage had been sold to Egyptians who murdered them and harvested their organs for corrupt transplant surgeons in Cairo. In addition, there were scores of unaccompanied and orphaned children, many of whom had been cruelly abused. Although most adult migrants were quickly transferred to more comfortable camps farther north, Italian Immigration officials constantly struggled to find spaces for minors. Marco had told her that many ended up stranded for weeks in crowded holding centers along Sicily's southern coast, where they were vulnerable to continuing abuse by other migrants.

In keeping with one of her primary assignments, Sarah assisted in the interrogations of four young Syrian men who had been singled out by Major Sander Dirksen, a NATO intelligence officer. Dirksen was a Dutch national seconded to the Italian Navy. The vast majority of both the rescued and the deceased migrants were sub-Saharan Africans fleeing conflict or poverty in their homelands, so the presence of these four Arabic men, all in their twenties, had attracted the officer's immediate interest.

The secondary screening interviews were conducted carefully and professionally, and Sarah's ready access to Homeland's resources contributed to their swift resolutions. Only one of the men spoke English. He had lost his wife to a phosphorus barrel bomb. Before her horrifying death, the couple had sworn to each other that, if one were killed, the other would carry their baby daughter far away from the conflict zone so she would have a chance to grow up in a peaceful society. Rather than spend months rotting away in a refugee camp, he had worked his way along the North African littoral, baby in arms, until he'd finally made contact with a Libyan smuggling group.

Now after weeks of hardship, he had failed. When their boat sank in heavy seas, his baby girl had been washed from his arms and lost in the Mediterranean. His frantic search among the survivors and the laid-out dead had confirmed that the infant's body had not been recovered. The man was inconsolable, barely able to speak. Under Sarah's gentle questioning, he explained that, before the war, he had been living in Homs, studying computer engineering.

"I wanted that degree. I thought it would help us to emigrate one day . . . to use the proper channels. To live in peace. In England. Or maybe even America! And now my Jada and our beautiful baby are gone! What do I work for? Where is my reason to live? Can you tell me that, American lady? What do I do? What do I do?" He wept without shame, and without hope.

One thing was pretty clear to Sarah: the young man was no jihadist.

The other three men were interviewed with the assistance of an Arabic-speaking interpreter supplied by the commander of the Carabinieri detachment in Agrigento. Their stories were similar, their gaunt faces a portrait of composite agony. Two of them were cousins traveling together—one had lost his parents in a bombardment, the other his entire family in the same attack. The last interviewee had two fingers missing from his right hand. He told of refusing military service, of being imprisoned and tortured, and of escaping only because a government helicopter had accidentally released a barrel bomb while taking off and the blast had destroyed most of the building where he was being held. He had escaped the government-controlled area and joined the White Helmets, a group of unarmed volunteers who spent every waking hour rescuing people from the smoking rubble in the aftermath of government air attacks. But when the warplanes began circling back to attack the rescuers, and government snipers started deliberately picking them off, he decided he'd had enough and fled the country. Now, weeks later, he sat across a table from Sarah, haggard with shame, hating that this self-possessed woman from America might think him a coward.

Not knowing that Sarah thought nothing of the sort.

Not knowing that she had never felt less self-possessed in her life.

After endless calls and database searches on the encrypted cell phone and laptop system Homeland had provided to Sarah, and after Washington had made direct contact with CIA sources on the ground in Syria, everyone was satisfied that the men's stories checked out. By the end of the fourth day, all of them were cleared to file their EU asylum applications.

That procedure would not be difficult for the Syrians because they could genuinely claim to be fleeing war or persecution, but, as Sarah learned, it would be almost insurmountable for many of the African migrants. Those deemed to be "economic migrants" would be summarily classified as illegal immigrants, served with refusal-of-entry documents, and told they had seven days to leave the country. Most of them, of course, were penniless and had no means of returning to their home countries. Some would end up being held in detention camps for weeks or months before being expelled at EU taxpayers' expense. Others would escape, go on the run, and end up working illegally in northern Europe, where jobs were more readily available.

Or living on the streets.

Or turning to crime.

The whole process was unedifying, chaotic, and immensely depressing.

Sarah's time at Porto Empedocle had left her feeling heartsick. She was more than ready to head directly back to Catania and bury herself in the more mundane aspects of her assignment.

But that was not to be.

At least . . . not exactly as she'd planned.

On the morning of the fifth day, she checked out of her hotel and returned to her car. After loading her luggage in the trunk, she noticed an envelope tucked under her driver's-side windshield wiper. It was addressed, in neat handwriting, to *"Signorina Lockhart."* Inside, she found a printed card, in Italian, inviting her to attend a special Mass being held in the church at the Italkali salt mine.

She was vaguely aware of this church. Over dinner with a pair of coast guard officers one night, between stories of capsized boats and rescues at sea, she'd been told that the Pope had once held a Mass in a nearby underground church—a house of worship that had been carved entirely out of salt, deep in a mine under the village of Realmonte.

Inscribed on the back of the invitation was a handwritten note: *"Ho informazioni."*

"I have information."

# 6

Half a kilometer inland from the shore of the Sicilian Channel, the dark, gaping entrance to the Italkali Corporation's Realmonte salt mine gave access to a broad tunnel that sloped deep underground, connecting the surface to twenty-five kilometers of chambers, drifts, and crosscuts stretching in every direction. The mine produced over a million tons of rock salt a year, most of which was shipped to northern Europe for winter road de-icing.

But the walls of the mine also offered an astonishing natural wonder—alternating dark and light layers of sedimentary rock salt laid down five million years ago, resulting in a vivid presentation of stripes, spirals, and concentric circles. At many of the interlacing tunnels' collars and junctions, the vast, mural-like phenomena dramatically called to mind the abstractions of optical-school artists from the 1960s.

In an immense gallery off the main tunnel, a kilometer from the surface, lay another attraction: a cathedral formed entirely of salt. Painstakingly carved out of those eons-old deposits were an altar, a bishop's seat, and finely executed frescoes—most prominent among them an elaborate relief of Saint Barbara, the protector of mine workers. The church was large enough to accommodate eight hundred people.

There were not that many worshipers at today's Mass. By Sarah's count, there were no more than two dozen souls—all that could be accommodated in the three Fiat Ducato passenger vans that had conveyed the congregation down the long, arrow-straight tunnel from the surface.

Sarah's grandmother had been Catholic by heritage only. She had been deeply embittered by her experiences in the Resistance, by her encounters with compromised priests who blindly supported Mussolini, hypocrites in cassocks who turned a blind eye to violence and persecution, some of whom even gave a raised-arm Fascisti salute at the conclusion of every Mass. After the war, Nonna had been determinedly nonobservant. Apart from an occasional wedding or funeral, as far as Sarah could recall the woman never voluntarily set foot in a church of any denomination in all the years she lived with her.

And so it was with Sarah.

Unfamiliar with the minutiae of the Catholic liturgy, she took a seat at the rear of the eerily bleached-out house of worship and tried to follow the lead of her fellow congregants. She had learned on the ride into the mine that they were all members of a Catholic charity based in Palermo. They had arrived in a large bus which had disgorged them on the shoulder of Via della Miniera, next to the mine entrance, and then driven away. The cathedral of salt was merely a waypoint in a three-day tour of religious attractions across the region. Sarah had arrived before their bus. When she showed her invitation to the driver of one of the Ducato transports, he had bowed his head, opened his vehicle's front passenger door, and wordlessly indicated that she should take the seat beside him.

Oddly, not a single question had been raised about her presence with the group.

She had read somewhere that Italian had replaced Latin as the language of services in Italian churches, but apparently the news had not reached this far underground. After forty-five minutes of breathing the brine-laden air of millennia, of standing and sitting and listening to repeated *Pater Nosters,* Sarah sensed that the end might be near. The priest, a thin man whose solemn face was a pale smudge against the equally pale walls behind him, held up the bread and the wine.

*"Agnus Dei, qui tollis peccata mundi, miserere nobis!"* Everyone around her chanted the response, and then rose to receive communion. Sarah remained in her seat.

Soon after, the congregation began filing out.

Sarah had been sitting next to the aisle that ran between the ranks of folding chairs that had been set out to form the pews.

She rose and stood waiting.

*Waiting for what?*

The priest approached.

"Miss Lockhart, remain, please," he whispered in English as he swept past. He positioned himself near the parked minibuses where, one by one, he thanked the parishioners as they filed aboard.

When the last transport had pulled away, the priest strode back to her side.

"My name is Gaetano Giardini." His spoken English carried only a faintest hint of an accent. He offered a hand.

"Pleased to meet you." She kept her tone neutral.

"You are not Catholic, Miss Lockhart."

"Correct."

"Good."

"Why?"

"Artificial respect hampers serious discussions."

If the man had intended to disarm her, he succeeded.

"Call me Sarah."

"I'm Gaetano." He smiled. "There. So easy. I do appreciate the informality of Americans. Such a relief."

"Did you leave that note on my car?"

"An associate." He gestured toward a small wooden structure in a side gallery near the church. "Come. She's waiting."

"She?"

"Yes."

They walked. He reached for a door handle.

"What is this building?"

"A facility for supervising mine operations. There are several of these throughout the mine. This one is not currently in use."

The structure's interior layout was not unexpected: a few chairs, a coffee machine, work clothing hanging on pegs, a drafting table . . .

And an old couch with one occupant.

A woman who appeared to be in her late thirties or early forties rose to greet her.

"Agent Lockhart," she said. "My name is Renate Richter. I work for the United Nations."

"This is a strange venue for a U.N. rep," Sarah remarked.

Sarah had inspected Richter's U.N. identity card and they were now comfortably seated on the couch, with the priest on a nearby chair. Coffee had already been brewed, ready for her visit. It had been offered and poured, but Sarah wasn't spending time drinking it. Her attention was fixed on the woman.

"My friend Gaetano here works in the Vatican secretary of state's office," Richter replied. Her precise English was delivered with a distinct German accent. "We are working together on an important assignment. I will let him explain."

"We are aware of your particular employment on behalf of your government here in Sicily," Gaetano began.

"And how is that?"

"You have been working at Porto Empedocle for the past several days," Richter interposed. "We are fully aware of your position with Homeland Security and your activities here and in Catania."

*Of course you are. This is Italy, after all.*

"All right."

Gaetano continued. "At the Vatican, it has come to our attention that fake baptismal certificates are being issued here in Sicily. We believe this practice is part of a larger industry."

"What larger industry?"

"I believe the English expression is 'baby laundering.'"

Sarah had heard of this industry before. She recalled once attending a session at the federal law enforcement training center in Georgia where a colleague from ICE gave a talk on an investigation into a black-market adoption ring operating between Guatemala and the U.S.

Sarah settled back in her seat. "I'm listening."

"We've come across a series of home study reports in the Palermo Juvenile Court files. Each report is a word-for-word facsimile of the others, with only names and dates altered. Every one of these files relates to applications by American couples to adopt Italian infants. American couples, I should tell you, who have never been to Italy."

"Adopting Italian infants who have never existed," Richter added. "These are fictitious children, with fictitious birth parents. The only logical conclusion is that these infants have been bought or stolen—perhaps in Italy, but, more likely, elsewhere in Europe. Our intelligence sources tell us—"

"What sources?" Sarah asked.

"U.N. sources. We do have our own networks."

"All right."

"Our sources tell us that these babies are being stolen—kidnapped—mainly from Syrian refugee families."

That struck a chord. "I remember seeing a Europol report. Something about thousands of unaccompanied children going missing."

"Fifteen percent of all the asylum seekers who have arrived in Europe so far this year have been unaccompanied minors. As far as we can tell, somewhere between five and ten thousand of them went missing after being registered by Immigration authorities. There's a growing body of evidence that unaccompanied children and teenagers are being lured away from the refugee encampments, abducted, and trafficked. That's a separate scandal, and it's a direct result of Europe's abysmal mishandling of the crisis." The tone of helpless anger in Richter's voice was unmistakable. She took a breath and continued. "But here is another statistic to think about: fifteen percent of female refugees are pregnant. Many of them end up in those refugee camps and give birth there. The cases Gaetano and I have been investigating involve, we believe, the abduction of babies from those camps—babies who are being sold to rich Americans who do not qualify as adopting parents, or have no patience with paperwork and waiting lists. These are couples prepared to pay substantial amounts of money for a black-market baby. We've seen these kinds of operations before—in Southeast Asia, for example, and Central America. The victim parents are always people without any means of recourse. They're desperately poor, or like here, refugees who have lost everything, constantly on the move, living on charity. People with no voice whose complaints to Immigration officials are met with indifference."

"We've identified a woman who works at the Juvenile Court registry in Palermo," Gaetano said. "She's in charge of filing the home study reports, and we think she is knowingly involved in this scheme. Her name is Carlotta Falcone."

"Then why come to me? Why not go to local authorities?"

"Only two countries in the world have failed to ratify the U.N. Convention on the Rights of Children," Renate replied. "Your country, and Somalia. Somalia we can understand—it has no recognizable government to ratify anything. So . . . what is your country's excuse?"

"I don't know how to answer that."

"I'll tell you. A majority of your members of Congress believe the ridiculous myth—spread by people like your right-wing evangelicals—that the Hague Convention is just a vehicle for the U.N. to interfere with the legitimate rights of American parents. *Interesting,* since none of the 192 other countries of the world have expressed such a misgiving. But that is a discussion for another time. We are asking for your help."

"Again . . . why my help?"

Richter was forceful. "You work for your country's so-called Department of Homeland Security, *yes*? What do you call it: ICE? Immigration and Customs Enforcement?"

"That's a separate—" A vision of Homeland Security's labyrinthine organizational chart flashed across Sarah's consciousness. "Never mind. Go on."

"You have access to vast intelligence resources. Use them for this! Find out how these babies are getting into your country."

Sarah stared at her.

*Me conducting an ICE investigation? Phyllis Corbin would go ballistic.*

She kept that thought to herself.

"Tell me how you think this works—and why you're so sure these babies are being sent to America."

"The only way it can work—starting with a network of 'recruiters' in the field. Basically they are criminals—thugs and kidnappers, with female accomplices—fraud artists to be used as persuaders in cases where they think they can just buy the babies with promises of a better life. But then they would need a corrupt employee at the Tribunale per i Minorenni, the Juvenile Court in Palermo—"

"Carlotta Falcone."

"Correct. Then they would need to pay off one of the Immigration officials at your consulate in Naples, and also an Immigration officer at the receiving port of entry in the United States."

"A lot of hurdles right there. I don't see how—"

"There are no Immigration officers posted to the American Consulate in Palermo. In such cases, your State Department's procedure is to have the consul himself review the applications and make his recommendations. *In every case,* your consul has recommended approvals of these so-called legitimate adoptions."

Sarah's mind called up the vivid image of a certain lemon-sucking bureaucrat. "You're talking about Anthony Nicosia?"

"That's him. He's been sending the completed files to Naples for finalization and the necessary visas."

"How do you know all this?"

"As I said, the U.N. has its sources."

"That's not an answer."

"That's all I am permitted to give you right now. Depending on your assistance, I may be able to give you more in the future."

"Okay. Now . . . answer this. As I recall, any air passengers leaving Italy for destinations outside the EU must pass through Italian Immigration when they exit. How are these babies getting out of the country?"

"The usual procedure would be for the adoptive parents to fly out from the U.S. to collect their child. But when these parents depart with their babies, Italian Immigration records would show that they had only been in the country for a short stay. Immigration officers know that under Italian law, foreigners cannot adopt a child unless they have been legally resident in the country for a minimum of one year. This is because, in Italy, true intercountry adoption protocols require that the prospective parents foster the child under Juvenile Court supervision for at least twelve months. It's called *affidamento preadottivo*—pre-adoption placement. So even if the baby's papers have a proper Convention adoptee visa, if the new parents try to exit the country through normal channels, the stamps in their own passports would expose them."

"So, the question is, how are they doing it?"

"We believe someone in your Immigration service is helping these baby smugglers. You're an investigator. We're asking you to investigate."

Sarah was silent. Richter and her Vatican companion sat watching, unblinking, waiting for a reaction.

"You're saying all this, but you're not showing me any evidence."

"We have no access to U.S. Immigration records, but Gaetano has copies of two baptism certificates from earlier this year."

The priest retrieved a small satchel from under the drafting table. He opened it and handed Sarah two photocopied pages. Standing over her, he pointed to the parish name on the top document.

"The bishop of the diocese merged that parish with a neighboring parish back in 2008. This certificate should bear the new name. It was not an isolated mistake. As you see, those certificates are dated more than three months apart, and both contain the same error. And, I checked. There are no birth records for these children. None." He heaved a sigh as he resumed his seat. "There are more. I've seen them, but I was unable to make copies without causing suspicion."

"May I keep these?"

"Yes."

Sarah rose. "Is there anything else you wish to tell me?"

"That depends on whether you agree to assist," Richter replied.

"I need to think about it."

"Please do so. May I have a telephone number? A secure line where I may call you?"

"I'm carrying a U.S. government phone. No offense, but I can't give that number to someone I've just met. Let me look into what you've told me. If you or Gaetano will give me a number, I will call you."

"You will call either way?"

"I will."

Richter handed Sarah a scrap of paper. "It's a Swiss number. It will find me."

"I have a car," Gaetano said. "I'll drive you to the surface."

"What about you?" Sarah was looking at Richter. "Are you staying down here?"

"We should not be seen together." She indicated an old dial telephone mounted on the wall. "The mine manager will come for me."

As Sarah and the priest were leaving, she turned back. "You could have gone to the Guardia with this," she said to Richter. "Or taken it to our embassy in Rome."

"We don't know who to trust."

"There is one Guardia officer I know you can trust."

"Marco Sinatra."

"Yes."

"You may be right. I hope you are right. But the fact is, you have just arrived in Sicily. We think that means you are untainted. We have told you about a crime that touches your country's honor, so we hope you will agree to help us. Discreetly. Quietly. Without 'calling in the cavalry,' as some of your more heavy-handed countrymen might do."

Sarah couldn't help but smile at that final remark. "I've been known to complain about that myself."

# LISA

# 7

Of the Collier County sheriff's eight separate patrol areas, district 7 was not exactly a premier posting for an ambitious cop. Fortunately for Detective Scott Jardine, he was permanently attached to the Special Crimes Bureau over in Naples, and this assignment had only been temporary. But it just happened that on that day, in late March 2015, Jardine was sitting at his temporary desk at the Everglades substation finishing up the paperwork on a parental abduction file. The case had involved an American woman who'd been married to a French citizen. Entangled in a bitter divorce, she'd been faced with contested custody proceedings in the French courts. In a panic, she'd fled back to Florida with her young son. In responding to an Interpol Yellow Notice, the State Department had specifically requested assistance from state and local law enforcement in South Florida. Jardine had finally tracked the woman and child to Everglades City. What happened next would be up to the lawyers. As far as Jardine was concerned, the case was cleared and he was more than ready to move back to his office in Naples.

But when the district 7 deputy showed up at the substation with a distractingly attractive, disheveled woman who had just reported *herself* missing, Jardine's curiosity had been immediately aroused. He'd heard the radio call, and he'd watched through the window as the officer walked her in from the patrol car. Even on ill-fitting wedge sandals, she moved with sinuous grace. As he studied her now, sitting across from him, there was something of the wild about her—and it wasn't just the soiled dress and unkempt hair that gave that impression. Those dark, almond-shaped eyes, when they locked on his, were like searchlights. Minutes into their interview, he'd had the strange sensation that he was in the presence of some mysterious, subterranean intellect.

He was intrigued.

The woman was claiming she had amnesia; that she didn't know how she lost her memory; that until today she could only remember waking up on a gravel road somewhere out in the bush. But now, she told him, memories were coming back—memories from before that awakening—memories of houses and faces, of seaports and ships and cranes and containers.

Memories of a uniform.

Memories of the military, or maybe the police.

And . . . memories of Italy.

"Italy?"

*"Mi ricordo che parlo italiano."*

He stared at her.

She spelled it out. "I remember speaking Italian. I realize now I always remembered it, but there was no context. No reason to speak it."

Detective Jardine was mystified.

"I was living with that man who tried to drag me out of the store."

Jardine glanced at Deputy Newman's notes. "Roland Lewis."

"I also remember . . . when Roland found me, I'd been in some kind of car accident."

"The amnesia . . . how long ago are we talking about?"

"I'm not sure. I think a couple of months. We've been living out in the Everglades. Or maybe . . . is there a 'Big Cypress'?"

"It's a national preserve. Part of the 'Glades."

"Today was the first time I've been anywhere near people. He always locked me in a special room when he went to get supplies."

Jardine's antennae went up. "Locked you in a room?"

"He said it was for my own protection." She bit her lip. "I believed him."

"Protection? The cashier said that little fight you had only lasted a second. She told the deputy you dropped the guy with one kick."

"I guess."

"She said it was like something you'd see in a kung fu movie."

The woman was silent, her expression impenetrable.

"Based on that," he continued, "it doesn't sound like it'd be too easy for anyone to lock you in a room."

"He said it was my idea."

"Your idea?"

"He said I was his fiancée. He said when he found me, I was sitting in the middle of a road. I remember that. It was a gravel road. It was near where the car wreck was. He claimed it had happened more than once, me losing my memory. He said he was hiding me so I wouldn't end up in an asylum. For a while, I believed him. But now I think he just wanted . . . you know. To use me."

"For sex?"

"Yeah." Her voice turned cold. "He's going to pay for that."

"We'll see."

"You know what did it, Detective? What kept setting off the alarm bells in my head?"

"What?"

"Personality." She sat forward, eyes burning. "Character."

"Explain."

"I reasoned it out. If you lose your memory . . . if you can't remember anything about your past, even your own name, that shouldn't mean you lose your personality. I mean, lose who you are . . . the kind of person you are."

"Makes a kind of sense."

"He kept telling me I was his fiancée. But after a while, after living with him out there, I started monitoring my own behavior. My thoughts. My reactions. And I began to wonder . . ."

Jardine got it. "You began to wonder how—"

"I began to wonder how a personality like mine *would ever agree* to marry a personality like his."

*This woman is smart,* Jardine thought.

"How much do you remember about your past?" he asked. "I mean, right now? I can tell you're not from around here. Your accent. Any idea where you're from?"

"Somewhere up north. I remember the leaves changing color in the fall. But that was when I was young. I remember an older woman looking after me. I remember calling her Nonna. That's what Italian kids call their grandmas. My past . . . it comes back in flashes, little pieces . . . you know, like a TV screen when the signal gets disrupted."

"Pixels."

"Yeah. But you know, I think I was . . ."

"What?"

"Might have been the navy, somewhere around here, but . . ." She was visibly struggling. "You know, I'm almost sure I was some kind of cop."

"This isn't making a lot of sense."

"I know I was someone else. Not some half-mental bimbo, living in the bush, engaged to that creep. I was definitely someone else. Some*thing* else. I need you to help me find out who I am."

"The deputy says you weren't carrying any ID."

"No. I don't even own a purse. Roland told me my name was Lisa. Lisa Green. But that never sounded right."

"Middle name?"

"He said 'May.'"

"So . . . Lisa May Green?"

"Yeah."

"Date of birth?"

"No idea."

"Be straight with me, Miss Green. Are you on drugs?"

"Not now. He had me on pills back at the beginning. I don't know what they were. Some kind of tranquilizer."

"Well, let's see what we can find out. Your friend Mr. Lewis isn't talking."

"Not my friend."

"I get it. The thing is, even though you demolished his knee, he refuses to press charges. Maybe that's understandable, based on what you've told me. The owner of the store doesn't want to press charges either. I guess she was impressed by her cashier's story. So, technically, you're free to go. On the other hand—"

"I don't want to go. I want to know who I am." The uninflected tone, the searchlight eyes—Jardine didn't know what to make of this woman.

"If you consent, I can take your fingerprints."

"Do it."

Jardine live-scanned her prints. He fetched her some coffee and fed the prints into the NCIC system. While he was waiting, he also ran "Lisa May Green DOB u/k." There were a few hits on the name—but the only one that matched the woman's apparent age was a Fort Myers woman who had died in a car accident three years ago.

After several minutes, there was a hit on the prints.

They matched a Customs officer who had gone missing in February.

The officer's name was Sarah Jane Lockhart.

But there was more.

While the detective was pondering this unsettling development, Lieutenant Powell, district 7's OIC, interrupted him. "Call for you, Jardine."

"Who is it?"

"FBI."

Jardine returned to his desk.

"You mentioned a car wreck. Where was that?"

"I don't know. When we left this morning, Roland told me we were driving on something called Loop Road. Does that mean anything?"

It did mean something. In early February, one of Jardine's fellow detectives had been called to investigate a collision at mile 7 on County Road 94. The road was a twenty-four-mile-long track through Big Cypress National Preserve known locally as Loop Road. A few miles of it were paved, but most of it was gravel, dirt, and potholes. Normally a vehicle accident would be something for the traffic unit, but this one had been different. An old jeep and a panel van had collided head-on and at high speed. No air bags, and no seat belts. Three dead, and no survivors. All of the deceased had been identified. The driver of the jeep was a local antigovernment redneck, well-known to the police. The vehicles had caught fire, and the van had been gutted so thoroughly that it eventually required a DNA database search to identify the other two bodies. They were both from up north, either New York or New Jersey, as Jardine recalled. The interesting thing was that they were reputed Mafia associates.

Jardine filed that last thought away for follow-up.

"You were right, by the way," he told her. "About your background."

"I'm a cop?"

"Close as . . . Your name is Sarah Jane Lockhart. You were a Customs officer in Miami. The report says you disappeared right after an overseas operation. And it says something else. Something I've never seen before."

"What?"

"Everything I've just said is redlined, and it came with a notice: '*Restricted—no media release. Report any contact to . . .*' No name. Just a phone number in D.C."

He let that sink in, watching her for a reaction. But she just stared into the distance, her expression concentrated, as if racking her brain for an explanation of what he'd just said.

After a few seconds, she turned back to him. "'Lockhart.' That sounds almost familiar." She studied his face. "Something's wrong. What is it?"

Apparently she was better at reading faces than he was.

"At first, you were presumed dead."

"At first?"

"You went missing on February sixth of this year. But on February twelfth, the Palm Beach Police issued a warrant for your arrest."

"Palm Beach? *Arrest for what?*"

Finally, a reaction.

Jardine took a deep breath before replying. "Two counts of first-degree murder, and one count of kidnapping."

The searchlights locked on him. "That can't be."

"You're the primary suspect in the murders of Kenneth and Darlene Eden of Palm Beach, and the possible kidnapping of a baby. I guess because of the kidnapping, and because you're a federal law enforcement officer accused of serious crimes, the FBI's involved. But an alarm must have gone off when I ran your prints, because they called me first. Agents are on their way."

"I didn't kill anyone." Sarah Lockhart spoke slowly, pronouncing every syllable. "And I sure as hell didn't kidnap a baby! And what does that mean—*possible* kidnapping?"

"I don't know." He rose from his chair. "I plan to check on that." He nodded to the female deputy he had earlier alerted to wait nearby. "Obviously we're going to be speaking with your Mr. Lewis. Meanwhile, I'm sorry, Ms. Lockhart, but . . ."

The substation had a single holding cell. It was unoccupied. Jardine locked her in, and the female deputy remained to keep an eye on her.

Nothing about this case made sense, Scott Jardine told himself, and he was determined to get to the bottom of it.

Lieutenant Powell was in his office. Jardine quickly briefed him. "Belrose and I want to talk to this Lewis guy. He's at Community, in Naples. Do you mind calling the boss and bringing him up to speed?"

"No problem. You go."

# 8

Jardine and his partner, Eric Belrose, headed for Naples Community Hospital, where Roland Lewis had been sent by ambulance. Belrose had accompanied Jardine when he'd doorstepped the woman who had abducted her kid from France. And it was a good thing he had, because the lady had become pretty hysterical during their interview. She was terrified they'd come to take her boy away, and it had taken some time to explain that they had only been assigned to locate her and the child. What happened next was for her own lawyer, the State Department, and the French authorities to sort out. Looking back, it probably would have been better to have had a female officer with them, but Eric had been a good fit because his grandfather had been a French *notaire,* he'd spent several summers in France when he was growing up, and he actually knew a bit about French legal procedure. He had handled the crisis well and Jardine was grateful for that.

Rolling west on the Tamiami Trail, Belrose braked for an otter that was humping its way across the highway from one swampy strand to another. "Now there's something you don't see every day," he commented as he flicked on their emergency lights to alert an oncoming car.

"What?" Jardine looked up from searching the contact list in his phone. "Oh, an otter."

"Yeah. About as rare as a panther these days. Haven't seen one of them in years." Belrose was a dedicated outdoorsman whose brother ran a swamp buggy tour outfit.

"Saw one today," Jardine said.

"Where?"

"She's sitting in our holding cell."

"Like that, huh?"

"Wait till you meet her." Belrose had been in a back office, working on another file, while Jardine was dealing with Sarah Lockhart.

Jardine dialed his phone.

"Who're you calling?"

"Mark Clifford."

Clifford was the detective who had investigated the collision on Loop Road. When he answered, Jardine skipped the small talk and got to the point.

"Remember that two-car wreck you attended on the Loop back in February?"

"Yeah. What about it?"

"I want you to pull the file. I'll be in later today to take a look at it."

"Why?"

"I might have something."

"What?"

"Maybe a passenger in the back of the van."

"The M.E. would've found something."

"Maybe he wasn't looking in the right place."

"What are you getting at?"

"Maybe someone *was* in the back of that van . . . someone who got out before the wreck went up in flames."

"No sign of anyone else at the scene."

"Did you actually look?"

Silence.

"Did you check the road surface in each direction?" Accusation crept into Jardine's voice. "Did you look for footprints? A trail of blood? Search the bush? Anything like that?"

"No." Clifford sensed he might have missed something, and now his back was up. "There was no reason to! Anyway, by the time I got there, a half dozen traffic cops had walked all over the scene."

"Well, I'd like to see the file anyway!" Jardine snapped.

"Help yourself! I'll leave it on my desk."

"Thanks." With an impatient stab of his finger, Jardine ended the call.

"What's with you, Scottie?" Belrose asked. "That didn't sound like you."

Jardine sighed. "I know. I'll apologize when I see him."

"Panther lady really got to you, huh?"

"Yeah. Guess she did."

He settled back in his seat.

To think.

When the detectives arrived at the hospital, Roland Lewis was about to be released. Jardine and Belrose found him in the ER, sitting in a wheelchair next to a bed. His left leg wasn't plastered, but judging from the bulge in his jeans, it was wrapped up pretty thoroughly. A pair of crutches was leaning nearby.

"They're letting you go already?" Jardine asked, after they'd introduced themselves. "I guess it wasn't as bad as the witnesses said."

"Depends on yer point 'a view," Lewis growled.

"We hear you don't want to press charges."

"That's right."

"Why is that?"

"My decision."

"And . . . your reason for that decision?"

"My decision," Lewis repeated.

"Okay. But maybe she wants to press charges. We hear you started the fight."

"She say that?"

"No. But the cashier saw it all."

Silence.

"Okay. What about this woman? Lisa Green? What is she to you?"

"Talk to her."

"We have. Looks like you might have a problem."

"Did she file any kinda complaint against me?"

"No."

"Am I under arrest?"

"No."

"So, end 'a discussion. Why don't you guys leave me alone?"

"How're you getting home?"

"I was just gonna call someone when you showed up."

"We can give you a lift as far as Everglades City, if you don't mind a quick detour on the way."

"What kinda detour?"

"I just need to pick up a file."

"Okay. Thanks."

They loaded Lewis and his crutches into the back of their unit and made a side trip to the sheriff's main office. Belrose stayed with Lewis while Jardine went in. Mark Clifford was nowhere to be seen, but the file was sitting on his desk.

Within minutes, they were back on the road.

For a while, they rode in silence. Jardine was doing a quick scan of the traffic file, but he spotted nothing beyond what he already knew. He set it aside for a careful read-through later.

He called back to Lewis. "Mind if I ask you something about Lisa Green?"

"What about her?"

"According to police records, a woman from Fort Myers named Lisa May Green died in a car accident three years ago."

Silence.

"Old flame of yours?"

A beat.

"I thought you said I wasn't under arrest."

"That's right. You're not."

"Then why the questions? Can't two women have the same name?"

"Sure. Let's just say you might be a person of interest in our investigation. We thought you'd want to cooperate with us up front and clear yourself."

"Clear myself of what?"

"Aiding and abetting a wanted fugitive."

"Fugitive? Who's a fugitive?"

"Looks like Lisa Green is."

"What's she wanted for?"

"Some heavy stuff. But here's an interesting thought: you might be the first person in the history of the State of Florida to be convicted of false imprisonment of a federal fugitive. How does that sound?"

Roland Lewis didn't say another word for the rest of the trip.

They made the turn onto Route 29 and headed south, toward Everglades City.

"Where do you want to be dropped off?" Belrose asked Lewis.

"Right Choice market."

"Hoping for a rematch, huh?" Jardine interjected. "I'd love to see that."

"My truck's there," Lewis muttered, clearly resenting Jardine's mockery.

When they pulled up in front of the supermarket, Jardine got out, opened the rear door, and helped Lewis out of the car. As he passed him his crutches, he said, "About that knee . . ."

"What about it?"

"How far do you have to drive?"

"A few miles."

"Your friend Lisa said you live somewhere down Loop Road."

"Yeah."

"How far down?"

"'Bout mile 8."

"That's over thirty miles from here. Your truck's an automatic?"

"Manual. Why?"

"Are you kidding? How're you going to drive it safely with your leg like that?"

"Not a problem."

"Sorry. Big problem."

"Meaning?"

"Meaning if you drive it now, my partner and I will have to report you as an unsafe driver. The last thing you need is a run-in with Highway Patrol. You'd better get it towed."

Jardine smiled as they drove away, leaving Roland Lewis staring after them.

# 9

"*Why didn't you call?*"

Jardine was furious.

While he and Belrose had been playing footsie with Roland Lewis, he'd lost his prisoner.

Unknown to him, back in the holding cell at the substation, a young woman's memories had been steadily filtering back. Slowly at first, then with gathering momentum, and finally in a dizzying cataract of sound and sensation and image, Sarah Lockhart had reentered her life.

When Jardine and Belrose returned to the office, they discovered that Sarah had been taken to the hospital.

"We were *at* the hospital!" Jardine was right in the female deputy's face. "Why the hell didn't you call us?"

"No, you weren't."

"Weren't what?"

"At the hospital. They took her to Regional."

"That's not an answer! What happened?"

"I went to the restroom. When I got back she was lying on the floor, covered in vomit. She was unconscious!"

"Okay. So you called an ambulance. But you didn't call us?"

"We didn't wait for the ambulance. She'd had some kind of seizure. She'd not only puked, she'd pissed herself. Evans and Fisk loaded her into the back of a unit and they met the ambulance on the way. It's okay, Scott.

She's under guard. The feds called again, and we directed them there. They'll take custody when she's released."

She still hadn't answered his simple question—*why hadn't she called him?* Exasperated, Jardine let it go.

"Did the lieutenant brief the boss?"

"Yes."

There was something very wrong with all this.

Something Jardine just wasn't ready to accept.

Belrose had known his partner for a long time, and he read his expression. "Want to head back to town, Scottie?"

"Definitely."

Striding toward their car, Jardine held out his hand for the keys. "I'll drive."

When they pulled out onto US 41, he said, "Lights."

Belrose activated their emergency lights, and they covered the next twenty-eight miles in twenty-five minutes.


At Physicians Regional Hospital in Naples, the paramedics had transferred Sarah Lockhart from the gurney to a bed in the ER. As they left, a severe-looking nurse appeared through the curtain. Sarah was lying perfectly still, apparently conscious, but nonreactive. As the woman took Sarah's vitals, her expression migrated from mild puzzlement to quizzical. She left the cubicle, drawing the curtain behind her, and marched off.

Sarah guessed she was looking for a doctor.

A doctor who would quickly expose her.

*Time to go.*

She rose to a sitting position and crawled to the end of the bed. She peeked out through the curtain. The sheriff's car that had transported her for the first part of the trip had kept pace after she'd been transferred to the ambulance, following it to the hospital. One of the deputies was still in the reception area, talking with a clerk. More like flirting with her, judging from the deputy's body language. The other cop was nowhere in sight, and Sarah's nurse had vanished around a corner.

She launched herself off the bed, scooped up her sandals, and ducked out through the curtain. She strode purposefully to the nurse's station. It was unoccupied. Her eyes swept the scattered clutter on the long desk. She spotted a set of keys.

A set of keys that included a key fob for a vehicle.

She snatched them and moved away quickly, putting distance between herself and the ER's main reception area. As she'd hoped, the row of examination alcoves led to an interior door. Some were occupied, but their curtains were drawn. When she reached the door, she knuckled a round steel plate to trigger the automatic door opener and slipped through the widening gap. She quickly pulled on her shoes. It took a few more minutes and one wrong turn for her to find her way out of the building. She circled the complex. When she located the staff parking area, she strolled through the ranks of vehicles, pressing the key fob at intervals. She was aware that there were probably security cameras trained on the staff parking lot. Any facility that employed night shift staff would routinely install such equipment. Nevertheless, she was confident she'd have enough lead time to complete the first part of her plan.

She noticed a Chevy Malibu's signal lamps flashing.

In less than a minute she was out of the parking lot and heading for US 41.

Seven minutes before they arrived at the hospital, Jardine got a call on his cell.

"Scott, this is Larry at dispatch."

Larry McClure was dayshift supervisor in the communications center.

Jardine had a sudden uneasy feeling. "Hi, Larry. What's up?"

"Thought I'd call you on your cell so you wouldn't hear it first on the air."

"What are you talking about?"

"Your prisoner . . . that Lockhart woman. She's gone."

"What do you mean, 'gone'?"

"I mean, vanished. Ducked out of the hospital. Gone."

*"What the hell?"*

"Yeah, I know. Those two deputies are gonna be in deep shit with the boss."

"They're in deep shit with me! But that's for later. Right now, we've got to find her."

"Bolo's going out in five seconds, but just thought you'd want to hear it from me first."

"Yeah. Thanks, Larry." He ended the call.

"More trouble?" Belrose asked.

"Big time."

While Jardine was learning that his enigmatic detainee, Sarah Jane Lockhart—wanted murderer, wanted kidnapper, and alleged amnesiac— had escaped custody, he had no idea that she had already passed him, heading east. When his police unit had appeared in the oncoming lane, grill lights flashing, she had dutifully slowed the Malibu and edged it onto the shoulder. It wasn't until forty minutes after his arrival at the hospital that Jardine learned about the stolen car. The hospital's security cameras had shown the woman leaving the ER, moving through the hospital's corridors, and out the main doors. On the film, she moved lithely and appeared fully alert. It was obvious that the whole "seizure" thing had just been an elaborate ruse. But for some reason, there were no security cameras focused on the nursing station, and the nurse who owned the Chevy had been so busy with a cardiac patient and his distraught family that she hadn't noticed her keys were missing.

Two and a half miles east of the Everglades City turnoff, Sarah spied the entrance to the Big Cypress Swamp Welcome Center. She'd noticed it that morning on her trip into town with Roland. She swung into the lot, parked, and strolled inside. It was a modern facility, with eye-catching exhibits, racks of publications, and a small souvenir shop. A fresh-faced young National Parks Service staffer was manning an information booth. The last thing Sarah needed was to be drawn into a conversation with anyone—especially while attired in vomit- and urine-stained clothing that was bound to draw unwelcome attention. She sidestepped out of the parks officer's line of sight and pretended to be engrossed in a collection of botanical specimens in a glassed-in display. Intermittently, her eyes scanned the racks of leaflets on either side of her position. She spotted what she was looking for on a turnstile of free brochures.

Back in the car, she unfolded it. As she'd hoped, it included a map of the preserve. It took her only a few seconds to spot Loop Road. Judging from the map's scale, the turnoff was roughly fifteen miles to the east at a junction called Monroe Station.

She drove on.

Passing a sign on the highway that read: MONROE STATION BACKCOUNTRY ACCESS PARKING 1/4 MILE, Sarah made the turn. She passed what appeared to be a derelict roadhouse and a public restroom and headed down a narrow, gravel road that ran dead south between an ever-higher border of cypress and sabal palms. Watching the odometer, and relying on memory—a point of no small irony, she remarked to herself—she drove fast for the first six miles, kicking up a plume of dust that obscured the road behind. When she hit the seventh mile, she slowed, watching for the secondary turnoff to the cabin. As she rolled along, she noticed a vehicle approaching from the other direction. It was a tow truck.

The driver gave her a friendly wave as he passed.

Another mile and the road took a bend to the left. And there it was: the gate with the misspelled sign.

She kept going for another quarter mile, looking for somewhere to pull off the road. She came to a widened stretch beside the next watercourse to the south. A sign read: SWEETWATER STRAND. The cypress trees that leaned over the stream were larger than most, bedecked in Spanish moss and thickly surrounded by ferns.

She left the car and walked back.

When she reached the gate, she slid around one of the rotting end posts that supported it and started up the driveway. Thick vegetation pressed in from both sides, but Sarah stayed close to one edge in case she needed to take cover. When she reached the clearing, she stepped into the brush and stood behind a tree, watching.

Thinking Detective Jardine might have anticipated her next move, she had half-expected to see a sheriff's car. But the only vehicle in sight was Roland's truck.

She waited, watching the windows for movement.

Minutes passed—five minutes . . . ten minutes. A horsefly attacked her arm. She pulled it off and crushed it against the tree.

She waited.

The first warning of movement was the sudden splash of daylight that appeared through the kitchen window. The front door, located on the far side of the cabin, had just been opened.

Had he just entered? Or had he just left?

In seconds, she had the answer.

He appeared around the near corner, leaning on crutches. He hobbled across the clearing, angling toward a pile of cut tree branches that lay against the brush about fifty feet from Sarah's position. Leaning and huffing, he yanked the branches aside, exposing the entrance to a forest trail.

Sarah knew that trail. A month or so earlier, when Roland thought she was napping, he'd slipped away. The snick of the closing front door had roused her from her doze. She spotted him through a window just as he disappeared into the woods. Curious, she had followed. A winding path led to a small clearing next to a deep section of Clearwater Strand. A plywood shed sat at the water's edge. The structure appeared to be considerably newer than their cabin. As Sarah emerged from the wood, Roland was in the act of locking the shed door. He herded her back to the cabin, explaining that the building housed the wellhead for their water supply and he'd just been checking the pump. The look on his face had told her that wasn't the whole story. But she'd had enough on her mind and she hadn't probed further.

Today, she followed him again. As he inched along on the crutches, she trailed behind, carefully and silently, staying well back. When the path grew brighter ahead, she stopped and waited, mentally timing his progress across the clearing to the shed.

Then she moved again. When she reached the end of the trail, he was nowhere to be seen.

Fifty feet away, the door of the shed stood open.

She moved in.

She stepped through the door into the windowless murk of the shed.

Roland was waiting. He was leaning on a single crutch. "Figured you'd be back," he said with a warped smile.

He had a semiautomatic pointed at her chest.

# 10

Sarah took a step closer.

"Who did you figure would be back, Roland? Lisa . . . or me?"

"Don't matter. Now I get to finish the job."

She knew that smug tone. He wouldn't pull the trigger until he'd proven to her how smart he was.

She risked another step.

"What job is that?"

"Turning you into soup." He waved the gun at a tall, stainless steel tank sitting on bricks in a corner. Next to it was a propane tank, its pressure line connected to a ring burner. A thick pipe with an in-line valve led from the bottom of the vat and out through the wall of the shed. "Sucker holds eight hundred gallons. Kept putting it off. Finding you out there, 'n those guys that hired me all burnt up. Looked like a win-win. Stupid me. Shoulda got on with the job." He smirked. "Thing is, the fuckin' was just too sweet."

Stepping closer, as Sarah had done, would have signaled her intentions to anyone who'd been properly trained. But lack of training was just another entry on Roland Lewis's long list of deficits. In one flash of movement, his wrist was an excruciating ruin and Sarah was holding the gun. She kicked his crutch out from under him and he went down. She trained the pistol on his groin.

"Yeah, stupid you."

She fired.

Roland bellowed with terror.

The 9mm slug blew a hole in the wooden floor between his legs, less than an inch from his crotch. Eyes bulging, he clawed at his pants, searching for blood.

She kneeled and jammed the muzzle of the gun against his testicles. "This one won't miss." Her voice was hard, her eyes obsidian.

"What do you want?" he croaked.

"Start with who hired you."

"I don't know their names!" She jammed the gun harder. "I swear! The Cubans came . . . said they'd subbed me out. No names, no questions. Paid me up front. Said two guys would bring a package the next night. Hadta bin them killed in that wreck you was in!"

"Cubans? You mean the Marielitos?"

"Yeah."

"You work for them?" Her eyes cut to the vat. "Doing this?"

"Yeah. Ain't pretty, but it pays the bills."

Sarah stood up. She tucked the gun into her belt.

Roland's rigid frame slumped with relief.

But not for long.


Roland was alive, but after the beating she'd just given him, he was in pretty bad shape.

She patted him down and took his phone and his wallet.

The next task was a bit tougher. There were several loops of rope hanging on the wall of the shed. She selected one of the longer ones, tied his ankles together, and then dragged him out of the shed and back up the trail to the cabin. She had to stop a few times to clear clothing snagged on exposed roots, but within fifteen minutes she had Roland Lewis's groaning frame through the door of the cabin. She dragged him straight to the safe room and locked him in.

*First things first . . .*

She stripped off her foul-smelling clothes and treated herself to a long shower. After she dried off, she picked through the single drawer of clothing she'd been wearing for the past several weeks. Some of the garments had been produced out of a battered suitcase that Roland claimed was the only one they'd had time to pack before he saved her from the shrinks. When she'd noticed they were a size too large, he'd said she'd lost weight after she got sick. Other clothes Roland had found for her during his forays into town. She'd been happy enough to receive them at the time, but recalling their condition when he'd produced them, she wondered if he'd stolen them from some charity group's collection bin.

Once she was dressed, she emptied all of the cash from Roland's wallet and pocketed his phone. Then she picked up his gun.

It was a collector's item—a Beretta M1934.

She'd recognized the weapon immediately when he pointed it at her. Her grandmother had owned one.

*Nonna. Thank God you're not alive to see all this.*

Sarah had no intention of taking the pistol with her. It was most likely stolen, and not knowing if it was associated with serious crimes, she couldn't take the chance of a ballistic match.

So she had two choices: toss it into the swamp, or leave it on the table to be found.

She split the decision.

She cleared the chamber, ejected the magazine and emptied it of cartridges. She pocketed the rounds. Then she wiped her prints off both the gun's frame and its magazine. Her prints might be all over the cabin, but there was no way she was leaving them on this suspect gun. She left it and the magazine on the kitchen table, along with the key to the safe room. She was tempted to leave Jardine a note, but then she had a better idea.

She'd call him.

She threw the ammo in the swamp as she walked back to her car.

Before she pulled away, she checked the map. It was about eight miles back to US 41 if she retraced her route, or seventeen miles through the backcountry if she kept going and intersected the highway farther east. One way was faster, but the other was less visible.

She chose the long way.

For the next forty minutes, she drove along the gravel track without seeing another vehicle. She switched on Roland's phone. She'd made it a point over the last few weeks to watch him whenever he opened it to play his incessant video games, so she'd figured out his passcode. For most of the drive, the phone was telling her there was no signal, but toward the end of the run, not long after the gravel turned back to pavement, the screen showed a few bars of service.

She pulled over, searched online to find the landline number for the Everglades substation, and made the call.

A bored voice told her Detective Jardine wasn't available.

"Can I take a message?"

"Tell him if he wants to speak to Sarah Lockhart, he can phone this number."

"What number is that, ma'am?" The voice didn't sound bored anymore.

"It's on the screen in front of you. Tell Jardine he's got five minutes."

Roland's phone rang in three minutes.

"Sarah?"

"Oh, we're on a first name basis now? Okay, Scott. Listen to me. I didn't kill those people."

"I believe you. Where are you?"

"Send an ambulance to Roland's place."

"Sarah!"

"He tried to kill me. I'll send you a full statement later."

"And that seizure of yours? What was—?"

"Make the call, Scott!"

Her tone of authority startled him. He dropped the phone, and she heard him giving quick instructions to another officer to dispatch an ambulance and a police unit.

He came back on the line. "The seizure? You faked it?"

"My grandmother fought in the Italian Resistance. She always said it was easier to escape from a fascist hospital than it was from a fascist jail, and the fastest way to get moved to a hospital was to frighten the guards."

"Your grandmother. So your memory's back?"

"Yes. And now I'm going to put it to use." She paused. "There's something you should know. When your deputies get to that cabin, they're going to find a Beretta pistol on the table. You might want to run it for a ballistics match."

"Match to what?"

"I don't know. But if Roland had it, it's probably been used in a felony. Oh, and by the way, I locked him in the safe room. The key's on the table next to the gun. Now, there's something else. *L'urna della morte.*"

"What?"

"The urn of death. There's a trail that leads to the water, downstream from the cabin. It starts on the southeast edge of the clearing—I marked the entrance with Roland's crutches. The trail leads to a shed on the riverbank. In that shed is a stainless steel vat. I drained it enough so you can see the bottom. Tell your people to take a look."

"What are you saying?"

"I'm saying I was going to be next. The only thing that saved me was my memory loss and that bastard's sick fantasies. By the way, he won't be using that sorry dick of his for a while."

"What did you do?"

"Taught him a lesson."

"Sarah, turn yourself in! Let me help you! That car wreck! You were probably kidnapped yourself, locked in the back of that van! The whole thing stinks of frame-up. Let me help you prove it!"

"It was more than a frame-up, Scott. I need to do this myself and I can't do it from a jail cell. You're a county cop. You won't get anywhere if you try to mess with the feds. But there is one thing you can do for me."

"What's that?"

"Those murders I'm accused of . . . find out if the detectives found a baby cam."

"What?"

"A video monitor. People use them to keep an eye on their baby when they're out of the room. I want to know if they found one in the nursery at the murdered couple's house."

"Are you serious?"

"Yes. Goodbye, Scott. And thank you."

"For what?"

"For helping me get my life back."

She ended the call. She got out and tossed the phone into a slough that bordered the road.

She got back behind the wheel and drove on.

She had already planned her next move.

# 11

Jardine and Belrose arrived at Roland Lewis's cabin ten minutes after Deputy Newman had used a bolt cutter on the chain at the gate and waved the ambulance in. After knocking on the door and receiving no answer, Newman and the paramedics had entered. Jardine had told the deputy about the locked room and the key on the table. They found Roland Lewis in the safe room, lying on the cot, covered in dirt, his face bleeding and swollen.

Sarah Lockhart had laid a royal beating on him.

When Jardine arrived, one of the EMTs said, "I'm not a doctor, Detective, but I'd say this guy won't be seeing out of his left eye for a while. And you should see his nuts."

"I'll pass. What about them?"

"Black and blue, and swollen like you wouldn't believe."

Jardine had a hard time feeling sorry for the creep.

Newman pointed out the Beretta and its empty magazine lying on the table, along with Lewis's empty wallet. Jardine took a quick look around while the paramedics were getting Lewis ready for transport, but he found little of evidentiary value. There were a few smears of blood on the floor between the front door and the safe room, but no visible signs of a struggle. The only indication that a female had ever lived in the cabin was the small pile of women's clothing on the bed and the empty dresser drawer sitting next to it.

As soon as they'd arrived, Belrose had located the trailhead marked by Lewis's crutches and headed down the path behind it. As the ambulance pulled away, he appeared at the cabin door.

"Scottie, we need the crime scene guys out here."

"What'd you find?"

"That shed by the river . . . that vat she told you about . . . it's there. Stinks to high heaven, and there's a bunch of teeth lying at the bottom. Gotta be a few hundred of 'em."

"Teeth? *Human* teeth?"

"Pretty sure."

"Show me."

Belrose led him across the clearing. "See the scrape mark?" He pointed to an intermittent string of furrows in the gravel and across the patchy grass. "They run all the way up the trail. Looks to me like she took him out down at the shed and dragged him up to the cabin."

They arrived at the shed. The door was wide open. Jardine immediately noticed the bullet hole in the wooden flooring and a couple of sprays of blood on one wall.

"Think you're right. The fight started here."

"I doubt it was a fight. Your panther lady's dangerous."

Jardine tugged a pair of latex gloves out of his pocket. He pulled them on and then lifted the lid of the huge stainless steel vat that sat in the corner of the shed. The smell from within made him recoil. Belrose was right—it was noxious. He couldn't quite place it. It was something like a cross between toilet cleaner and a slaughterhouse he'd once visited.

Belrose handed him a Maglite. Shining it downward, he craned to look.

It was just as his partner had described—a mass of discolored teeth, lying in an inch of milky liquid at the bottom of the vessel.

He dropped the lid and backed away.

"My guess . . . this guy's been dissolving bodies in acid and dumping them into the river," Belrose ventured.

"He's a fucking *pozole* man."

"*Pozole?*" Belrose was not only mystified by the word, but startled to hear Jardine use the f-word. Jardine seldom swore like that.

"It's a kind of Mexican soup. That's what the drug cartels call it. Great way to make their rivals disappear. They have guys who specialize in it."

"So you're saying the only thing that saved that lady from an acid bath was this guy taking advantage of her amnesia so he could screw her?"

"Yeah. Looks like that."

"Then if she hadn't done that number on him, I mighta done it myself."

# SARAH

# 12

The Tribunale per i Minorenni in Palermo was located on Via Principe di Palagonia. Sarah had figured that the best time to stake out the court building would be on a Friday afternoon, and her instincts paid off. At precisely 4:30 P.M., she spotted Carlotta Falcone among a mob of court officials spilling out the main door. She almost missed her. Her target was a string bean of a woman, a dark-eyed brunette with narrow, precise features, angling through the crowd. The only photograph Sarah had to identify her had been secured with Marco's help. She'd persuaded him to pull up Carlotta Falcone's Transport Ministry driver's license file, while at the same time managing to avoid giving a straight answer to his curious questions.

She'd enlisted Marco's help right after she'd called the Swiss number Renate Richter had given her. After a few odd-sounding clicks, the line had rung once.

"This is Renate."

"This is Sarah. I'm in."

"Very good. I will tell Gaetano. How will you begin?"

"With Falcone."

Sarah had told her Italian team she had official business in Palermo— an explanation for her absence that, while not a straight-out lie, was not the truth, either. Her activities in Palermo were not exactly "official," although they had the potential to become so.

She had expected to follow Falcone on foot, but was caught off guard when the woman stepped into a waiting taxi.

Caught off guard, yes, but not flat-footed. Sarah had positioned herself on a bench across the street. A dozen feet away, parked behind a sidewalk newsstand, was her rented Vespa. She pulled on her helmet, fired up the scooter, and slid into traffic. Keeping a few cars between her and Falcone's taxi, she followed the vehicle as it worked its way north on Via Palagonia, and then swung east on Via Principe di Paterno. As each succeeding intersection rolled by, it crossed her mind that the cab was heading in the general direction of the U.S. Consulate. It wasn't until the vehicle circumnavigated a final block and pulled to the curb on Via Vaccarini that she realized that was exactly where Carlotta Falcone was heading.

On reflection, she wasn't really surprised. As Renate Richter had said, in every suspect case, Consul Nicosia had recommended approvals of the adoptions and issuance of the required visas. Sarah had already noticed that Falcone was carrying a messenger bag along with her purse. She idled her scooter past the taxi just as the woman stepped out. She took a good look at the bag. Its bulk and the way it hung heavily from the woman's shoulder suggested that it contained papers.

*This particular Juvenile Court file clerk must be paid pretty well,* Sarah thought grimly, because Carlotta Falcone's calfskin bag bore the logo of a world-famous designer. On Worth Avenue or Rodeo Drive, that particular bag would sell for over five thousand dollars.

Unless, of course, it was a knockoff.

Life was filled with little ironies.

As she rolled on to the next intersection, Sarah watched Falcone in her side mirror. She saw her stride directly to the main door of the consulate building and enter.

She pulled over, dismounted, and walked her Vespa across to the broad median that, inexplicably, divided the two sets of northbound lanes of Via Marchese di Villabianca. After parking the scooter under a tree near a bus shelter, she took off her helmet and sat on the bench to wait.

She didn't wait long.

Falcone reappeared on the sidewalk in less than ten minutes. She turned west, crossed Via Villabianca on the same crosswalk Sarah had just used, strode past her without a glance, and positioned herself at the curb. She was either waiting for a prearranged ride or planning to hail another taxi. She was still carrying the messenger bag, but now it hung loosely on her shoulder.

With her target standing less than ten feet away, and no one else within earshot, Sarah decided on a move she hadn't planned.

She stood up.

"Carlotta Falcone."

The woman spun around, her facial expression a muddle of puzzlement and fear.

"How do you know my name? Who are you?"

As a test, Sarah replied in English. "I'm the person who knows what you have just done. And I am the person who will stop you."

Carlotta Falcone went pale. She turned and fled into the traffic. Tires screeched and horns blared as she weaved across the thoroughfare and disappeared into the streets beyond.

Sarah didn't attempt to follow. She wasn't concerned that she'd lose track of her quarry. She already knew where she lived.

And in that short exchange, she had established two things: that Carlotta Falcone understood English, and that she was unquestionably guilty of something.

The address on Carlotta Falcone's driver's license was an apartment building off Via Torremuzza, in the historic Arab section of Palermo known as La Kalsa. Although still showing signs of wartime bombing, with some streets marred by peeling doors, grubby staircases that led nowhere, and the acrid smell of rotting masonry, the entire quarter was in the midst of an intensive revitalization program. After decades of neglect by Mafia-influenced city administrators, honest and imaginative investors had finally gained traction. Over the last few years, La Kalsa had been slowly transformed into a haven for urbane residents and popular wine bars.

*I suppose the hip address goes with the five-thousand-dollar bag.*

Sarah completed her survey of the rows of wrought iron balconies behind the screen of cotton trees that lined the street front. Lights were on in most of the apartments, and the faint odor of frying oil drifted on the still air. Nevertheless, she doubted that Falcone had made her way home in the fourteen minutes it had taken Sarah to ride her Vespa to this location. She located an observation spot in Piazza della Kalsa, the small park across the street from the apartment building, and settled down to watch.

This time it was a long wait.

It was nearly eleven when a taxi pulled up in front of the apartment block. Sarah spotted her target when the driver turned on his interior light to make change. A minute later, when she opened the door to her building, Sarah silently stepped in behind her.

"It was stupid of you to run," she said in Italian, as the door clicked shut. "You could have been hit by a car."

Carlotta Falcone's features went pale. Her body swayed. Sarah caught her just before she collapsed. Her breath smelled of wine. Sarah kept a grip on one of her bony arms while she scanned the post boxes on the wall of the tiny foyer. "Number 11. I have a few questions. Shall we go?" Trembling, Falcone directed her toward a flight of steps. They climbed to the next floor and treaded along a narrow passageway.

Falcone finally spoke. "Who are you?"

"My name is Sarah Lockhart. I'm a United States Customs officer."

"United States? How can you be . . . here?"

"I work with the Guardia."

*Which is sort of true.*

"The Guardia! Are they here?"

"Nearby. Shall I call them?"

The bluff worked. "Oh, no! Please!"

Carlotta stopped in front of a polished door. Keys jingled in her hand.

"Do you live alone?"

"With my grandmother."

"Does she know what you've been doing?"

"No. Please! You can't tell her!"

"Does she speak English?"

"No."

"Where will she be? I mean, right now."

"Probably in bed."

"Okay. Let's go in."

The apartment was not what the building's well-kept exterior had led Sarah to expect. A few dingy rooms, sparse furnishings, and a pervading sick-room smell mixed with undertones of ground coffee.

And, to complete the picture, there in the parlor sat a wizened old woman watching the news on a small television set.

Carlotta whispered to Sarah in English, "What shall I do? Please help me. Can I tell her you are a friend?"

Sarah's eyes were locked on the old woman. "Tell her I'm an American you met this evening. You asked me back for a glass of wine so you can practice your English."

It was done. During Sarah's introduction to Signora Clara Falcone, she pretended to stumble over the Italian salutations. At the same time she noticed, with a flinch, that the old lady was missing the thumb and index finger on both of her hands. The remaining fingers were wrinkled, almost clawlike, appendages.

After fifteen minutes or so—after wine had been ceremonially poured, and after Signora Clara had briefly joined in a three-way chat that Carlotta made a fluent show of translating—the old lady tactfully announced that she was going to bed. Carlotta helped her out of her seat and over to her bedroom. A few minutes later, she shut the bedroom door and rejoined Sarah in the parlor.

Sarah was ready to get down to business, but her changing perspective of Carlotta Falcone prompted a few preliminary questions.

"Are you comfortable to speak with me in English?"

"That would be best," Carlotta replied, her eyes sliding to the bedroom door.

"Are you supporting your grandmother? I mean, financially."

"Yes."

"How old is she?"

"Eighty-nine."

"Do you have a husband? Children?"

"I have no family. Just my Nonna."

That simple statement resonated with Sarah. It was an exact replica of her own early life.

"Does your Nonna have a pension?"

"Not enough to live on." Carlotta's voice rose. "After the war, the politicians pretended there had been no civil war. They ignored her injuries, and they refused her the war disability benefits. They forced her into silence. She worked in a laundry until she could not work anymore."

Sarah had already guessed the truth.

"Your grandmother fought in the Resistance."

"Yes."

"Her hands . . ."

"She was captured. And tortured. Not by Germans. By Italians. The Fascisti who never paid for their crimes." The bitterness of a fading generation lived on in this middle-aged woman's voice.

Carlotta stopped talking. She sipped her wine and sat very still, staring at Sarah.

Sarah knew why.

"You're waiting to find out what I know."

"Yes."

Sarah felt a trace of admiration. The woman was suddenly showing some backbone.

"Someone is supplying you with fake baptismal certificates. Based on those documents, you are creating fictitious Juvenile Court files and forged home study reports, along with forged court approvals."

There was no reaction, so Sarah went in with both feet.

"You are delivering those documents to Anthony Nicosia, the United States consul here in Palermo. In fact, that's exactly what you were doing when I followed you." She pointed at the messenger bag that was now sitting on a small desk behind Carlotta. "You were delivering fake adoption files to Mr. Nicosia in that bag right there."

Carlotta sat still and wooden faced.

"How much are you being paid to commit these crimes?"

That got a reaction.

"It is for adoptions of lost children! There is no other way to get them out of that orphanage! They can go to America! How can that be bad?"

"'Lost children.' You believe that?"

No answer.

"How much are they paying you?"

Carlotta hesitated. "One thousand euros."

"For each file?"

"Yes."

"Cash?"

"Always."

"How many files have you created?"

"I'm not sure. Many. Thirty. Or forty."

"*Who* is paying you?"

"Two men, at different times."

"Names?"

"That's all I can say."

"Why?"

"I . . . I could be . . . These people . . . this is Sicily, Sarah Lockhart! Do you know what that means?"

"You mean, the Mafia."

"I don't know for certain. But yes, maybe. I cannot take a chance. My Nonna . . . she needs to be comfortable, she needs her nurse's visits, her medicines."

"You did all this for your Nonna?"

"We could never live here on what I am paid. And now that you have come, now we will need to move. There are cheaper parts of the city, but they are dangerous. Drug dealers, illegal migrants. At night, people cannot go outside."

"If your Nonna's care is so important to you, why did you spend thousands of euros on a designer bag like that?"

"It's not mine. The consul gave it to me. I only use it to deliver the files to him."

"Why? Why a five-thousand-dollar bag to carry documents?"

"He told me it's not real. He said he has a . . . he called it a 'source.'"

"A fake bag to carry fake documents?"

"It is for security."

"Explain."

"When I am carrying that bag, I can go straight into his office without being searched."

Sarah was beginning to wish she'd been tape-recording this bizarre interview.

"You mentioned an orphanage. Where is it?"

"If I tell you, what can you do for me?"

"You're looking for a deal?"

"I have watched your American television shows."

Sarah had already been thinking about how she could steer around making more trouble for Carlotta Falcone and her grandmother.

"Okay. Help me understand. Do you know where these children come from? Before the orphanage?"

"I'm not sure. Unwed mothers . . . dead parents . . ."

"You were never told?"

"No."

"You just understood that if you helped with the adoptions, the babies would go to America."

"That is what they told me."

"You must know that whatever 'deal' I make with you, the Guardia, and your Italian prosecutors, they are not bound by it."

"If they come to see me one day, will you help me with them?"

Sarah thought about that. "I will keep your name out of my investigation for as long as I can, but you must understand that eventually, your involvement will become known."

"Yes. I understand."

Sarah took a notebook from her pocket. After a moment of writing, she tore out the page and handed it to Carlotta. "Those are my contact details in Catania, and also at the U.S. Customs office in Miami, in the United States. Keep that paper in a safe place. If the Italian police eventually come to see you about this, tell them to call me. I will do everything I can to help you."

Carlotta breathed a sigh.

"In return, Carlotta, I want you to do two things for me."

"What things?"

"First, I want you to promise me that if you receive any more of those baptismal certificates, you will call me. Immediately. Do you agree?"

"Yes."

"Second, I want you to tell me where they keep these babies."

"They were all from the same orphanage. It is called Piccoli Angeli."

"Little Angels. How comforting. Where is it?"

The woman went silent. Sarah wondered if their "deal" was about to collapse.

"Near Randazzo, on Strada 89."

"Write down the address."

# 13

A week later, after once again telling her Italian team that she had business in Palermo, Sarah drove to Randazzo (*Rannazzu*, as the Sicilianu dialect pronounced it), an ancient *comune* located on the northern slopes of the dominating feature of the landscape, Mount Etna. Ominously, Randazzo was the Sicilian town closest to the volcano's brooding summit and its active central vent.

The "orphanage" was a long, low, gray stone building roofed in cracked and broken tiles, set well back from the main road. It was located off Strada Provinciale 89, some distance east of town, nestled in greenery next to the Fiume Alcantara, the fast-moving river that flowed down to meet the Ionian Sea ten miles south of Taormina. The building wasn't easy to identify, but Carlotta's pencil-drawn map had helped.

Standing with her back to the smoking specter of Etna, Sarah's first impression was that it would be difficult to put the building under surveillance. While she was assessing the possibilities, a trickling of running water intruded on her thoughts. She noticed a thin stream passing through a narrow stone culvert under the highway a few feet from where she stood. Following the path of the stream uphill, she spied a mountain road carved into the slope above, and, passing under its roadbed, another culvert.

It was a broad, vine-covered watercourse with a yawning black entrance that looked like the entrance to a mine.

Sarah returned to her car and began retracing her earlier route from the town center. Less than a minute of driving brought her to the turnoff she was seeking. The road led higher on the mountain and directly to the culvert she had spotted. She continued for a quarter mile, parked on the shoulder, grabbed her jacket and binoculars, and hiked back. With no traffic in sight, she slid down the slope, pushed her way through a thicket of broom, and ducked into the channel under the road. The passage was almost head-height and the rivulet running through it barely two feet wide. She settled on a conveniently placed boulder near the downstream exit. The screen of shrubbery and the impenetrable darkness of the culvert made her effectively invisible to anyone on the roadway and property below.

Even in that damp redoubt, her nostrils picked up a faint whiff of sulfur in the air.

*Etna non dorme mai.*

Etna never sleeps.

She began her vigil.

By late afternoon, after nearly six hours of standing and sitting, numb with the chill from her damp surroundings, Sarah was getting ready to call it a day. From time to time, she'd detected a whisper of movement through one or another of the three small windows visible from her position. Three times, she'd seen a middle-aged woman dressed in pleated slacks and a matching jacket emerge from the main door and walk to the east end of the building. There she'd entered a small structure that was set against the end wall of the main building, remained within for several minutes, and then returned.

She'd seen no evidence of children of any age.

Without more to go on, she'd need Carlotta's full cooperation, and a long, confessional talk with Marco—and probably with some fastidious, pouchy-faced public prosecutor—to secure a *decreto di perquisizione,* the Italian version of a search warrant.

She was about to force her way back out through the shrubbery and return to her car when movement caught her eye. The wrought iron gate that blocked entry into the building's long driveway suddenly began to swing open, obviously activated by an electronic command. Then she saw a car approaching on the main road. A gray sedan with tinted windows. It slowed, turned in, and continued onto the property, rolling to a stop near the front door of the building.

Sarah retreated into the darkness of the culvert and raised her binoculars.

The driver's door of the vehicle swung open.

A male figure stepped out.

Conrad Nelthorp.

He circled the car and opened the off-side rear door. Someone inside handed him a large red-and-white chevron-patterned soft-sided bag. He stepped back and a woman got out.

The woman was holding a baby.

Carrying the bag, Nelthorp led the way into the building. He walked straight in without knocking.

Sarah waited, frozen in place, trying to process what she had just seen. Minutes passed. Finally, Nelthorp reappeared. He was alone. He returned to the car. It rolled back down the driveway to the highway and turned east.

Sarah clawed her way back up to the road and sprinted back to her car. She got in and lead-footed it, heading east, hoping the road she was on would offer an intersection that would take her back to SP89.

It did, but by the time she rejoined the highway, Nelthorp's car was nowhere in sight. She reasoned that if he was heading for Autostrada 18, the main artery that ran north–south along the eastern shore of the island, he'd have cut over to the fastest route, Strada Statale 120. Risking a speed camera, and not really optimistic about regaining contact, she took a chance and put her foot down.

Fifteen miles later, the gamble paid off. Just north of Piedimonte Etneo, the last *comune* on SS120 before the A18 interchange, she spotted a gray sedan stopped in a line of vehicles waiting at a rail crossing. Back at the culvert, she'd identified Nelthorp's car as probably a German make, maybe an Opel, but she couldn't be sure. The car she was looking at now matched what she remembered, and as the traffic started moving, she took a chance and followed, maintaining contact but keeping a few cars between her and the target. She'd expected it to take the A18 south, but when they reached the coast it took the north ramp, heading in the direction of Messina. When it made the hard turn into the ramp, she was close enough to confirm that Nelthorp was behind the wheel.

On reflection, it almost made sense. At Messina, Nelthorp would have a choice of ferries to the mainland, and . . . maybe he was thinking . . . no chance of running into a certain American Customs agent.

*Look behind you, smart ass.*

Sarah trailed his car for a few miles, toying with the idea of sauntering up to him when he eventually stopped, just to see the expression on his face. She quickly rejected the idea. She'd seen enough. She took the next exit and headed back to Catania. As she rolled south, her mind was replaying a conversation she'd had three weeks earlier.

*"How often do you come to Sicily?"*

*"Once a month. Sometimes twice."*

*"Call me next time you're in town."*

*"I will. But I'm here now. So what is it? Need more time to background me?"*

*"Something like that."*

*"Thought you'd done that already."*

*"Never hurts to recheck your work."*

By the time she reached home, Sarah had made a decision. She knew that the time would come when she would be obliged to share her investigation with Marco Sinatra.

But that time was not yet.

She needed to think about her next move.


Within a few days, that next move was handed to her.

She was deep in a discussion with a port worker at the ferry terminal, which was located near the southern end of the port facility. While they were talking, the 9:30 A.M. ferry from Naples was discharging vehicles. Late in the unloading process, the port worker interrupted their conversation.

"Hmm . . . there they are again."

Sarah followed his gaze. Two identical white panel vans were driving off the ferry, one directly behind the other. Neither bore any commercial markings or insignia.

"What do you mean?"

"Every month or so, those two vans come off that ferry. I've never seen them go back on. They must leave from some other port."

"Sorry, but why is that—?"

"Watch."

The vans eased along the exit lanes marked on the jetty, but then, instead of exiting left onto SS114 with the rest of the traffic, they both swung right onto the port road.

"They always take the long way through the port."

The narrow lane the vans had accessed ran north, inside the security fence, and through the container area. The main exit from that sector was almost a mile away, and the port speed limit was 10 kmh.

So why take that route?

Sarah's car was parked nearby. "Maybe I'll just take a look. Talk to you later."

"Something else . . ."

"What?"

"They were here last week. I don't usually see them that often."

Sarah jumped in her vehicle and followed. She caught up with them just inside the port's northern gate. They were both parked off to one side, next to the Catania Nautical Club. As she drove past, a woman got out of the passenger seat of the lead van. She was carrying a baby and a large, soft-sided bag.

It was the bag that riveted Sarah's attention.

She'd seen that red-and-white chevron pattern before.

The woman started walking toward the gate.

Sarah rolled out through the gate and parked in front of the on-site car rental office. She watched for the woman to pass. After she did, she got out of her car and followed. She kept her in sight as she crossed the main highway at Via Cali, walked east, and then turned into a small piazza across from the Guardia di Finanza's main office.

She watched the woman approach a car, open a rear door, and get in.

It was a gray Opel with tinted windows.

The vehicle drove away.

Sarah immediately retraced her steps back to the port to check on the vans.

They were both gone.

When she returned to her office, the receptionist told her that Signor Nelthorp had called. The woman's mouth twisted with mild amusement as she added, "He said he would be in Catania tomorrow and he would like to buy you dinner."

"Did he mention where he would be staying?"

"At the Villa Romeo. He will be arriving very late tonight—"

Sarah had a pretty good idea why.

"—but he said you could call him at the hotel before nine o'clock tomorrow morning, or anytime on his *cellulare*. He said you have his card."

# 14

The Hotel Villa Romeo was located on Via Platamone, less than half a mile from the northern gate to the port.

*Villa Romeo?*

Maybe Nelthorp had been fantasizing about some imaginary romantic finale to their dinner date.

At eight thirty in the morning, Sarah stood against a locked iron gate in an alcove two doors down from the hotel entrance. She called Nelthorp's room. He was in, and he sounded delighted to hear from her. They agreed to meet at eight that evening at Hosteria del Panda, a seafood restaurant he swore would not disappoint.

"Rates high on TripAdvisor. You'll love it, believe me!"

After the call, she stayed in position, waiting and watching.

A few minutes after nine, Nelthorp walked out of the hotel.

She tailed him. He began his stroll by pretending to window-shop. To Sarah, his attempts to check if he was being followed were amateurish. Although she was fully aware of her capacity to turn heads when it suited her, she had long ago learned to become invisible when invisibility was needed. She knew how to become just another anonymous face on a street, bland and unremarkable.

Sometimes, all that was needed was a prop—like a bicycle.

Today, it was shabby clothes, sunglasses, a knitted cap, and a collapsible hand cart stuffed with groceries.

Twice, Nelthorp looked right at Sarah Lockhart and failed to see her.

Eventually he ducked into an espresso bar. A few minutes later, Sarah ambled slowly past the establishment's broad window. Its awning cast just enough of a shadow that she was able to make out Nelthorp sitting at a back table. There was another man with him.

Counting off seconds, she ambled to the next corner, then reversed course. She passed in front of the bar again. This time she was able to identify Nelthorp's companion. It was Elias Terenzi, one of the young Italian Customs officers who had been flirting with her. Sarah knew he was supposed to be on duty today, but right now he was wearing civilian clothes.

As she watched, Nelthorp slid something across the table. Terenzi quickly pocketed it.

Sarah moved down the block, crossed the street to a bus shelter, and waited. When the two men emerged from the bar, they immediately separated. Nelthorp walked west, then made a right at the first corner, probably heading back to his hotel. Terenzi crossed the street and headed in Sarah's direction. As he neared her position, she leaned forward and made a show of digging through the contents of one of her grocery bags. Unseeing, Terenzi breezed right past her.

Sarah followed.

After a couple of turns, it was clear he was heading for the port.

At the next corner, Sarah came upon an old woman dressed in black. She was sitting on a tattered blanket. A wooden bowl in front of her contained a few coins. Sarah stopped, parked the grocery cart next to the old woman's bony figure, and said, *"Per te, Nonna."*

The woman's eyes widened. *"Grazie! Grazie! Dio ti benedica . . . !"* Gnarled hands reached to clutch Sarah's.

Sarah smiled. She put a finger to her lips, and walked on.

Keeping her distance, she followed Terenzi into the port. She was puzzled when she realized he was heading straight for the Green Channel—the sector where containers were stored after being screened and cleared for loading on a U.S.-bound ship. He strode down a row of dry cargo containers as if he knew exactly where he was going. When he stopped at one particular tier of twenty-footers, Sarah sidestepped into a narrow passage.

As she watched, Terenzi placed a high-security bolt seal on the container. Her first thought was: *Why isn't it already sealed?*

Her quarry turned to look around. She pulled her head back just in time to avoid being spotted. After a few seconds, she heard his footsteps approaching. She backed into the gloom and waited until he had passed. When she finally risked another look, he was gone.

She moved directly to the container he'd tampered with. She checked the ISO code painted high on the door. She felt sure this container was one that she had inspected a few days before. One that she had personally sealed. She examined the security bolt. It bore the CBP stamp and an alphanumeric serial number. She took out her phone and photographed the ISO code and the security bolt number. Then she headed for the office. As the only female officer in the Customs headquarters, she'd been provided with a small locker in the women's restroom. She ditched the cap and sunglasses, changed clothes, and went to her workstation.

Terenzi was the only officer in the operations area. He'd changed into uniform and was sitting at his cubicle a few stalls away from her own. She smiled a reply to his cheerful *"Buongiorno,"* logged onto her computer, and shuffled papers, killing time. Eventually Terenzi stood, stretched, and headed down the corridor that led to the men's toilet.

As soon as she heard the door close, Sarah moved quickly to the supervisor's office. Deputy Director Zago spent the first half of every day out on the docks, after which he would invariably take a two-hour lunch before settling down in the afternoon to do paperwork. Today was no different from any other, so there was little danger of him walking in on her while she was searching his desk. She quickly leafed through the records in his out-tray, looking for her own work from the previous day. It took less than a minute to find the inspection she was looking for—it bore the same bolt seal serial number as the one she'd just seen Terenzi place on the container.

She pocketed the document and went back to her desk.

Sarah had sealed that container late in the afternoon two days ago. Since then, someone had cut off the seal, probably tampered with the cargo, and then, she assumed, Terenzi had been paid off to reseal it with the same number. There was only one explanation of what she had witnessed: Conrad Nelthorp was involved in some kind of smuggling operation, and he was covering his tracks with counterfeit CBP bolt seals.

This was just another example of the vulnerability of the Container Security Initiative program. Once a U.S. Customs officer had cleared a container into the Green Channel, its cargo was effectively already in the United States because the vast majority of those containers landed stateside without further inspection. American officers posted overseas were relying on the integrity of the local Customs personnel, but in many countries, these were low-paid officials who were susceptible to bribery.

In Italy, as Sarah had learned from office talk, and during one evening's long discussion with Marco, there were certain conditions that made corruption more likely among Customs officers than within the Guardia. Customs was not a police force in the strict sense, so its officers did not earn certain police benefits, and therefore effectively earned less than their counterparts in the Guardia or the Polizia di Stato, the State Police. Customs often worked on joint operations with the Guardia, causing many Customs officers to resent the pay differential when they realized they were doing the same work for less pay. On top of that, career advancement within Customs was slower than the other agencies.

Whatever the background, and whatever Terenzi's reasons for what she had just witnessed, the time had come for her to act. When he returned from the men's room, she told him she had an errand to run, and left the port to track down Marco.

She found him in his office, across the piazza from where Nelthorp had collected the woman with the baby.

# 15

Major Marco Sinatra was wearing overalls and wielding a heavy-duty bolt cutter when Terenzi appeared at his side. There was an edge in the Customs officer's voice as he asked Sinatra what he was doing.

"Ask our American friend."

Sarah stepped into view from behind the container, where she'd been waiting since Marco had sent a trusted port worker to tip off Customs that the Guardia was conducting an investigation in the Green Channel.

"You sealed this one yourself!" Terenzi told her, just as Deputy Director Zago and Customs Officer Morelli arrived on the scene.

Marco handed her both ends of the severed bolt. She examined them closely.

"That's really strange," Sarah said, replying to Terenzi.

"What is?"

"I did seal this container. So imagine my surprise when I watched *you* seal it again this morning"—she held up the pieces of metal—"with this counterfeit seal. Would you like to explain that to us?"

Terenzi swallowed.

"*Vieni!*" Marco called, and a pair of uniformed Guardia NCOs stepped into view. They quickly took Terenzi into custody.

Zago and Morelli stood gaping as their fellow officer was led away.

Marco and Sarah opened the container. The cargo facing them looked the same as Sarah recalled it, but that didn't mean anything.

Due to the positioning of the container tier, the doors couldn't be opened wide enough for a forklift, but it didn't take long for a team of port workers to empty the first three rows of crates. What they discovered was that the last five feet of the container—350 cubic feet of space—was filled with a much different cargo than the one listed on the manifest.

Over a hundred boxes of auto parts.

*Durasteel* auto parts.

Nelthorp was only pretending to run an investigation for the American corporation that had hired him. Behind his client's back, he was profiting from the same counterfeit auto parts trade that the company had hired him to stop. But there was no way he could run this operation on his own. Sarah concluded that the intelligence her department had received, indicating that a counterfeit goods ring was operating through Catania and that it had a stateside Mafia connection, was probably correct. Nelthorp must be in the pay of an American mob family.

The whole thing was almost unbelievable, but Sarah couldn't think of another explanation.

And what about the baby laundering? Infants that had been purchased, or, more likely, stolen from their parents. Infants who were then adopted out, no doubt for a big price, on the pretext that they were legitimate orphans.

Nelthorp was neck-deep in that racket as well.

The time had come to tell Marco everything she knew. When they finished with the container, Sarah took him for a walk on the docks.

"What doesn't fit is the Mafia itself," she added, when she'd finished. "Nothing I ever read about the so-called Five Families ever gave me the impression that they would stoop to trafficking in children."

"I never would have guessed . . . *sei una romantica!*"

Sarah almost laughed. "Me? A romantic?"

"Listen to me." Marco's tone was grave. "There might have been a time when these crime families had standards. Some lines they would not cross. No more. The Camorra, up in Naples . . . they've been forcing Nigerian women, and even young girls, into the sex trade. They came to Italy to work on the tomato farms, and the farms went broke. The old Mafias all across the south—the Sacra Corona Unita in Puglia, the 'Ndrangheta in Calabria, and the Cosa Nostra here—they all conspire with the Egyptians and the Libyans to exploit the migrants. These gangs have no standards at all, Sarah. They are all swine. Their American cousins will be no better."

Sarah was silent, processing what he had just said.

"I have sent officers to Nelthorp's hotel to arrest him."

She grabbed his arm. "No!"

"No?"

"If there's time to stop them, just get some plainclothes officers to watch the hotel. I have an idea."

Marco made a call on his cell. He caught the team leader just as they were getting out of their cars. Sarah heard the order to stand down, move the cars, and post a watch on the hotel's front and rear exits.

When he finished, he disconnected and looked her in the eye. "Tell me."

# 16

As highly rated restaurants go, Hosteria del Panda's premises could not have been more unprepossessing—undersized, hunkered below two floors of shabby apartments, and located in a characterless neighborhood of home furnishing outlets and lottery shops. To add to the charm, it was flanked on one side by a renovation project clad entirely in plastic and corrugated steel.

But that was in the daytime. By night, with soft lighting, and magnificent ceramic urns blocking street-side parking next to exquisitely set sidewalk tables, the entire prospect was transformed into a warm and inviting venue for diners.

At 7:50 P.M., three hours after they had finished documenting two more containers packed with fake Durasteel auto parts, Sarah and Marco were two streets away from Hosteria del Panda, sitting in an unmarked Guardia cruiser. They were monitoring radio traffic. They knew Nelthorp had left his hotel ten minutes ago. The Villa Romeo was not much more than a quarter of a mile from the restaurant, so he was on foot. One of Marco's men was keeping him in view. Four other officers, male and female pairs who were fluent in English, had already reported in. Posing as diners, one couple was seated inside the restaurant, and the other outside.

It had taken some doing, but Marco had managed to persuade one of his regular prosecutors to authorize a one-party consent intercept. In other words, Sarah was wearing a wire. Even more interesting, the microtransmitters were embedded inside ceramic beads on a pair of tiny stud earrings.

"And if my ears weren't already pierced?" Sarah had asked when Marco handed them to her.

"We could have fixed that," he'd replied, grinning, as he held up a hole-punch that was lying on his desk.

*"Subject has arrived. He took the last empty table outside—the one closest to the corner. It had a reserved sign on it."*

Sarah reached for the door handle. "That's my cue."

"Talk to me while you walk, so we know the signal is clear."

She did, and it was.

Nelthorp was facing the street corner, his back to the rest of the diners seated along the sidewalk. His table was the only one in partial shadow because the frontage lighting didn't quite reach to the corner. She pretended not to see him as she strode toward the restaurant's main entrance. He called out to her. Feigning surprise, she altered course.

He rose and offered a cold hand. "I came a bit early so I could argue with the owner if I didn't like the table he was holding for us. I didn't."

"Where was it?"

"Inside, right beside a table set for eight. Thought you'd rather be out here."

*You reserved this table, you jerk. Why lie about something so unimportant?*

Sarah sat. They ordered wine. When their glasses arrived, Nelthorp declined the waiter's *antipasti speciali* suggestions and set his menu aside.

The warm, firm grip she remembered, the salesman's tones, the gleaming teeth—all the moving parts of Nelthorp's normal charm offensive didn't seem to be meshing.

Something was wrong.

Sarah glanced past his shoulder. The two outside Guardia officers were three tables away, with the female facing her. If something went sideways, the inside pair would be no use at all.

She tried small talk. "So, how was your day?"

"Really?"

She shrugged and tried a questioning smile. "You invited me, Conrad. What did you want to talk about? Or is this supposed to be a date?"

That foray seemed to break through.

He sighed. "Date? Haven't had one of those for a long time." The sigh seemed staged. He went on, answering her first question. "My day? The usual. Catching up on paperwork while I waited to meet a source." He sipped his wine. "Didn't get much from him . . . almost a waste of time."

"Almost?"

"After our meeting, he went on his way. Then I discovered something. He was being followed."

*Damn!*

Sarah realized she was on a knife edge.

But she had been here before. She maintained her engaged, faintly warm expression, showing just enough concern to look mildly surprised. Although she was looking straight at Nelthorp, her peripheral vision was watching for body language three tables over that would signal that the conversation was coming in clearly and her two outside minders were alert.

She detected no movement.

"You're sure he was being followed?"

"We went in separate directions, but after a few seconds, I decided to double back and follow him. Basic countersurveillance—making sure he wasn't being tailed." He paused. "He was . . . by a woman who looked a hell of a lot like you."

*I'm not going to get any more out of this guy, Marco. Take him!*

Buying time, Sarah dove straight in with a hastily improvised deflection. "Are you talking about Elias Terenzi?" she asked sharply.

"Yes."

"Then that was me. So what are you saying? *You're* the one who's been using him? You couldn't get Homeland's intel out of me, so you hired Elias to spy on us? Is that what you're saying?"

The uncertainty on Nelthorp's face told her she'd scored. He'd been worried she might be closing in on his smuggling racket. Instead of running for it, he'd kept their dinner date to find out how much she knew. And she'd just implied she didn't know anything.

Which meant he didn't know Terenzi was in custody.

But Nelthorp's eyes were telling her there was something more.

He glanced at his watch.

"I'm sorry. You're an attractive woman. I thought we could be friends."

"What changed your mind?"

In the background, barely noticeable, the approaching sound of a whining engine.

Nelthorp leaned forward, his hand grasping her wrist. "Not 'what,'" he hissed. "*Who!* Dominic Lanza."

She heard chairs scraping on the pavement behind him.

*About time, Marco!*

That exasperated thought was lost in the sound of screeching tires and a loud bang. Sarah twisted in her seat. A van had mounted the curb and halted directly behind her, flattening a street sign in the process. Two men dressed in black leaped out of the side door. One man held a machine pistol. He yelled, *"A terra!"* and sent a rattling burst of gunfire over the heads of the seated diners. Against the resulting backdrop of screams and toppling furniture, the other man snaked a thick arm around Sarah's neck and yanked her bodily out of her chair. Covered by a second burst of gunfire, he dragged her to the van and shoved her headlong through the open side door. He jumped in after her while his companion unleashed another spray of gunfire.

But they'd misjudged their victim.

In the two seconds it had taken the first thug to launch himself into the interior of the van, Sarah had regained her feet. He rushed at her, arms wide.

Mistake.

Lashing upward with an open palm, she destroyed his nose. With a bellow, he toppled against the back of the passenger seat, spraying blood. When the gunman stepped into the van, he walked straight into a violent kick that launched him back out the door. He landed heavily on the pavement outside. His machine pistol clattered away, sliding to rest in the middle of the street.

The driver twisted in his seat, a pistol in his hand.

Sarah leaped out of the van.

As shocked diners gawped and the Guardia cover team fumbled for their sidearms, the man on the pavement struggled to rise. Sarah took him out of the fight with a violent kick to the jaw.

The van's engine screamed. Tires spun and poured smoke, the vehicle rocked and twisted, but it remained stationary, its front axle hung up on the stub of the street sign it had just destroyed.

Sarah sprinted for the machine gun.

With a wrench of tearing metal, the van shot forward. The driver swung the wheel, aiming straight for her. She sprang out of the vehicle's path, but its side mirror clipped her shoulder, sending her sprawling. Tires slithered and squealed as the van spun into Via Torino and disappeared.

Within seconds, all four Guardia officers converged on her, forming an armed shield. As they helped her to her feet, she stared back at her table.

Nelthorp had vanished.

## 17

"Your shoulder?"

"A bruise. No serious damage. What about Nelthorp?"

"No sign of him on the street. We checked his hotel room. It was still registered in his name, but there was no trace of him. Our people were there within ten minutes of the incident, so it looks like he'd already emptied the room before he came to meet you."

"Probably right after he spotted me tailing Terenzi. What about the gunman?"

"His name is Alberto Motta."

"Cosa Nostra?"

"Possibly. Probably."

"Do you know the name Dominic Lanza?"

"Lanza . . ." He was thoughtful. "An old name. I think from near Caltanissetta. One of the big landowners near there."

"Mafia?"

"The landowner? Perhaps, at one time. He is an old man now, and lives quietly. I have heard, or maybe I read, that some of the family moved to America. A long time ago . . . before the First War." He looked at her. "Why?"

"Nelthorp said that name a few seconds before the van showed up."

"I didn't hear that."

"It will be on the tape. This Motta guy . . . is he talking?"

"Not much. You broke his jaw. He's in surgery."

"Oh, right. Sorry."

"Sorry? I'm not. Anyway, it doesn't matter. If he is Mafia, their *soldati* never talk."

They exited the hospital.

"That gun. It was a MAC 10. That's an American weapon."

Her friend wrapped a protective arm around her. "We nearly lost you, young lady."

There was genuine emotion in the big man's voice. Sarah stopped.

"I've been in worse situations, Marco. I would've handled them."

"No. You don't understand. You'd have been dead before the van left the city, and we would never have found you. Those people have too many places to hide a body." He went silent for a second. "*Lago della Morte.* Have you heard of it?"

"Lake of Death? Sounds like something from a horror movie."

"In a way, it is. It's near Palagonia. It's not actually water—it's concentrated sulfuric acid. It's fed by two subterranean channels. Both are sources of $H_2SO_4$ from volcanic activity."

"So . . . not a place for water sports."

"It's no joke, Sarah. I've read the reports. Standard procedure for the Cosa Nostra . . . someone gets in their way, make him disappear. Forever. The usual routine is to garrote the victim and then drop the body into the lake. It only takes a few days for a corpse to dissolve completely."

"And you think that was the plan for me."

"Think of it this way: Nelthorp didn't know Terenzi was already locked up, and he didn't know we'd found his shipments. He wouldn't have come to the restaurant if he did. No, he saw you following Terenzi, cleaned out his hotel room, and called his contact—probably a local *capodecina*. They decided it was time to make you disappear before you got too close."

"Then why not do it quietly, so no one would know what happened? I mean, think about it. A U.S. Customs agent vanishes in Sicily? Snatched off the street in front of a dozen people? The FBI would be all over it, but if I disappeared into thin air, they wouldn't know where to look, or who to suspect. Why the theatrics? Those gorillas might as well have painted *Mafia Hit Squad* on the side of that van."

"That was a message for us. The families have a long tradition of intimidating our judges and police. The big display was to encourage our officers to . . . how do you say it? . . . drag feet when your FBI showed up."

"Okay, I guess you know the landscape. But I don't think Nelthorp was too happy about it. It was written on his face."

"He was worried he'd made a big mistake. He was thinking he could be next."

"You caught that from the audio? I'm impressed."

"Not me. Bruno Luzi, the agent who followed him from his hotel. He was keeping watch from the Merola showroom across the road. He had binoculars and a live audio feed, and he's fluent in English. He could see Nelthorp's face right up to the second the van blocked his view."

"Then why the hell didn't he come running?"

"Don't go hard on him, Sarah. It wasn't his fault."

*"Not his fault?"*

"He and Merola's security company had their . . . um . . . wires crossed, as you say. When he ran for the door, he set off the alarm, and that automatically sealed the building. The *stupido* security dispatcher forgot he was there and called the Carabinieri to report a break-in." Marco chuckled. "He came to me while the doctor was checking you over. He wants to apologize and buy you a drink. He thinks you're totally cool."

"Totally cool?"

"He loves American TV."

Sarah sighed.

And then she laughed.

After everything that had happened in the last twelve hours, it felt very good to laugh.


Sarah knew she had a call to make. A long overdue call. Apart from the regular inspection data that was dispatched electronically, and a verbal and written report on the four days she'd spent interviewing migrants at Porto Empedocle, she hadn't been briefing her supervisor back in Miami on everything she'd been up to lately. Old habits die hard.

Phyllis Corbin was at her desk.

"Nice of you to remember us."

"I've been busy."

"This is not a dating relationship, sweetheart. Why am I reading about you in *The Washington Post*?"

"You're not. They kept my name out of it. And no one got a photograph."

"Okay, let's see . . . 'WOMAN TURNS TABLES ON KIDNAP SQUAD. *AP Catania,*

*Italy . . . Violent incident . . . shocked diners . . . woman, believed to be an American . . . one thug left unconscious . . .'* et cetera, et cetera. Care to explain?"

"Long story."

"No time like the present."

Sarah decided to start with the counterfeit goods investigation since . . . well . . . since that was one of the real reasons she was in Sicily. She tagged on the restaurant incident at the end, playing down the theatrics.

"Okay, so three containers so far?"

"That's right."

"And you're thinking these vans are coming in by ferry, they're parking them out of sight somewhere within the port area, and then transferring the loads into pre-inspected containers overnight?"

"Looks like it."

"What about the overflow? The legit shipments they off-load to make room?"

"My guess is they're loading them into alternate twenty-footers and leaving them for us to inspect and clear. Someone's obviously messing with the paperwork, creating split shipments. My guess is that was one of Terenzi's jobs."

"There'd have to be a few port workers in on that. One Customs officer isn't doing that all on his own."

"You're right."

"This Terenzi . . . is he talking?"

"Not yet. The last I heard, he was demanding a lawyer."

"And Nelthorp. He's in the wind?"

"So far."

"We'll contact Interpol and get a Red Notice issued. Now, here's what I want you to do: seal up those containers, register the bolt numbers on new paperwork, and let them load the ship."

"Let them go?"

"Yes! We'll arrest the ship when it arrives at MIA. We'll get a lot more cooperation from that Greek shipping company once we've seized one of their ships."

"Anything else?"

"Send me a full written report via the usual channel. And keep your head down! I don't want to read about any more of your exploits in the media."

"Okay. Uh . . . boss?"

"What?"

"There's something else."

"Should I be glad I'm sitting down?"

"Yes."

"Tell me."

Sarah knew the baby laundering investigation wasn't exactly within her remit. If anything, it was a matter for ICE and the FBI. Something told her she'd better not get into too much detail about her extracurricular activities with her sometimes prickly boss. So she kept it brief, just hitting the highlights. She repeated what she'd been told by Renate Richter and Father Giardini, and, without naming names, that there were allegations of involvement at the consulate in Palermo and maybe a U.S. Immigration officer in Naples.

She finished with the tie-in. "And here's the thing . . . Nelthorp might be involved."

"Nelthorp?"

Leaving out the long sequence of surveillance, interrogation, and yet more surveillance she'd been conducting, she told her about the woman with the baby who got out of one of the smugglers' white vans, and about following her and seeing Nelthorp drive her away.

There was a long silence on the line.

"Boss?"

"Unbelievable."

"If you'd met him, you might not think so."

"Obviously we can't ignore this! Write up what you have and send it to me. Don't copy anyone. I'll speak to the ICE supervisor, but I doubt he can spare anyone to send over there. At least not right away. He keeps sniveling about how he's stretched to the limit, as if it's just his branch that's hurting and not the rest of us. In the meantime, I need you to get back to work on those migrants. The Italian Coast Guard just picked up two more boatloads. Washington is raising hell about making sure there are no crazies hiding in the crowd. They never stop reminding us that if they get into Europe, it's only a short step onto a flight over here."

After a few more perfunctory instructions, Corbin ended their call.

The last part of the conversation gnawed at Sarah. Infants were being stolen from their parents, but Corbin's attention was elsewhere. It was all, "The mission, the mission."

*"Sometimes you can commit an injustice simply by doing nothing."*

Nonna again.

No, Sarah wasn't going to let this go.

# 18

Richard Bird was an old friend from her high school days. Like Sarah, he'd never been part of the high-octane popular set. The two introverts had discovered each other during sophomore year—outcasts drawn together by affinity and, occasionally, for self-defense. An initial fumbling romance had been too awkward to promise a future—at least from her point of view, though not from Dickie's. But he had accepted the situation, and their bond of close friendship had endured until graduation and for a year or two beyond. Eventually, they had lost touch—only to be reunited a decade later in an encounter that had almost cost them their lives.

These days Richard was a State Department analyst. He was also one of the few people on the entire planet that she trusted completely. She called his direct line.

"Dickie Bird! How's it going?"

"How many times have I told you not to call me that?"

She sensed the sprig of welcome behind the crankiness. "But, Dickie, I miss you."

"Don't even start! You haven't called me in months."

"I've been away."

"Where?"

"Out of the country. Still am."

"Where?"

"Not on this line."

"Name?"

"Sarah."

She heard him expel a heavy breath. "I'm never going to understand you, am I?"

"Can we talk?"

"Number 3 in ten."

Number 3 was his private, *private* cell phone. She waited ten minutes, then called.

"Hi."

"Gálvez Park?"

"Yup."

Sarah pictured her friend in the little park behind the Harry S. Truman Building, sitting on the bench near the statue of Bernardo de Gálvez, the little-known Spanish general who had come to the aid of the Americans during the Revolutionary War. It was one of Dickie's favorite spots.

"I'm in Sicily."

"Should I ask why?"

"Assignment."

"U/C?"

"Partly."

"How can you be 'partly' undercover?"

"Two files, three jobs. And I stumbled onto something."

"Stumbled, or waded right in?"

"A bit of both."

"What do you need?"

"How much time do you have?"

"I took an early lunch. Go."

"Have you ever heard of baby laundering?"

"Baby . . . what?"

She told him the whole story.

"Just a minute! These goons that tried to grab you . . . you're saying the mob? You mean like, *bada-bing, bada-boom*? That kinda mob?"

"Yes, Dickie. That kinda mob."

"Jeez, girl! You need to get out of there!"

"Dickie—"

"I know, I know. Comes with the job. I just wish—!"

"I need you to look into a few things. Can you do that for me?"

"Will I get whacked if I do?"

"You couldn't resist that, could you?"

His laugh sounded a bit strained. "What do you need?"

She told him.

Ninety minutes later, he called back.

"Here's the short version: When it comes to intercountry adoptions, Italy has never been a sender nation. What I'm saying is zero adoptions from Italy by Americans—*none!* I checked all the way back to 1998."

"But . . . ?"

"But . . . that changed two years ago. And I'm not talking two or three adoptions a year. Since the spring of 2013, it's totally spiked."

"How many?"

"Forty-one."

*Forty-one! Almost two a month.*

"So, no U.S. adoptions from Italy for fifteen years, and all of a sudden it jumps to twenty a year? Why hasn't somebody at State noticed the change? Why is this thing still under the radar?"

"Probably because Italy's an Adoption Convention signatory—that's the Hague treaty that covers child protection and intercountry adoptions. No one worries about Convention country files because they're supposed to be righteous. The State Department focuses on places like Guatemala and Cambodia where baby-stealing keeps hitting the news."

Sarah chewed on that for a second. "Thanks, Dickie. I really appreciate it. Keep this to yourself. I'll get back to you."

"Don't go after those guys yourself, babe. Call in the troops."

"What troops? I'm on my own here. The U.S. consul's implicated, and the rest of our CBP guys are posted over on the mainland. Apart from Marco, I don't even know which locals I can trust."

"Then Miami should send you some backup."

"They seem more interested in screening shipments. It's like they care more about counterfeit goods than counterfeit children."

"Exceptionalism."

"What?"

"Same old bullshit. America is unique. America is superior to all other nations. America supports international law, but only as long as Americans are exempt from it. They're probably thinking, what the hell, if this is happening, these kids are getting a huge break in life. They get to grow up in the greatest country in the world instead of some foreign hellhole."

"I have no idea what they're thinking, Dickie. All I know is I'm supposed to be working the Green Channel and screening half-drowned refugees while babies are being bought and sold on the black market like exotic pets. If nobody else wants to get involved, I guess it's up to me."

# 19

Autumn is historically the wettest season in Sicily, and this year was no exception. A week ago, from her lair inside the culvert, Sarah had mentally mapped out the most secure route to the rear of the orphanage. Tonight, she was following that route in heavy rain. It was nearly one in the morning when she finished picking her way by penlight along the igneous margins of the Alcantara Gorge. Leaving the river behind, her path took her through an olive grove and up the broad, soggy slope of a vineyard that was still dense with unharvested table grapes. The rush of the downpour masked the rhythm of her squelching steps.

But it couldn't mask a memory . . .

A memory that came down with the rain . . .

With gritted teeth, she trudged on.

Her target was the small outbuilding set against the east wall of the main structure. At first, watching from the hillside above, Sarah had thought it might be a utility room, or maybe a laundry. But the well-dressed woman she'd watched repeatedly enter and leave hadn't been carrying a laundry basket. During her most recent surveillance, earlier today, she'd noticed that the orphanage's power and phone lines from the street terminated at a single point under the eaves of the annex.

Whatever it was, she'd decided to take a look.

When she reached the grime-covered window in the back wall, her suspicion that the annex might be an office was confirmed. It contained a desk and chair, a landline telephone, and a rusting filing cabinet.

A lamp on the desk had been left on. Right next to it lay a file folder.

Marco had promised his help, and she knew he was sincere. But now was not the time to worry about finicky prosecutors, search warrant applications, and the near certainty that Marco's superiors would report Sarah's activities to Miami.

She rounded to the front of the annex. She'd noticed during her surveillance that the woman wasn't consistent about locking the door.

It opened.

She stood still and studied the floor near the threshold. The tiles exhibited muddy evidence of recent entries. A few extra footprints wouldn't be noticed. She stepped inside and shut the door.

*First . . . check the exits.*

There was only the one door, and a single window in the rear wall. It was small, barely large enough for her to crawl through in an emergency. Fortunately, unlike the windows in the main building, it didn't have bars. She tried the window latch. It released easily. The frame was designed to swing out from the bottom. She tested it.

Satisfied, she stepped to the desk and opened the file folder. It only took her a few seconds to realize that it was an adoption file.

A *complete* adoption file.

Every step in the paperwork Renate Richter and Father Giardini had described to her was right there. The female adoptee's fictitious baptismal name was Gisella Pelizon. The adopting parents were a couple named Eden. On one document, the words ANTHONY NICOSIA, CONSUL, UNITED STATES OF AMERICA appeared in type beneath a scrawled signature. Immediately below that was another signature above a name she didn't recognize, but a title she did: BENEDICT J. HUNTER, ADJUDICATIONS OFFICER, UNITED STATES CITIZENSHIP AND IMMIGRATION SERVICES.

A small piece of notepaper stapled to the inside front cover of the file caught her attention. It was only two short lines of handwriting, but it suddenly made everything clear.

It was the key piece in the puzzle.

She used her phone to photograph the note.

She was about to photograph each document in the folder when she heard it.

The sound of braking tires sliding on gravel.

The sound came from right outside the door.

She quickly slid the file back to its original position, darted to the window, and launched herself out. For a nerve-jangling second, her coat pocket caught on the latch, but she managed to free herself. She heard a car door slam as she slid headfirst onto the soaking grass behind the annex. Springing into a crouch, she pushed the window frame down. It hung loosely, leaving an open gap about an inch wide.

Just in time.

A blaze of light spilled out through the window.

Quickly regaining her feet, Sarah risked a quick look. The office door stood wide open, and the room was bright from the glare of headlights.

A silhouette was standing at the desk.

It was the middle-aged woman she'd seen before. As Sarah watched, she picked up the folder and shoved it into a voluminous purse. She was about to switch off the desk lamp, but her hand stopped in midair.

Sarah pulled back.

Again, just in time.

The light through the window diminished. A hand appeared, pushing the window outward. Sarah retreated quickly around the closest corner. Long seconds passed. Finally, she heard the faint scrape of the latch. She waited. She heard the office door close, heard a key in the lock, and then a car door slam. She eased to the next corner in time to see the car rolling to a stop at the entrance to the main building. The woman got out and opened the rear door closest to the building. Immediately, a younger woman appeared carrying a baby wrapped in a blanket. She ducked into the rear compartment. The driver locked the building. She got back behind the wheel and drove away.

Sarah hadn't been able to get a fix on the make of the car. All she knew for sure was that it was a white, late-model four-door with a plate number that began with the letters EM.

She watched the taillights flare at the end of the long driveway and then swing east. She had a damned good idea where the car was headed.

She faced a choice. Force her way back into the office and search the desk and filing cabinet . . . or start running.

She ran.

It took her ten minutes to get back to where she'd left her car.

She got in and drove like hell for Catania.

# 20

The general cargo freighter *Atromos III* was built in 1990. At 340 feet, she was well within the five-hundred-foot limit on vessels permitted access to the port, but with over twenty feet of draft, she was close to the limit of vessels able to go alongside at Catania's primary cargo pier. It was nearing peak tide, and the captain was a cautious man. He was getting ready to sail.

"What are we doing here?" Marco asked. "Those containers went aboard last night, just as your Homeland people asked. I watched them being loaded myself."

He was standing at Sarah's side, watching the *Atromos III*. The activity under the floodlights on the dock made it plain that the vessel was being readied for departure. Sarah had roused him from his bed and persuaded him to meet her on the roof of a Port Authority suboffice next to the fuel dock. She'd been standing there in the dark for half an hour before he finally showed up.

"The harbormaster's notice board says that ship is scheduled to sail at six ten."

"Makes sense. They'd want the advantage of the tide. But that's not an answer. How do I explain to Marta why I abandoned our bed at five o'clock in the morning so I could meet with you?"

"Does Marta have an issue? About you and me?"

"No. And I want it to stay that way."

"We're waiting for a white car. If it shows up before that ship sails, it will prove my theory."

"What theory?"

"That the stolen babies are being transported to the U.S. on Ikaria ships."

"Why haven't you mentioned this before?"

"I wanted to be sure."

"And what makes you sure now?"

"This." She handed him her cell phone. "I photographed that at one o'clock this morning. It was stapled to an adoption file."

Marco studied the words in the photograph.

ATROMOS III

BANCHINA F. CRISPI 0530

"Okay. This ship, this pier"—he checked his watch—"and this time. And the white car?"

"You're going to be angry with me."

"Maybe. Probably. Speak."

"I went back to Randazzo."

"When?"

"Last night."

"To the house where you think they keep the babies."

"I was right. They do. Carlotta Falcone called it an orphanage, but it's just a warehouse. What American criminals would call a stash house."

"You broke in?"

"No. But there's a small building next to the main one. It's being used as an office. The door was unlocked. I took a look."

"Sarah—!"

"There was a folder on the desk. It contained all the paperwork for an American couple to adopt a baby. A little girl. I was getting ready to photograph the whole file, but then a car showed up." As she was speaking, movement on the pier caught her attention. "*That* car."

Marco turned to see a white Renault rolling slowly along the quay from the direction of the Via Cali entrance. It came to a stop at the bottom of *Atromos III*'s gangway.

The driver popped the trunk and got out. It was the middle-aged woman. A crew member started down the gangway. She had a quick word with him and then he went to the trunk and unloaded a large suitcase. The vehicle's rear door opened and the younger woman Sarah had seen earlier emerged. She was holding a small bundle wrapped in a blanket. Even from this distance, they could see it was a baby. Without a backward glance, both women started up the gangway. The seaman rolled the suitcase around to the open rear door, retrieved a chevron-patterned bag from the backseat, and lumbered up the steps behind them.

Marco comprehended what he had just seen. He reached for his phone. "We'll arrest them right now!"

"No, Marco."

"What do you mean? That's a kidnapped baby!"

"We've only identified some of the people involved. Nelthorp, the consul, Carlotta Falcone, an Immigration officer in the Naples consulate, and those two women down there."

"And Elias Terenzi."

"Probably. But we don't know who's involved at the U.S. end. If you arrest everyone now, it will be much harder to roll up the entire operation."

"You want us to let that little baby go?"

"Too many loose ends, Marco! I need to coordinate with Miami. We need to find out who's landing the babies in the States. My information is that over forty of them have been sent already. Some bogus adoption agency in Florida must be involved. And we need to figure out how many of Ikaria's captains are in on the scheme." She gestured at the freighter. "There's no way that captain doesn't know what's happening on his ship. While we're working on all that, your people should just keep a watch on the suspects we have. Carlotta Falcone probably knows more than she told me. She needs to be handled carefully. If the Lanza family is behind the fake auto parts, then they're behind this business as well. Offer Carlotta Falcone witness protection and start interviewing her. Use her as a *pentito*."

"Sarah, I can't approve something like this! I'd have to take it to a prosecutor—and he'd probably have to take it to a judge."

"You're thinking about that baby."

"Of course I am! You're a hard woman, Sarah. That's some mother's child."

The words seared.

They seared, and they struck home, and the anguish of remembered loss tore through Sarah Lockhart like a tsunami.

That old pain again . . .

*That old rain again . . .*

It took a supreme act of will, long practiced, to force it down.

"Marco! I'm just trying to think strategically. Do you think those two women know where the baby came from? Do you think they can tell us how to find her parents?"

"Probably not . . . if she came off a ferry in one of those white vans."

"So, if you arrest them and take custody of the infant, where does that get us? The baby ends up in a real orphanage, and our investigation is no further ahead. This way, the baby will still be well cared for, and we'll be able to arrest everyone on both sides of the Atlantic."

Marco didn't answer.

"Even if we find Nelthorp, I doubt he'll be able to identify that baby's true parents. These baby-smuggling rings use 'recruiters' to find the babies. They don't ask any questions."

Marco didn't answer.

"How about this? Let the ship sail, keep everyone here under surveillance until it arrives in Miami, and then make your arrests. Just keep the roundup quiet. Keep it out of the media. That will give us time to figure out the other end of the chain, get the baby back, and pool our resources to find her parents."

On the ship, the older woman reappeared on the gangway. As they watched, she returned to her car. There was increased activity on the quay.

"The younger woman stayed aboard," Marco said.

"Her job is to look after the baby until they get to Miami. Which means she must have clearance to land in Miami as well. That means some organization like a private adoption agency has made sure the nanny's precleared."

"A corrupt Immigration officer at the port?"

"Exactly right."

Marco thumbed his phone.

Sarah's eyes narrowed. "What are you doing?"

"Calling the gate." He put the phone to his ear. "Sergio? Marco Sinatra. Yes . . . listen, please. A white Renault is coming toward you. Woman driver . . . that's right. No, leave her. Just get the license number. *Grazie*."

*Atromos III* lifted her gangway, dropped lines, and eased into the channel.

They kept watch until the freighter passed the breakwater.

"Sicily is an island that is not island enough," Marco pronounced sadly as they trudged across the roof toward the ladder. He answered her questioning look with a melancholy smile. "Old saying."

# 21

After logging on to a website that tracked over one hundred thousand vessel movements worldwide, Sarah established *Atromos III*'s estimated date of arrival at the Port of Miami.

They had ten days.

She called Phyllis Corbin.

"Lovely that you called, dear girl, but when I asked for more frequent reports, I meant in writing."

"Some of what I'm going to tell you can't go in a report."

"Why?"

"Because I don't know who else is reading them."

A pause. Then, "Okay. I'm listening."

*Start easy . . .*

"The containers are on their way. They're aboard the *Atromos III*. She's due at Miami on the fourteenth."

"Okay."

"And, there's a baby on that ship."

Dead silence.

"Did you hear me?"

"Yes. Go on."

Carefully omitting Dickie's involvement, Sarah related everything that had happened since their last conversation.

"Unbelievable."

"You said that before."

"No! Unbelievable that you're running around in the middle of the night on the territory of a foreign ally, breaking into buildings, chasing a case that's outside your authority. And unbelievable that you're doing all this while another boatload of migrants is landing at Syracuse! *Or do you even know that?*"

Sarah had had enough of this.

"Unbelievable?" she shot back, white heat in her voice. "It's more unbelievable that you don't seem to give a damn! This is human trafficking, Phyllis. *Hu-man traf-fick-ing!* If you can't be bothered with it, maybe it's time I called someone *higher up the fucking food chain!*"

"I do give a damn!" Apparently rattled by Sarah's fierce reaction—or by her threat to go over her head—Corbin's tone immediately softened. "I'm sorry! I really am! But you need to understand, we're getting it from all sides here. Terrorism. Illegal immigration. The politicians are climbing all over us. Counterfeit goods? The lobbyists are all over the politicians, and the politicians pass on the aggro. It never stops."

With an effort, Sarah calmed her own tone. "I'm sorry, too. And I get it. I do. I know how Washington works and I know you're always getting political pressure. But we have to do something. My Guardia contact has agreed to coordinate with us. They'll hold off making arrests, to give us time. If we do nothing, how is that going to look?"

"Okay, we'll do this: I'll get onto the ICE investigator I've been talking to. We'll fix it so the Immigration officer who goes out on the pilot boat will clear everyone—crew, nanny, baby. Once the ship's alongside, we'll do a random inspection of the cargo, find the fake goods, arrest the ship, and detain the captain. Meanwhile, ICE will put a tail on the nanny and see where she delivers the child."

"I can help! Bring me home."

"We need you there. I'm sorry. The baby's name . . . what did you say it was?"

"I didn't. It's Gisella. Gisella Pelizo . . . no, Pelizon." She spelled it. "I think there was a middle name, but I don't remember it."

"What about the parents?"

The first names hadn't registered, but Sarah clearly recalled the adopting couple's surname.

*Eden.*

But now she hesitated. Always hold something back, Nonna had taught her. Always keep a key piece of information to yourself.

Never give up control.

More than once during Sarah's notorious previous assignment, that advice had proved its value.

"Sorry. Didn't get a name. I only had a second and then I had to bail."

"Okay. I'll keep you advised. Meanwhile, get your ass down to Syracuse." A pause. "Sorry. Will you *please* get your ass down to Syracuse?"

"Yeah. I will."

She hung up.

Sarah left for Syracuse the next morning. The drive on the autostrada only took an hour, but the teeming mass of humanity in the migrant compound presented her with the daunting prospect of long days and little time for rest. She'd intended to commute from home, but by the end of day one she surrendered to reality, shopped for a few essentials, and booked a hotel room. But whenever she had a waking moment to herself, which wasn't often, all she could think about was the baby on the ship.

Eight days later she returned to Catania, exhausted by long hours of emotional encounters with the human flotsam of civil war and social chaos.

It was late when she reached her apartment, but she took a chance on upsetting Marta and tried Marco's cell number. It went straight to voice mail.

She went to bed, but her mind refused to shut down. There was something she'd forgotten to ask Dickie. It was still suppertime on the East Coast, so she turned the light back on and tried calling him.

Before she could get a word in, he started jabbering.

"You know those names you emailed? The kids on those certificates the priest gave you—?"

"Yeah."

"Well, their paperwork did come here, and the department sent out certificates of citizenship, but I can't match those kids to any travel manifests on any incoming flights on the dates they officially entered the U.S. Not only that, none of the adopting parents traveled to Italy. They never left the country, and yet those kids are now living in the States. The question is: *How did they get here?*"

"They didn't come by air, Dickie. They came by sea, through Miami."

"What?"

She gave him a quick summary of events since they'd last spoken.

"I don't get it. Why ship babies on freighters? Why take days when it can be done in hours?"

"Chain of custody."

"What do you mean?"

"Think about all that fake paperwork—an Italian court order that was obtained by fraud, the consul's endorsement, the visa issued by the Immigration officer in Naples. If these people are smart, they'll want to make sure nothing ends up in the Immigration database. They'll want to maintain custody of every baby—*and* all its paperwork—and keep it inside the organization. So there's got to be an Immigration officer at the Port of Miami who's on the payroll, to make sure both the baby and the nanny get cleared and the child gets passed on to the new parents. That way, when the parents apply for the child's citizenship, they'll send certified copies of the paper file to State. Italy's a Convention country, so how many department clerks are going to bother running a computer check to see when and where some kid arrived in the country when they've got copies of the adoption papers and the visa sitting right there on the desk?"

"I see what you're saying."

"Dickie, there's something else I want you to look into."

"What's that?"

"Have you ever heard of Dominic Lanza?"

"No."

"He lives in New Jersey. He's supposed to be some kind of mob boss."

"As in, Mafia?"

"Yes. There's nothing on him in the Homeland database, and when I crawled through the internet, all I found was one long article full of rumors and a couple of gangland fanboy sites full of hero worship. If there's ever been a serious investigation of this guy, it went nowhere and the FBI aren't talking about it."

"I'll see what I can find out. But I want you to understand one thing."

"What?"

"I won't hack the FBI. Not even for you."

"Got it."


The next morning, Marco was waiting for her at her workstation. His eyes were red-rimmed and he looked exhausted.

"I tried calling you last night," Sarah said.

"Had my phone turned off. I just got back and saw the missed call."

"Back from where?"

"Palermo. I've been up all night."

"Why? What's going on?"

He dropped a newspaper on her desk.

Sarah stared at the headline.

STATI UNITI CONSUL TROVATO MORTO

"Nicosia's dead?"

"I thought that was why you called me," Marco said.

"No. When I got back from Syracuse, I just wanted to check in with you before I went to bed." She quickly scanned the story. "Suicide? I find that hard to—"

Marco stopped her with a warning gesture. She looked around. Customs officers were watching them with undisguised interest.

"Let's go for a walk," Marco said.

He led her to the far end of the Nautical Club dock.

"He went off the balcony outside his office. The fall killed him. It was made to look like he jumped."

"You're saying he didn't."

"We think he was thrown."

"Physical evidence?"

"A dislocated shoulder. Not caused by the fall. Marks in the skin of the same arm, as if it was held in a strong grip."

"That's it? Is that enough to—"

"The pathologist says yes."

"Do you have a time of death?"

"7:23 P.M. A man was standing at an ATM, around the corner on Via Villabianca, when the consul struck the pavement two meters away. The bank machine's camera fixed the time."

"I remember his office faced Villabianca, but the building entrance is on Via Vaccarini. That made it easy for whoever did this to get away. All the commotion would have been on the other street."

"There's more. That Immigration officer at the consulate in Naples . . ."

"Benedict Hunter."

"He didn't show up for work today." Marco laid a big hand on her shoulder. "You know what this means, Sarah."

"The Mafia knows we're on to them. They're eliminating witnesses."

"I'm assigning two men to protect you." He saw her expression. "No arguments. And we're moving up the timetable. We picked up Carlotta

Falcone and her grandmother early this morning. They're being moved to a safe house on the mainland." His mouth twisted. "The old woman was a lot calmer about it than Carlotta."

"Somehow that's not a surprise."

"We have officers watching the stash house, as you call it. The white Renault is there. Our prosecutor obtained a search warrant and a Polizia Stradale car is on its way to deliver the warrant to the team leader. I just pray they don't find any babies when they go in."

"With all this activity, some journalist is going to start connecting the dots."

"We can isolate Consul Nicosia's death. Pretend to treat it as a suicide while we investigate it as a murder. We can make any other arrests look unrelated. Our prosecutor has agreed to this approach. But there are no guarantees. Your investigators may not have much time after that ship arrives. You must warn your supervisor. I'm surprised she hasn't called you already about the consul's death. As you can see, it's in the news."

"When did the story hit the wire services?"

"I don't know."

Sarah pulled out her phone.

"Are you calling your boss?"

"No. I want to check something first." She logged on to a search engine. After a few seconds, she showed the screen to Marco. "Corbin has a digital subscription to *The Washington Post*. She's always checking it for breaking news. This story hit the wires at ten minutes after ten our time last night. That was four ten yesterday afternoon in Miami."

"You're saying she would have seen the story while she was still at her office."

"Yeah. But she didn't call me."

"Meaning what?"

"Meaning it's time Phyllis Corbin and I had a little face-to-face."

# 22

Sarah's apartment was in the Edgewater district, just north of Miami's downtown. She called Marco as soon as she got out of the shower.

"I'm heading out in a minute. Bring me up to date."

"Carlotta hasn't told us any more than she told you. She knows the consul was murdered and she's terrified. She thinks they're coming for her next."

"Is she right?"

"There is no way to know. Just to be safe, we're moving her and her grandmother again. We're taking them up north."

"Good. What about Elias?"

"He seems more afraid. His *avvocato* has told our prosecutor that he will admit that Nelthorp paid him to switch the container loads, and to install the fake bolts. But he will only admit to those three containers we found. He insists Nelthorp never told him who he was working for. He says he will tell us the names of the port workers who helped him shift the loads, but only if the prosecutor gives him full immunity. He insists he knows nothing about baby smuggling."

Sarah could feel frustration tightening her throat. "What about the orphanage? The search warrant? What did you find?"

"The Renault woman was there. She was alone. Her name is Sonia Sturzo. The building is a converted stable. It is now a three-bedroom residence. One bedroom is set up to be a nursery—it has three cribs and lots of supplies for babies. Based on what you said about seeing Nelthorp with two different nannies and babies, I thought we'd find one when we searched. But the nursery was empty. Sturzo told us she uses her home as a shelter for unwed mothers. She claimed she receives support from a Catholic charity. We checked. She was telling the truth."

"A Catholic charity? Father Giardini won't be happy to hear that."

"When our officers told her she had been seen helping a woman with a baby board a freighter in Catania, she admitted that she had driven the woman there. She said the girl had been staying with her, and had asked for a ride to the port. She said the girl told her that the captain was her brother and he was taking her to stay with relatives in Genoa. She refused to say any more without advice from a lawyer."

"What about her office? There was a filing cabinet. Tell me you found something!"

"*Niente*. No adoption files. Just the usual household paperwork—utility bills, bank statements, personal papers—and expense records for the charity that supports her."

"She was warned. She knew you were coming."

"It can only be that."

"Thank you, Marco. I'd better get going."

"To see your supervisor?"

"Yes. The ship was due in port this morning."

"Good luck. Call me if you need anything."


CBP's Miami field office was housed in a functionalist concrete building on SE 1st Avenue, in the shadow of the Metrorail. Sarah's sudden appearance in her section's outer office was barely noticed. Every agent in the room was glued to a television mounted on the wall. On the screen was a street scene milling with law enforcement personnel. A huge truck held center stage, its front bumper jammed against the driver's side of a sedan—a vehicle that was, in turn, shoved tight against a concrete wall. The sedan's windows were riddled with bullet holes.

A reporter's voice-over was supplying the details.

"*. . . used this stolen refrigerator truck as a battering ram to intercept the vehicle and then execute its occupants. Channel 6 News has learned that the target vehicle was carrying a Port of Miami Immigration officer who had just been arrested for corruption. Witnesses say two men jumped from the truck, sprayed the vehicle with automatic gunfire, and then fled the scene in a car* *driven by a third man. The prisoner was being transported to Homeland Se-curity's field office near Dolphin Mall. He and his escorting officers died at the scene. Immigration officials have refused to comment on the reason for the officer's arrest. They will only say . . ."*

It took Sarah about three seconds to realize what had happened.

She felt a hand on her shoulder. She turned.

"We've been waiting for you to show up."

Phyllis Corbin was accompanied by a stiff-backed man in a dark suit. His "I'm-a-G-Man" posture was somewhat undermined by the jowly cheeks and the sag of a soft belly over his belt.

"This is Special Agent David Kemp."

"ICE?"

"Yes."

She looked at Corbin. "You know about the consul in Palermo?"

"I saw the press."

"You saw the press and you didn't call me." She read Corbin's face. "Right. You knew I'd be coming."

"I know you pretty well by now. We flagged you on the system. I'll deal with your insubordination later. Come with us."

Sarah was in no mood for Corbin's attitude. She followed them into Corbin's office, and as soon as the door was shut, she turned on her boss.

"That officer who was arrested. He was the one, wasn't he?"

Kemp gave the answer. "Yes."

"Where's the baby?"

"She and the nanny weren't on the ship when it docked," Corbin replied.

"What do you mean? I saw them go aboard! I saw the ship sail!"

Kemp said, "The officer our people arrested—his name is Selwyn Bailey. We figure he sent them ashore on the pilot boat."

Sarah exploded. "The pilot boat? What the hell is the matter with you people? I handed you this on a platter. The Italian police bent over backwards to give us extra time!"

"Watch your tongue, little girl!"

Sarah wheeled on Corbin. "What did you say?"

Kemp intervened, raising his voice. "I know who you are, Agent."

"What the hell has that got to do with anything?"

"Your name's got too much profile," Corbin said, her tone suddenly conciliatory. "It attracts too much attention. I'm sure you understand that. We can't take the risk that it will be leaked."

This had a familiar ring. "Just a minute! *We* can't take the risk? Who's 'we'?"

"Washington has a new assignment for you—they want you out in L.A."

"That's bullshit! I only booked my flight yesterday. Maybe you knew I was coming, Phyllis, but nothing in this department happens that fast. I'm being sidelined. Why?"

Corbin looked uncomfortable.

"Tell me!"

"These adopting parents. The ones from before, who already have their babies. The word is, some of them may be . . . prominent."

"Black-market adoptions cost big money. So what you really mean is *rich* and prominent."

Reluctantly, Corbin gave a nod.

"And, from the look on your face, politically connected. As in . . . Party donors?"

"All these people believed their new baby was an orphan. It's not as if we can take the kids away and return them to their parents."

"You don't know what they believed. And you don't know that their parents can't be traced. The European police are interviewing witnesses, working their way back up the line."

"The thing is, this needs to be handled carefully. You have a certain . . . reputation. Washington doesn't want you in the middle of it. They don't want the kind of attention you could generate if your identity became known."

"Became known how?"

"Maybe by a judge ruling that you have to testify in your own name," Kemp said.

Sarah was angry. Very angry. But, unlike many people, her rage helped her see more clearly. She knew she wasn't going to win this argument.

She stared at Kemp, who was just sitting there.

Waiting for something.

She looked at Corbin. "What do you want? From me?"

"Agent Kemp is in charge of the investigation. The conference room's clear. Go with him. Walk him through everything that happened in Italy. Give him your Guardia contacts. We've agreed that you're just here to brief him, not to provide a formal witness statement. None of his team will be present. When you're finished, go home. Take a break. You're on paid leave until the paperwork for your L.A. transfer is finalized."

"And my 'insubordination,' as you called it?"

"We'll keep that out of your file."

*There's that "we" again.*

The writing was on the wall, plain to see.

Sarah knew she had no choice.

So, she pretended to concede.

Pretended . . . because now she knew her instincts had been right and she *had* to finish this case. If that meant exposing cowardice in Washington—and chicanery in Miami—that wasn't her concern.

Pretended . . . because her only concern was making sure this barbarous network of baby peddlers didn't get a chance to start up again.

She went along with Kemp to the conference room. The blinds were already closed. She did as Corbin had asked and launched into a detailed briefing.

"This LaGuardia, is it—?"

*Christ! Is this clown for real?*

"It's a police force, not an airport! It's called the Guardia di Finanza. They're responsible for all financial crime and smuggling investigations in Italy."

"Okay. Got it."

She had already decided to keep Marco's cell number to herself, so she gave him the main number for the Guardia's office in Catania.

She walked him through everything she knew about the baby-smuggling case, step by step, just as she had lived it.

Word for word, just as she had related it to Marco.

She only held back one word.

A name.

*Eden.*

# 23

It took a couple of days, but Dickie came through. Again.

"You didn't give me much to work with."

"That's never stopped you before."

"I think I deserve a French kiss for this one."

"Because you never got one when we were kids."

"That's right."

"My lips are chapped."

"Always the excuses."

"They could be healed by the next time we get together . . . depending on what you've got for me now."

Dickie laughed. "I thought about those parameters you gave me: last name Eden, rich older couple; no kids; significant financial support for a serving congressman or senator; probably living in Florida or the Southeast."

"That's right."

"I thought of a few more. Statistics show that conservatives seeking to adopt tend to request boys to carry on a family name. This couple accepted a girl, so they're probably registered Democrats."

"Okay."

"And they would have tried to adopt through the usual channels before turning to the black market, so you're looking for a Mr. and Mrs. Eden who suffered serial rejections by their home state agencies."

"Not necessarily. Some people just have no tolerance for red tape."

"True, but these folks are liberals, remember? They created most of it. Anyway, I found them. Their names are Kenneth and Darlene Eden. He's fifty-one, she's forty-two. Second marriage for both of them. He made his first fortune when he was twenty-one in that leveraged buyout boom back in the eighties. These days he's heavy into green energy. But he's had two drunk driving convictions, and the wife once did eight months at Lowell Correctional for forgery. Since the beginning of this year, three different Florida adoption agencies have rejected them on medical and good character grounds. I'll need to do more work to get the details on the medical grounds."

"No need. You're saying they applied in Florida?"

"Yup. Want their address?"


As the seasonal home to a few dozen American billionaires, along with a handful of post-1990 Russian oligarchs, Palm Beach was well known as a prestige address for the moneyed few. Despite that reputation, the Eden residence on Chilean Avenue was modest by the standards of any wealthy couple. The house was a stuccoed, flat-roofed tribute to understatement, enhanced only by a touch of ornate ironwork and a terracotta fountain on the manicured front lawn. The single concession to affluence was a late-model Mercedes parked on the redbrick driveway.

It was just past eight in the evening when Sarah knocked on the door.

She heard footsteps inside. Then, silence. She sensed a suspicious eye examining her through the peephole. A second passed. Another.

She held up her badge.

The door opened, revealing an exquisitely dressed woman. Slender figure, green eyes, blond hair, pert mouth . . . if this was Darlene Eden, she was aging well.

"Darlene Eden?"

"Yes."

"My name is Sarah Lockhart. I'm with the Department of Homeland Security."

"May I see that badge, please?"

Sarah showed it to her.

"This says 'Customs and Border Protection.'"

"Look at the crest below that. Homeland includes both Customs and Immigration. I'm here to talk to you about an Immigration case."

Sarah didn't miss the woman's nervous swallow. Dickie had found the right people.

"May I come in?"

The woman peered past Sarah, searching the night. "You're alone?"

"Yes, Mrs. Eden. This is an informal visit."

*Was that a flash of relief?*

As Sarah stepped into the foyer, a man wearing pressed slacks and an open-necked dress shirt materialized in an archway to her right. She recognized Kenneth Eden from a photo she'd found on the internet.

"Darlene? What's going on?" He saw the look on his wife's face. His eyes slid to Sarah, then to the badge that she hadn't put away. "And who are you?"

On the drive up from Miami, Sarah had decided on two alternative approaches, gentle or merciless, depending on the reception she got. Kenneth Eden's instant belligerence made the decision for her.

"Sarah Lockhart, Mr. Eden. I'm from Homeland Security. I want to ask you about a baby girl who was kidnapped from her parents. You know her as Gisella Pelizon."

The couple's stunned reaction removed all vestiges of doubt.

Wordlessly, Kenneth Eden led the way into the living room.

"Kidnapped?" Darlene Eden asked in a whisper.

"Yes. From a refugee camp in Eastern Europe."

"Oh, Kenny! Oh, no!"

"Please tell me where the child is."

"I had cancer. I'm cured, but the radiation made me infertile. They said I can't have a baby because the cancer might come back. *It wasn't fair!*" Darlene finished in a flood of tears.

Sarah decided not to inflame the situation by pointing out that there had been other grounds to reject them, so she just repeated her question.

"Where's the baby?"

"We don't have her," Kenneth Eden replied as he put an arm around his sobbing wife. "The agency said there'd been a delay."

"I'm sorry, but I find that hard to believe. We know for a fact that this child arrived in Miami four days ago."

Kenneth Eden's response was gruff. "We're not lying! You're welcome to look through the house."

"Lead the way."

The couple walked her through every room, ending the tour in an alcove adjoining the vast master bedroom. It had been fitted out as a nursery.

There was a wrought iron crib with an elaborate canopy.

The crib was empty.

Sarah stared into it. Crisp, unused mattress. New, neatly folded bed-clothes. Patterned baby girl sleeper, with tasseled cap and booties.

All waiting for a squirming little tenant.

*Here comes the rain . . .*

*No . . . !*

"Agent?" Kenneth Eden was standing at her side. "What's wrong?"

Sarah's jaw tensed as she fought off the invasion of memory.

*You will not!*

*You will not let the rain come!*

Her eyes locked on a baby monitor perched on a table next to the crib, its lens trained on the empty mattress. Her brow darkened.

"A baby camera, and no baby?"

Darlene Eden was immediately defensive. "We wanted everything to be ready. Wouldn't you?"

They returned to the living room. The couple sat side by side on a couch. Sarah took a chair facing them. Kenneth Eden's belligerence had faded into visible unease. He'd been pale and silent during their circuit through the house, leaving it to his wife to do most of the talking.

Now he asked, "Should I be calling my lawyer?"

Sarah had already resolved to show her hand, in the hope that they would give her the information she needed.

"That is your right, Mr. Eden. But before you do, please understand that I'm not here to squeeze confessions out of you, or make arrests, and I'm not recording our conversation. I saw the shock on your faces when I told you Gisella was a stolen child. I'd like you to listen to what I have to say. When I'm finished, if you prefer not to answer questions, I will understand. I will immediately leave your home so you can make your arrangements for legal advice before other investigators come to see you."

Darlene Eden clutched her husband's arm. "That sounds fair to me."

"And me. Go ahead."

"Have you ever heard the expression, 'baby laundering'?"

"Oh, God!"

Sarah spent ten minutes giving them a broad outline of how baby laundering worked, and explaining, in rough outline, why she was certain that the little girl they'd adopted was a product of that illicit trade.

"As to Gisella's custody, I'm not able to predict what will happen in the end. It may be that there will be no way to trace her parents and she'll be left with you to raise. But it also may be that you will be disqualified for the same reasons you were rejected by those other agencies."

"You know about the other . . . issue?"

"Yes."

"Those convictions were a long time ago, for both of us. We were in our twenties. Anyone who had bothered to look at our lives since then would realize . . ." Kenneth Eden didn't finish.

"Assuming Gisella's parents can't be traced, I would personally hope that you and Darlene could be left alone to raise her. But if that happens," Sarah added gently, "you will have a terrible burden to bear."

"Knowing that one day we would have to tell her the story of her life."

"Yes."

Kenneth Eden took a deep breath. "You want to know how we arranged the adoption. You want to work backward from us to that freighter."

"That's right."

"The agency is called Engender," Darlene said.

"Engender, LLP, to be exact," Kenneth added.

"Where's its office?"

"We don't know. An agency rep called us. He said he understood we'd had a problem adopting. We figured his firm must monitor the other agencies' rejections. He came to see us twice. He did everything out of his briefcase. Made it really simple—nothing like those other people we dealt with."

"How much did he charge?"

"A hundred thousand up front, another hundred on delivery."

"So you knew you were buying a baby."

They both looked uncomfortable.

Kenneth finally answered. "Admitted. But we also thought we were adopting an orphan. We have the money, and it was a fair price to pay just to get out from under all the red tape."

"And not have our old run-ins with the law and my medical history stop us from having a child!" Darlene added heatedly.

"But, why would you trust this man? A door-to-door baby salesman?"

"He gave us some names and telephone numbers. We talked to other couples. Solid people, some prominent enough that we'd heard of them. A few of them have their own pages on Wikipedia. They said they'd done it, and it was all good—that we were saving an orphan."

"I'll need this rep's name—and those other parents' names he gave you."

Sarah's phone rang. She checked the screen. It was Marco. She was about to answer when Kenneth and Darlene Eden suddenly stiffened, looking past her, instant terror in their eyes.

She heard a whisper of movement.

Her hand went for her weapon, but it never arrived.

The blow came from nowhere.

Oblivion . . .

# LAURA

# 24

Laura Pace parked her stolen car in the back row of the crowded parking lot of the Miccosukee Resort and Casino on Route 41, slotting it between a blowsy '83 Cadillac DeVille and a hulking Land Cruiser. She briefly considered stealing the Caddie, but figured she'd only attract unnecessary attention. People expecting to see a white-haired old man driving the vintage land yacht might remember seeing a young woman behind the wheel.

Always drive plain vanilla.

People forget plain vanilla.

She went for a walk.

Circumnavigating the vast parking lot, she inventoried its sporadically placed security cameras and flagged a promising candidate for her next stolen ride. Maintaining an unhurried pace, she entered the casino through the main doors, wandered past half an acre of clamorous slot machines, and located a coffee bar. She bought a latte and then left the building through a different exit. Carefully navigating her way back through the parking lot, keeping to the CCTV blind spots, she reached her target vehicle—a '95 Camry with rust-chewed doors that was parked behind the hotel's kitchen. The car made "nondescript" sound like a compliment. The fact that the owner had left it unlocked was a bonus feature. Hot-wiring presented no challenge to a girl who had grown up in Newark. She was rolling out of the parking lot in under two minutes.

It was a half-hour drive from the casino to her apartment on NE 27th. She guessed the place would be staked out, and she was right. Her first clue was a pair of silhouettes in an unmarked Crown Vic parked down the block from her building. The second was the Miami PD blue-and-white emerging from NE 27th Terrace, the grandiloquent name assigned to the narrow alley behind her building.

She checked the Camry's dash clock: 10:20 P.M.

Her address was on file, and Phyllis Corbin and a few other CBP officers had known where she lived. Now that the word was out that Sarah Lockhart had been detained in Everglades City, and then, within hours, had escaped from a hospital in Naples, the investigators were obviously betting she'd head for home. In other words, despite everything Homeland and the FBI knew about Laura Pace, aka Sarah Lockhart, they actually thought she'd be dumb enough to return to her apartment and get caught doing it.

She figured the marked unit was probably assigned to area patrol, which would give her enough time to dump her ride at the soccer field on the other side of Highway 1 and walk back.

Before she left the Camry, she grabbed the tire iron from the trunk.

A circuitous route brought her to the north end of the alley. She ghosted past her own building and hopped the fence into the rear garden of the private home next door. In two steps, she was standing under the lean-to roof that sheltered her neighbor's barbeque pit.

Almost invisible in the murky darkness, she waited.

Finally, she heard it.

The marked unit was rolling through the alley. It slowed when it reached her building, tires crunching on the broken asphalt. After several seconds, it drove away.

Laura tucked the tire iron into her belt and vaulted the fence that divided the neighbor's property from her building's rear yard. She ducked into the shadow of the garden shed, and in seconds she was crouched on its roof. With a few quick strides and a leap, she launched herself across the ten-foot space between the corner of the shed and her apartment's second-floor balcony.

It took her less than a minute to jimmy the sliding door and slip inside.

The place smelled musty, and she knew instantly that it had been searched. From the look of things, it had been searched more than once.

But not, she hoped, as thoroughly as it should have been.

She strode directly to the front hall closet and pulled out her vacuum cleaner. She released the housing that enclosed the disposable bag. Under the bag, right where she had left them, were three strapped bundles of twenty-dollar bills—six thousand dollars in cash, with random serial numbers.

Before she'd left for Italy, Laura had sold her car and made arrangements with her bank to keep her utility bills up to date. Mortgage payments weren't a problem, since she owned her apartment outright. In fact, she owned the entire building. She could thank the now dead and conspicuously unlamented Colonel Muammar Gaddafi for that, if for nothing else. The only good thing that had ever come out of the Pan Am 103 disaster was the millions of dollars in compensation the Libyan dictator had been strong-armed into paying to the families of the victims.

The tenants in the other three apartments paid their rent by direct deposit into her account. But she knew it wouldn't be long before the FBI showed up at her bank armed with a warrant to monitor her account, so it was just as well she'd gotten in the habit of keeping a supply of cash on hand for emergencies.

Although running from the law wasn't the sort of emergency she'd had in mind.

Tucked under the strap of one of the cash bundles was a Virginia driver's license bearing Laura Pace's—and Sarah Lockhart's, and Lisa Green's—photograph.

A driver's license in the name of Barbara Faye Hyatt.

Laura had operated in deep cover for over a year before taking down one of the longest-serving members of the United States Senate, along with the mayor of San Francisco and a prominent Chinatown gangster. When the operation began, the senator's involvement wasn't even suspected. Because of the inherent dangers of her assignment, Laura had been provided with two quick-escape IDs. She'd never had to use them, but the lessons of those months spent undercover had not been forgotten. When she'd turned in her go-bag after the arrests, she held back one of the undeployed identities. The joke was that, by then, Homeland had become so big, so unwieldy, and so fiercely obsessed with terrorism that no one had even noticed.

A joke, yes, but a depressing one if you gave it any thought.

There were a few other little treasures tucked under the vacuum bag: an orange plastic card embossed with three printed words: WIND PIÙ VICINI, a Walmart Visa money card—which was basically a reloadable prepaid debit card—in the name of Barbara Hyatt, a ziplock bag filled with quarters, and a cell phone.

Laura had bought the phone in Arizona last spring. It was one of three prepays she'd bought, each purchase a week apart, and each purchase from a wireless store in a different state. In each case, she'd paid extra for an eighteen-month expiry date on the credit balance. She'd programmed the first phone to automatically forward all calls to the second one, and the second to the third. Then she'd destroyed the first two phones. If she needed someone to call her, she only had to give that person the first cell number. As far as the caller knew, he was calling area code 541 (Oregon). Unknown to him, his call was actually forwarded to a number in area code 307 (Wyoming) before ringing finally on the phone in her hand—registered to a number in area code 928 (Arizona). Outgoing calls would be more difficult, but there were always pay phones. That's what the quarters were for.

When in doubt, go low-tech.

She pocketed her haul and shoved the vacuum cleaner back in the closet.

She went looking for her old knapsack. She didn't have to look far. Every drawer in her bedroom dresser had been pulled out, and the empty knapsack was lying on the floor. She stuffed it with the bundles of cash and then picked through the mess on the floor until she'd managed to assemble two complete changes of clothes: short jacket, ripped jeans, and a plain old T-shirt for mucking around, and black slacks, a cashmere pullover, and dress flats if she ever needed to be presentable. There were thrift stores all over Florida—she could buy secondhand clothing if she needed it and stay off shopping mall security cameras. She kicked off the ridiculous sandals Roland Lewis had bought her and pulled on her favorite Merrell boots—they were tough, well broken-in, and added an inch and a half to her height. She pawed through drawers until she found her old Timex watch, and she strapped it on.

She moved to the kitchen and opened her junk drawer. The key ring she was hoping to find was exactly where she'd left it. As any cop worth his salt knew, you can tell a lot about people from the contents of their junk drawers. It isn't always scissors, pens, and household knickknacks. Sometimes it's also randomly stowed receipts, medications . . . or extra sets of keys. In other words, objects that could tell you something about your quarry. It baffled her that none of the searching officers had bothered to investigate the two keys on that ring.

She slung on her pack and headed for the balcony. In the living room, she stopped for a few seconds and took a look around. The pale solitude of this apartment had sometimes oppressed her, but it had been her sole sanctuary from the job and the press of hurrying humanity. With a pang, she realized that she had no idea when, or if, she would ever return.

She stepped outside and slid the balcony door shut. After climbing over the railing and dropping silently to the ground, a few strides took her to the garden shed's door. Using one of the keys on the ring, she unlocked the shed and disappeared inside. Seconds later she reappeared, wheeling her 2006 Yamaha XT225.

Simple, clean, stripped down, and fast.

Even better, it wasn't registered in her name. It was registered to Silvana Pace, lately of an address in Lake City, Florida—an address that didn't exist.

She wondered if the agents sitting in the sedan down the street would ever figure out that Laura Pace had come and gone right under their noses.

She opened the chain-link gate into the alley, wheeled the bike through, carefully shut the gate behind her, and rode away.

# 25

There was a time when phone booths were everywhere. They were ubiquitous on urban streets and in suburban shopping malls, and could always be found outside a convenience store. But those times were over. In an age of cell phones and text messages and VOI apps, pay phones were becoming scarce. But even in 2015, there were still a few holdouts—in airports, train stations . . . and bus terminals.

There were two phones mounted on the outside wall of the Greyhound terminal in Fort Lauderdale. It was close to midnight when Laura got there.

She knew it was a long shot, but she called the Everglades substation and asked for Detective Scott Jardine.

He was in.

"Hi, Scott. Working late, I see. Is that because of me?"

It took him a second. "Sarah?"

"Who else?" No sense confusing the man with her real name.

"Where are you?"

"You know I'm not going to tell you that. Did you find out what I asked?"

"I'm starting to hear stories. Rumors. Nothing official. About your . . . history."

"You're wasting time."

"You promised to send me a statement. About what happened with Lewis."

"I said I would, and I will. Eventually. You're stalling, Scott. Are the feds standing over you?"

He hesitated—just long enough to signal to her that they were.

"No."

"I asked you to find out one thing. Do you have the answer?"

"There was no monitor in the nursery. No cameras anywhere in the house. And no cell phones."

"Thanks. I'll call you again."

"When?"

"When I have something to tell you."

She hung up the phone, jumped on her bike, dropped south three blocks, and swung onto Route 842, heading east. She stayed just below the speed limit. The last thing she needed was a traffic stop. Two miles later, she stopped at Walmart and loaded fifteen hundred in cash on her card.

It was coming up on 5:00 A.M. when she rolled into Clewiston, Florida, population seven thousand, give or take. It shouldn't have taken that long, but staying off toll roads and using secondary highways and back roads had racked up the miles.

Clewiston was a textbook rendition of Anytown, U.S.A., squatting safely behind the Herbert Hoover Dike on the southern shore of Lake Okeechobee. The broad, empty lanes of US 27 brought her to the Executive Royal Inn, near the center of town. Despite the grandiose name, it was a simple, one-story motel with a dozen or so units, no different from hundreds like it on every secondary highway in the country.

In other words, it suited Laura perfectly. She pulled in.

The greeting sign she'd passed on the way into town had read CLEWISTON: AMERICA'S SWEETEST TOWN. Laura vaguely recalled that the nickname dated to a time when the local area was the sugarcane capital of America. Its honeyed sentiment failed to animate the check-in clerk who finally appeared after several long rings on the night bell, but Laura welcomed the woman's sullen indifference. She had no interest in being noticed. She'd chosen Clewiston for its location. Equidistant between Palm Beach on the Atlantic and Fort Myers on the Gulf, the town placed her an hour away from either coast, with the added bonus of a labyrinth of county roads in every direction in the event she needed an escape route.

She checked in as Barbara Hyatt and used the Walmart card to pay for five days in advance.

"Since you're checking in this early, you'll have to pay for last night."

"I understand."

"There's also a hundred-dollar damage deposit, for extra cleaning in case you smoke in the room," the unsmiling woman intoned. "It'll be refunded to your card."

"That's fine."

Despite the building's unremarkable exterior, her unit, the one closest to the office on the western end of the complex, turned out to be larger than she'd expected. It had obviously been recently refurbished. She took in laminate flooring, spotless bed linens, and solidly functional furnishings. A minifridge and microwave completed the package. Satisfied, she hung out the Do Not Disturb sign, checked that the interconnecting door to the adjacent unit was secure, and went straight to bed.

# 26

Before Laura left Walmart the night before, she'd called Dickie on a pay phone. It was after midnight, but she knew he was addicted to the late-night talk shows.

It was a cruel call to make, but it had to be done.

Her voice almost unhinged him. Pain and relief and anger all poured into her ear.

"LAURA? THANK GOD. *I thought you were dead! I thought those mob bastards had—I know you didn't kill those people. I didn't know who I should talk to. I didn't know what to—*" His voice caught in his throat, and the outpouring ended in a deep sob.

Laura felt sick.

Sick for Dickie, and disgusted with herself.

Dickie was her oldest friend. Her truest friend. She knew he loved her. She knew he'd always loved her. There had been a time, while she was undercover, when he had willingly risked his life for her.

In the years since, she'd sometimes played on his abiding love for her own ends. She knew that he knew that . . . and that he was resigned to it.

But the belief that he'd lost her forever had ripped him apart.

Laura's stomach knotted with shame.

"Dickie . . . Richard. I'm sorry. I can't imagine what this did to you. I have a lot to tell you. I've . . . I've been . . ."

*No, don't you play that card! Comfort him!*

"I've been held as a prisoner . . . since February sixth."

*Coward!*

Silence. Then a snuffle. "A prisoner? What happened? Where are you?"

"I escaped. But now the mob *and* the feds are looking for me. I'm going to give you a phone number. Memorize it and call me at noon tomorrow from somewhere private. Somewhere away from your office. Can you do that?"

"Noon my time?"

"Yes."

And now, in her motel room, her burner phone vibrated at exactly twelve noon.

Laura didn't recognize the number.

"You're using a prepay."

"That's right. And you're not in Oregon."

"There's something I need you to do."

"Just like that, huh? *NO!* Not before you tell me everything. What happened, what's going on now, and where are you?"

"It would be better if you didn't know where I am. I don't want you to have to lie."

"I'm going to lie anyway. Lie my fucking head off! Anyway, no one's on to me. I'm walking through Bunker Hill Park, talking to you on a phone that I bought an hour ago. It's going under the hammer as soon as we finish this call, and I'll buy another one. "

"Good."

"Two months ago, you were a federal agent working in Sicily, and now you're a murder suspect. Trust is a two-way street, Laura, so if you want my help, start talking."

Laura knew that tone. He had every right. She'd pushed him too far, too often.

"I didn't murder that couple."

"I know that! I never believed you did. But if you want me to put my ass on the line for you, *again,* tell me where you've been for the last few months, why you're a murder suspect, and what you're planning."

"How much time did you buy with that phone?"

"A hundred minutes for state to state."

"Okay. Find a bench, sit down, and listen."

It took her twenty-seven minutes to bring him completely up to date from their last contact, when he'd given her the lead on the Edens. He listened silently and didn't interrupt her once, not even when she told him about the amnesia. But she could tell from his breathing that he was living every minute of her story.

When she finished, he said heatedly, "Okay, the first thing I'm going to do is hack into every illicit cell phone in whatever jail that Lewis guy's in and offer fifty grand to the first inmate to stick a shiv into him!"

"Can we leave that for later?"

"If we have to. But I'm angry, Laura. *Really* angry!"

"So am I, Dickie."

"What do you need?"

She explained.

"Even if the brand they used had CVR," he replied carefully, "most storage plans only run seven to thirty days."

"CVR?"

"Cloud video recording. The monitor uploads through the home wireless provider. The parents can watch their child in real time, or download to review later. A lot of people like that feature because they can use it to capture stills for family albums, and if the camera is concealed, it also gives them a chance to keep an eye on nannies and babysitters."

"So you're saying that even if you could identify the brand, any video footage of that night will be gone."

"Not necessarily."

"But you just said—"

"Nothing's ever 'gone,' Laura. Purged, maybe, but not gone. Leave it with me."

"But how do we find out the brand? I can describe what I saw—the lens was like an eyeball on a black stand—but there must be dozens of brands that look like that."

"These people had money and they lived in Palm Beach. So they probably bought it at one of those high-end tech stores on Worth Avenue. These things all come with an automatic warranty, and all that information is stored electronically these days. We know their names, and when they expected to get their kid. If there's anything to find, I'll find it."

"Okay. And Dickie . . . remember the code?"

"Yeah, I do."

It took some effort, but by the following morning Dickie had hacked every tech outlet in Palm Beach, found the sale, identified the brand, and determined what storage plan the Edens had paid for. He kept Laura up to date on different burners he'd picked up, while she kept a low profile in her room, living mostly on takeout and watching the street.

That in itself was a problem. There would be no surer way of drawing attention to herself than by staying in her room 24/7, sending the maid away when she knocked. So on the first morning, she found a used bookstore and bought a couple of old textbooks on federal civil procedure and contract law. She told the day manager, a smiling and polite East Indian gentleman, that she was studying for very important exams and needed to be left undisturbed as much as possible. He arranged for her room to be serviced each morning at nine o'clock while she went for breakfast at a nearby diner. She left the books on her room's small desk, along with a couple of pens, a colored highlighter, and a notepad scrawled with legal gibberish plucked at random from the pages of the textbooks.

It took Dickie all day to drill through the baby cam manufacturer's system and recover the purged footage from the night of the murders.

He called just as she finished her Sunshine Sushi Selection Supper, which was basically a weird Japanese-American version of a Happy Meal.

"Hi."

"Do you have Wi-Fi where you're staying?"

"Yes."

"Can you log on with that phone?"

"Yeah."

"Okay. I'm going to give you an email address. The password is *redemption,* all lowercase. Go to Drafts. I've left a video link there. Watch it, but don't forward it anywhere."

She could hear the relief in his voice.

"Tell me!"

"Just watch it, Laura. I'll call later."

As prepared as she thought she was, the video was a shock.

There was Agent Lockhart with the now-dead couple. Her heart froze as she watched herself staring into the crib. As eager as she was to see what Dickie had already seen, once again the rush of memory froze her attention. She missed several seconds of the footage and had to run it back. There she was, all brisk and professional again, asking the sharp question.

"A baby camera, and no baby?"

There were the Edens' faces again, discouraged, resentful, apprehensive. She remembered that exact moment. She remembered struggling with herself, behind the cop façade, deciding how to deal with them, how to connect with them, how to handle this delicate situation when they returned to the living room.

Eleven minutes later, by the time stamp on the film, two darkly clad figures walked past the crib without pausing. She couldn't see faces, but she saw thick male bodies. By pausing and replaying a few times, she identified the grip of a handgun in the nearest man's hand. A minute later, there was the faint sound of a shriek . . . a few seconds of silence . . . then two loud gunshots. A few minutes passed. Suddenly one of the males reappeared. He stared at the baby cam, then reached for it. His hand filled the frame. The screen went gray . . . then, black.

Laura recognized the man.

His nose was still taped.

He was the thug who had snatched her off her chair at the restaurant in Catania.

She now had a good idea what had happened: While one man held his gun on the Edens, the other pistol-whipped her from behind. Then they'd taken her service weapon and shot the couple. When they left the house, they'd taken her, the camera, and the Edens' cell phones. It had never occurred to the investigators that there might have been a baby monitor in the nursery, so no one had followed the leads that Dickie had now followed, two months later.

They'd dumped her in the back of that van and drugged her. They'd been taking her to Roland Lewis, probably for a friendly little gang rape, just before they finished her off and dropped her into Roland's handy-dandy soup vat. But they'd both been killed in the collision that had robbed her of her memory, and Roland had seen his chance to turn a one-off rape and murder into a sex slave fantasy.

Her phone rang.

Area code 301. Bethesda, Maryland.

It could only be Dickie.

"I picked up another burner, but I'm not sure I needed to."

"I watched the video." Laura's voice shook.

"Yeah. I almost threw up. But that does it, Laura. You can clear yourself."

"Not yet."

"What do you mean? That video—"

"There's something I have to do first. And I'd rather not turn myself in and end up in a cell while some state attorney reviews 'fresh evidence.' I know how the system works."

"Laura, it's a slam. You'd be out in a few days."

"More like a few weeks. And then what? Even if the mob doesn't have me killed while I'm in custody, as soon as the FBI finish taping my statement I'll be transferred to some field office in Alaska. They'll bury me because no matter what I did, no matter what I uncovered, and no matter what happened to me back in February, I'm an embarrassment. I brought them clear evidence that this thing involved a corrupt U.S. consul, dirty Immigration officers, and mob connections, but they spent so much time passing the buck back and forth between CBP and ICE and USCIS that the whole thing came down on their heads. I'm not *just* an embarrassment because of what I know about the baby-smuggling operation. I'm an embarrassment because I'm living proof that they knew and they failed to stop it. They'll never let me finish this investigation, and I think I know why."

"Why?"

"Because it might lead higher."

"Higher in Homeland?"

"Yes. Or straight to some politician."

Dickie was silent for a second. "What are you going to do?"

"Stay out here and blow this thing wide open."

"All by yourself?"

"I've got you, Dickie."

"You do. But I'm not much good on the street."

"I get that." She was thoughtful. "That video link . . ."

"Yeah?"

"If I give you a name of a cop, could you find out if he has a private email address?"

"Try me."

It didn't take long. He called her back.

"Your detective friend doesn't use his name or even his initials in his email address."

"But you found him."

"Hey, this is me, remember? His email address is a telephone number."

"How does that work?"

"Easy. It's 2395552312@comcast.net."

"239 . . . that's the area code for—"

"—yeah, the whole southeast corner of Florida—Everglades City and Naples included. It's not a landline, and the number's not assigned to the sheriff's office, so I figure it must be Jardine's private cell."

Laura was silent.

"Laura? What's the plan?"

"You sound like you're enjoying this."

"I am. Kinda. It's you, remember? What do you want me to do?"

"You're sure that's him?"

"I am. But there's one way to be certain."

"Call him."

"Yeah."

"I'll need to find a pay phone."

"No, don't use any phone in that town unless you're planning to get on your bike and hit the road right after you make the call. We don't know what your trackers' capabilities are."

"So, what are you suggesting?"

"I'll make the call."

"*You?*"

"Yeah. Listen. There's an all-night coffee shop in Alexandria. It's twenty minutes from here. It's got free Wi-Fi and the signal's strong. There are no security cameras, inside or out. I'll drive there and park across the street. They change the password every few days, but it's printed on the till receipt. I'll buy a coffee, go back to my car, and make the call. I'll say, 'Is this Scott Jardine?' If he says yes, I'll tell him to check his emails and hang up. I'll forward the link to him, along with your Oregon number, and then deep six the phone in the Potomac."

"That works."

"Okay. Now give me the license number of your bike."

"Why?"

"So I can make sure no one's running it."

She gave it to him.

"Good. Talk to you later."

"Dickie . . ."

"What?"

"Thank you."

"You're welcome. And I still want that kiss."

After he hung up, Laura picked up the orange card she'd retrieved from her vacuum cleaner. The logo on the card read WIND PIÙ VICINI.

"WIND More Neighbors."

WIND was an Italian telecom provider. When she was in Sicily, she'd bought one of their twenty-euro prepaid SIM cards. When she got back, she'd added it to the collection in her vacuum cleaner because . . . well, you just never know. She popped out the embedded chip and loaded it into her phone.

Dickie had said don't make any calls from Clewiston. But he hadn't said don't make any calls from Italy. She dialed a number she had memorized months earlier.

It was answered on the third ring.

"*Ja? Wer ist das?*"

"You could be a little more polite, Renate."

There was a pause.

"Well . . . Laura Pace."

"You know my name?"

"Yes. I thought you were dead."

"I nearly was. Not that you sound very concerned."

"I was, but then came the alarm."

"What alarm?"

"Your fingerprints. And then the stolen cars. So I knew you were fine."

"I was on the run from the Mafia *and* the FBI, but you knew I was fine?"

"I am aware of your abilities."

"The prints, the stolen cars . . . how did you know any of that?"

Renate didn't immediately reply. Laura could hear the sound of rapid typing in the background. "You're calling from an Italian number, but I see you're not in Italy."

*What the hell?*

"And how exactly do you know that?"

"You're in Florida. Clew-i-ston? Have I pronounced it correctly?"

Laura took a breath. "Don't let the FBI get its hands on that software."

"They have it, but they need a warrant to use it. But in your case, they will have no trouble getting one. I would advise against using that SIM card again."

"I need some information."

"First, tell me what happened."

"Where are you right now?"

"Rome."

"Rome? Hell, Renate! It must be—what?—three in the morning? I'm sorry. I wasn't thinking."

"Four. And I was awake. So tell me."

"How much time will twenty euros give us?"

"Summarize."

Laura did.

"You said you needed information."

"Dominic Lanza. He's a New Jersey Mafia boss. I think he's behind all this. I'm guessing you can help me find him."

"That would be unwise."

"Trying to make me disappear was unwise. I intend to explain that to him. In person."

"The intelligence I have points to a different organization being involved."

"Don't believe it! Nelthorp was working with Lanza on two parallel rackets—fake auto parts and stolen babies."

"I'm saying you are wrong. Do not risk your life on a false premise. Mr. Lanza is not the enemy. The time on that SIM card will expire in six minutes. Give me a number to call you back."

Something about the woman's tone rankled Laura.

And made her suddenly and deeply suspicious.

She ended the call.

She removed the chip from her phone, and smashed it under the heel of her boot.

# 27

Just after 1:00 A.M., Laura's phone rang.

Jardine skipped the formalities. "How did you get my email address?"

"Is that important?"

"No. Maybe."

"I have resources."

"Why am I not surprised?" More a droll statement than a question.

"You're calling this number, so I'm assuming you watched the video."

"Yes! Are you ready to come in from the cold?"

"No. Are you at work right now?"

"Yeah. I'm off at eight in the morning."

"But you're alone?"

"I'm sitting in my car."

"Good. This call ends now."

"What?"

"The first thing you do in the morning is buy a prepaid SIM card. Then call me back on this number."

"How's that going to help? If the feds ever get suspicious of me—"

"Destroy the card after the call. Do it, and call me back."

His 8:30 A.M. call woke her up.

"Sarah, you need to come in! I'll do everything I can to protect you."

"I will come in . . . but not until I'm ready."

"I can make the car theft charges go away! Just tell me where you dumped the beater you stole from the casino."

"How do you know that was me?"

"Because I'm not stupid."

"How do you know I dumped it?"

"Because you're not stupid."

"Maybe we could start a club."

The lame joke only frustrated him. "Sarah! For God's sake, let me help you! That video footage tells the story. I need to give it to Turnbull, the FBI lead. It'll put things in a whole different light."

"No. I want you to sit on it. Wait . . . did you say Turnbull?"

"Alan Turnbull. He's a real pain. Do you know him? He's never mentioned that."

"We met once. And if he's on the case, it's a problem."

"Why?"

"He and Phyllis Corbin, my boss at Customs . . . they're close."

"Close, as in . . . ?"

"Yeah. That close."

Special Agent Alan Turnbull worked at the FBI's Miami field office. Laura only knew this because a year ago she'd been invited to the dedication ceremony for the FBI's gigantic new office complex in Miramar. Corbin and a few agents from her office, and a few from ICE, had attended. She'd noticed Corbin standing next to one of the Feebee agents. The body language was obvious. Curiosity aroused, she'd eased her way toward them through the crowd. She noticed their fingers were partially entwined behind his pant leg. Corbin's quick release and sidestep when she spotted Laura approaching confirmed her initial impression. Trapped, Corbin had been forced to introduce her to Special Agent Alan Turnbull, a man who appeared to be several years her junior. "Old friends," Corbin had said.

*Sure you are,* Laura had thought.

As she now recalled, Turnbull's most noticeable features were an exaggerated jaw and a self-important manner that didn't quite mesh with his otherwise colorless presence.

"Which means it's even more important that I stay out here," she told Jardine.

"More important than clearing yourself of a double murder?"

"Yes."

"How could it be?"

"There's more to this, Scott. A lot more! I need freedom to operate."

"What freedom, Sarah? You're a federal fugitive!"

"And how close are they to catching me?"

A pause. "Point taken. So, why did you send me that video link?"

"Insurance. I need one person inside law enforcement I can trust."

"You're saying you trust me?"

"Am I wrong?"

"Just me? No one else? What about Homeland? Customs? What about your old boss? If she's close to Turnbull, she could—"

"I can't take the chance. This case . . . it's not what you think."

"Then what is it, Sarah? Help me understand."

"That's not my name."

"What do you mean? Your prints, the warrant—everything comes back Sarah Lockhart!"

"They're avoiding publicity."

"Who's 'they'? It's a murder case. Murders attract publicity."

"Are you forgetting the 'restricted' notice that came up when you ran my prints? How much media coverage did those murders get?"

"Uh . . ."

Laura had already run an online search. Of course the story of the killings could never have been completely suppressed, but somehow Homeland had kept it small.

Very small.

Even more disturbing, they'd managed to keep it local. A truncated report had appeared in the back pages of *USA Today* and in a few other national papers, and then was mentioned no more. There was nothing about the suspected killer being a federal agent, and not a word about the victims being shot with a law officer's service weapon. The reports did mention that the FBI had joined the investigation, but that was put down to the fact that the case involved the suspected kidnapping of a child. If the press had sought and received any explanation of the *suspected* modifier, it had not found its way into their finished reports. All the public had been told was that a woman named Sarah Lockhart was being sought for questioning.

"I think I remember something in the press. Can't say for sure."

"My point."

"So, who is Sarah Lockhart?"

"A computer file."

"A computer file charged with two counts of murder?"

"That's right."

"So what were they planning to do if you were found and arrested?"

"Let's see . . . if I'm cleared before a trial, transfer me to some anonymous field office or pension me off early."

"And if you weren't? If it went to trial?"

"They wouldn't be able to hide my identity any longer, and they'd be facing a media shit storm."

"I'm not getting this. Why would—?"

"Scott, my real name is Laura Pace."

It took a few seconds for Jardine to absorb what he had just heard.

"Holy shit."

"My name was leaked after those arrests. But my photograph wasn't."

"I remember. The press hated that." The detective actually sounded excited. "Wait a minute! I do remember a picture—"

"From my tenth-grade yearbook. I look a bit different now."

"How did you manage to—?"

"By staying off Facebook, and making sure all public records were purged. Now . . . do you understand?"

"I'm beginning to."

"Scott. Can I trust you?"

"That depends. Tell me why I should trust you!"

"Because your instincts are telling you I'm innocent, and you always follow your instincts."

"How do you know that?"

"Intuition. Women have intuition; men have instincts. That's how we manage to survive each other."

An exasperated sigh. "Okay. What do you need?"

"Nothing right now. I have your number, and you have mine. Don't call me; I'll call you."

"What are you going to do?"

"Visit a mob boss."

"What?"

"His name is Dominic Lanza, and he's behind all this."

"Laura—"

"I'll explain next time we talk. Meanwhile, I need to make some coffee, and you need to destroy that SIM card."

"Yes, ma'am." He paused. "But I want you to promise me something."

"What?"

"When this is all over, I want to know everything."

"You will."

"No, not just about this. The senator. I want to know what really happened."

For the first time in a very long time, Laura Caterina Pace allowed herself a smile. No wonder Scott Jardine had sounded excited when she'd told him her name.

He was a Laura Pace fanboy.

# 28

Laura had hung out the Do Not Disturb sign before she crashed the night before, and the maid had respected it. But she'd left her phone on. After her conversation with Scott Jardine, she checked for missed calls, thinking she might have slept through the ringtone.

No missed calls. Her jaw tightened with worry.

Knowing Dickie, he would have called her by now.

She quickly showered and dressed. She was about to take a risk and call him when her cell rang.

"What happened? Why'd you take so long to call?"

She listened, waiting for the warning words. Long ago, they'd agreed on a code. If he was in trouble, calling her under duress, calling with a gun to his head, he would say something about an upset stomach in the first few seconds: "Sorry I didn't call . . . my stomach was acting up." Or: "I might have to cut this short . . . my stomach's bothering me."

"No worries. My stomach's fine." He laughed. "It was my boss. He was crawling down my neck about a project I'd promised him for yesterday. How did it go with Jardine?"

She told him.

"You should've let him help you!"

"Not yet. What did you find out about Lanza?"

"Not much. Lots of rumors." Laura heard rustling papers. "He's a businessman who lives in Florham Park, New Jersey. He's supposed to be connected to an extinct San Francisco crime syndicate, but that's never been proven. He's supposed to be the head of a so-called East Coast Lanza crime family, but that's never been proven either. There's pretty good evidence that his uncle, Tommaso Lanza, who died in '91, was linked up with some crooked construction union people back when Nixon was president. But if this organization even exists, it operates way under the radar. The FBI doesn't know what to do about Lanza because they've never been able to infiltrate his organization, assuming there's one to infiltrate, and they've never been able to turn one of his soldiers, assuming his employees are soldiers."

"Dickie, I read all this myself online."

"I figured. But there's one thing I've found that's not on the internet. It's in an intel report I found in the State Department's database. It was passed to us from the FBI."

"Tell me."

"Two years ago, Lanza and one of his assistants visited Sicily for a week. There were two other people with them—an old guy, maybe an old friend, and a young woman, probably some kind of nurse because the old guy was pretty frail. They landed at Catania in a private jet. Interesting thing: the flight plan showed the jet arriving from Florida. Anyway, during the week they were there, eleven members of one of the Cosa Nostra families in Palermo went missing. None of them has ever been found."

"What's the connection?"

"The Italian anti-Mafia police said there's some kind of long-running feud between this Palermo crime family and the Lanza people, who come from somewhere farther inland. Their immigration records showed that Dominic Lanza had only visited Italy a few times in forty years, and his last visit was something like twenty years earlier. So, after all that time he suddenly shows up, a bunch of these local mob guys disappear, and then he flies home. The Italian cops thought it was too much of a coincidence. They passed the info over to the FBI in case they might be able to help with the investigation."

"Any sign that the investigation got anywhere?"

"Nothing I could get my hands on."

"What's the name of this Palermo family?"

"Just a sec . . ." She could hear the whisper of turning pages. "They're called the Mazzaras."

"Spell it."

He did. Laura was silent.

"Laura?"

"Hmm?"

"What's next?"

"It's time I took a ride."

"Where to?"

"Florham Park, New Jersey."

"Not a good idea!"

"I'll stay in touch. Love ya."

"Laura!"

She disconnected.

The rented two-bedroom townhouse tucked in the back of the complex on Delano Street wasn't fancy, but it suited Scott Jardine just fine. It was close to the highway, and only thirty minutes from work. There were times when that half-hour drive was more than he wanted to face after a long shift, but he'd had a good reason for making the recent move. It was exactly halfway between the district 7 substation and the sheriff's main office in Naples.

As tired as he was after a full shift, and then four extra hours on an emergency call out, he wasn't so bushed that he missed the warning.

Movement inside his condo.

At this time of the year, the angle of the setting sun sent shafts of light through his patio doors, straight down the meridian of his railcar-narrow living room, and into his kitchen. He'd left in such a hurry this morning he'd forgotten to close the patio drapes.

A shadow had flickered across the inside of the slatted bamboo drop shade on his kitchen window.

He kept walking, rounded the end of the building, and climbed the trellis to his bedroom balcony. He had his key ready to unlock the sliding door, but it was already unlocked and open a few inches. There was no sign that it had been jimmied.

*Did I leave that unlocked?*

*Shit, I did!*

He removed his shoes and drew his weapon. Moving silently, he crossed his bedroom and then crept down the carpeted stairs to the main floor.

The first thing he noticed was that the drapes were now closed.

The second thing was the compact frame of a man with a tattoo on his neck examining titles on his bookshelf.

Jardine stepped into the open and leveled his weapon.

"Hands on your head and turn around slowly!"

The man did exactly as he was told. Jardine took in the dirty-blond hair, the angular face, the crooked smile . . . and the leather edge of a holster under the open jacket.

"Who are you, and what are—?"

"Please put your weapon away, Detective."

A taut-faced woman was sitting at his kitchen table. She looked to be in her early forties.

"Who are you?"

"My name is Renate Richter." She held up an identity card. "I work for the United Nations. This is Rolf Karppa. He works with me."

"Well, Mr. Karppa is armed, and he's in my house."

"We're not here to cause harm. We're here about a mutual friend."

"Who's that?"

"Sarah Lockhart. Please put your gun away."

Jardine hesitated, then holstered his weapon.

"Please join me."

Jardine walked over, pulled out a chair, and sat. He studied Renate's identity card, and handed it back.

"Okay. Why is the U.N. in my house?"

"From your reaction, I see that Sarah has not mentioned my name."

"No, she has not mentioned your name, and neither has Laura."

"You know this. Good. That will save us time. Now . . . you will recall her concern about a baby monitor."

"I've seen the video."

"Have you shared that video with the FBI investigators?"

"No. But you can tell her that the only reason I haven't is because I don't know how to explain where I got it."

"I think, more importantly, you have withheld it because she asked you to."

"That's right. And I still don't understand why."

"You must be patient. You will have a lot more evidence to show your federal authorities when this operation is over."

"What operation?"

"The one we would like you to join."

Jardine glanced at Rolf Karppa, who was now standing near the window looking faintly dangerous, like an unexploded grenade.

"Listen. I believe Laura is innocent. I do. But aiding and abetting a fugitive? That will get me arrested."

"No, it won't."

Jardine leaned back. This strange woman had him flummoxed. All he could think to say was: "You sound pretty confident."

"I am. I'm here to tell you everything we know about this case, and about Laura herself. When I'm finished, I'm confident that you will want to help."

"Does she know you're here?"

"No, she does not."

Seconds passed.

"I'm listening."

Thirty minutes later, Jardine went upstairs and quickly packed a duffel.

# 29

It was over twelve hundred miles from Clewiston, Florida, to Florham Park, New Jersey—in other words, a tough eighteen-hour ride if Laura did it in one run. But that would also mean taking I-95, a route that had lots of tolls and lots of cameras. She resigned herself to a three-day grind, sticking to state highways and staying off the interstate system. Instead of trying to figure out her route on a tiny cell phone screen, she returned to the used bookstore where she'd found her stage prop law books and bought an old Rand McNally road atlas. She'd make her move early the next morning—up at four, on the road before five.

Just before six that evening, she went to find some takeout. She remembered seeing a Mexican restaurant when she rode into town. It was about a half mile away. Since she'd be sitting on her bike for the next three days, she decided to stretch her legs and go on foot.

Walking back with a boxed order of enchiladas, she noticed a black Escalade nosed in at the eastern end of the motel complex. Other than her motorcycle, there were no other vehicles in the lot. When she'd left for the restaurant, there'd been two pickup trucks and a VW Beetle parked in front of various units.

She dropped in at the office to buy a newspaper. The clerk who had checked her in three days earlier was on duty. The woman was just as indifferent as before.

As she exited the office, her phone rang. It was Dickie.

"Better get rid of that bike . . ."

"Why?"

"Somebody ran your name on DAVID."

DAVID was the Driver and Vehicle Information Database maintained by the Florida Highways Department.

"All they'd find is the car I sold before I went to Italy."

"They also ran 'Silvana Pace.'"

Laura stopped in her tracks. Only she and Dickie knew the bike was registered in her deceased grandmother's name.

At least, until now.

"When was this?"

"Yesterday."

"Who ran the search?"

"I'm working on the tracker code, but it was definitely federal. They've got access to your file, so they'll know about your Nonna. Someone must have taken a shot in the dark."

"Thanks, Dickie. Call me when you know."

She disconnected. As she moved slowly toward her room, her eyes swept the parking area. There was nothing to see except the Escalade, which was parked at the end unit a hundred feet away. As she approached her door, she studied the curtains covering her double windows. They were closed tight, with a deliberate ripple in the cloth exactly where she had left it. She set her newspaper and food package on the pavement next to the door. Then, as quietly as possible, she unlocked her bike and rolled it into the breezeway that separated her unit from the motel office. If she needed to make a fast getaway, that passage led straight into the alley behind the motel. She strolled back to her door and slotted in her key card. When the panel light clicked green, she shoved the door hard and stepped to one side.

With a bang, the door juddered off the wall and started swinging back.

Ready to sprint, she risked a quick check.

Her room was empty.

She scooped up her dinner and the newspaper, ducked into the room, and locked and chained the door.

She removed her jacket and was just about to hang it up when, directly behind her, the door to the adjoining room swung open.

She spun around.

Scott Jardine was standing there.

"Hello, Sarah. Sorry . . . Laura."

"Scott? How did you—?" She moved toward him.

He drew his service weapon. "I've heard all about the hapkido moves, Laura. They won't stop a bullet. You're under arrest."

"Where's your SWAT team?"

"Didn't think I'd need one. You won't hurt me."

"And you won't shoot me."

"So we're even."

"You're sure about that?"

"Yes."

"Why?"

"Because I'm the only cop on your side and you know it." He circled behind her, holstering his weapon.

"Are you planning to cuff me?"

"Do I need to?"

He had her, and he knew it.

"God damn you, Scott! I trusted you!"

"Best investment you ever made. Let's go." He nudged her toward the adjoining unit.

*Something's not right. . . .*

"What's really going on here?"

"I'm arresting you so the FBI can't. That's all I can tell you right now. But first, there's someone you need to meet."

Laura stepped through the doorway.

The first person she saw was a tall, pallid-faced man with a receding hairline. He was standing just inside the adjoining door. Wary and watchful.

He looked nothing like a cop.

"Thank you for joining us, Ms. Pace," a calm male voice said from the far end of the room. "I've looked forward to meeting you."

Sitting in a chair by the window was an older man with a shock of iron-gray hair and a grave and unmoving face. He was wearing a blue blazer and holding a coffee mug in one hand.

Laura recognized Dominic Lanza from a grainy photograph she'd found online.

Dumbfounded, she wheeled on Scott Jardine.

"*You're* part of this?"

Jardine looked vaguely ill. "Yeah. But for a good cause. Just listen."

"Do have a seat, Ms. Pace." Lanza indicated a chair that was positioned near his own. "My colleague and I are not here to harm you. To help you feel safe, Detective Jardine volunteered his services as—shall we say—our mediator."

"You're Dominic Lanza."

"I am. And the quiet gentleman behind you is my assistant, Carlo Barbieri."

Her eyes blazed. "You had me kidnapped, framed me for murder, and sent me to die in a swamp . . . and now you want mediation?"

Jardine interposed. "What did I say, Laura? Please just listen."

"There is something you need to understand, Ms. Pace," Lanza said. "I was not responsible for your earlier abduction. But I believe I know who was. I would be grateful if you would hear me out."

Laura gaped up at him. He looked absolutely sincere.

Her mind struggled with competing concepts.

*You're listening to a mob boss. These people extort. They lie. They kill.*

*Scott Jardine—a police detective you respect—arranged this meeting.*

She strode over to the offered chair and sat down.

Across the room, Jardine and Barbieri took up positions against opposite walls.

"First," Lanza opened, "my apologies. I was made aware that you had certain plans for me. Plans based upon a misconception about my role in your recent hardships. I realized it was important for us to meet and clear the air. But, being aware of your formidable skills, it was necessary to take somewhat elaborate measures to secure your attention. For that, we can thank Detective Jardine."

Laura was reminded of a few things about Dominic Lanza that she'd picked up online. College educated. Extremely intelligent. One daughter, living in Texas, married to an architect. If Lanza was head of a criminal organization—and this small experience tended to confirm that—the internet had also been right about the man's legendary manners. The only dissonant note was the dropped left eyelid with which his impeccable diction was delivered.

Resigned, and now deeply curious, she nodded acceptance of his apology.

"I am aware of your former profession, and of the investigation you were conducting in Italy. I don't mind telling you this right now: Mr. Nelthorp did have a business relationship with me, but only for auto parts. I say this in the presence of Detective Jardine because I know that is not why he is here, and because he kindly allowed Carlo to search him, so we know he is not wearing a recording device."

"Auto parts. You mean the shipments from Catania."

"Yes. Obviously, I don't appreciate your interference in that enterprise. But I do admire your tenacity."

Laura wasn't quite ready to accept the admiration of a mob boss, polite or otherwise. She responded with silence and a level gaze.

"But you must understand. My organization has never been involved in baby stealing. *Traffico di bambini* is an abomination."

She was tempted to point out the moral schizophrenia of being disgusted by baby laundering but not by the possibility of babies dying in car accidents caused by defective brake pads, but obviously this was not the time.

"Nelthorp hid that side of his business from me," Lanza continued. "He was working with another organization . . . the one that tried to kill you."

"Which time?"

"What are you saying?"

"In Catania. Back in January. I was at a restaurant with Nelthorp. We were sitting at a sidewalk table. He said he was sorry; he'd thought we could be friends. I asked him what had changed his mind. He said, 'Not what. Who. Dominic Lanza.' A second later, a van pulled up and a couple of hoods tried to grab me. He knew they were coming."

"That was you?"

"What does that mean?"

"It means I read the newspapers. The articles mentioned an American woman who turned the tables on some kidnappers."

"I had backup. We got one of them, but his partner and the driver got away. My point is, Mr. Lanza, Nelthorp gave me *your* name seconds before I was attacked. And those men who got away were the same men who grabbed me in Palm Beach and murdered the Edens."

"Which supports my point, Ms. Pace. When Nelthorp used my name, was your investigation closing in on him?"

"Yes."

"And did he suspect that?"

"I'm sure he did."

Lanza nodded knowingly. "He dropped my name in case you were wired."

"I was."

"And . . . in case anything went wrong, which it did. His partner was making sure everything came back on me."

"Partner?"

"Antonio Mazzara." He saw the recognition on her face. "You know that name?"

"I saw certain intelligence reports," she lied. "In Sicily."

Dominic grunted. "Then you'll know he's been running the Mazzara organization from an Italian prison for the last fourteen years."

Laura's answering nod was another lie.

"He has crews in Sicily and over here. The Brooklyn branch is run by his nephew, Gustavo. They use one of the old New York families for cover and stay out of sight. And it fits that they'd try to shift attention onto me. Antonio hates me."

"Why?"

Lanza smiled. "You'll have to wait for my memoirs." He rose from his chair. "We'll be leaving now. Good luck."

Laura made a quick decision. "Before you go . . . I want to show you something."

"What?"

"A video. Detective Jardine has already seen it. It's on my phone"—she gestured toward the open door to her unit—"in my jacket."

Jardine went to retrieve the phone.

She logged on and the screen came to life. There they were again . . . the two men brushing past the crib . . . the shriek . . . the gunshots . . . the thug reaching for the monitor, his ferret eyes and acne-blotched face filling the screen.

"Stop there," Dominic said.

Laura froze the screen.

Barbieri was standing behind them. "Boss . . ."

"Danny Quintavalle," Dominic muttered.

"He works for Mazzara," Barbieri explained.

Laura noticed the expression on Lanza's face. "There's something else. Something you're not saying."

"You're very perceptive."

"What is it?"

"Quintavalle used to work for us. We've been looking for him."

"That sounds ominous."

"It can be, Ms. Pace. If circumstances require."

*At least he's not hiding it . . . even with Scott listening.*

"Well, Mr. Lanza, you can stop looking."

"Why?"

"Because he was killed in a head-on collision on February sixth. I was there."

Jardine's phone pinged. Lanza shot him a sharp look. Jardine glanced at a text on his screen. "You gentlemen will want to leave now."

"We understand," Lanza said. "Thank you, Detective."

And then they were gone.

Jardine led Laura back into her unit.

"Okay, Scott. Explain!"

"Explain what?"

"Are you kidding? That meeting! You being here! How did—?"

"Later! Grab whatever you need. We need to move fast."

The urgency in his voice, the concern on his face—suddenly she knew. From the initial shock and puzzlement of witnessing him "mediate" a meeting between her and a Mafia padrone, her comprehension now graduated to a whole new level. Scott Jardine was risking everything—his career, maybe even his life—for her.

Risking everything for Laura Pace, a woman he barely knew.

*Don't argue! Go with it!*

There wasn't much to pack and Laura was ready in minutes. He led her through the breezeway to an unmarked police unit that was parked in the alley behind the motel.

She tugged at his arm. "My bike's gone! I left it right here."

"Taken care of," he replied cryptically. He opened the front passenger door. "C'mon. We're running out of time."

Jardine peeled out of the alley and swung on to Route 27, heading south with his make-believe prisoner seated next to him.

"If I'm in custody, why didn't you put me in the back?"

"That might be noticed."

"By?"

"By busybody citizens."

He remained closemouthed for several miles.

Finally, fed up with his silence, she tried again. "Ready to explain all this now?"

"Just wait."

"Where are we going?"

"You'll see."

"My motorbike. What happened to it?"

"It's safe."

As they sifted down a forty-mile-long straight stretch of US 27, heading for its intersection with Interstate 75, she tried again. "This silent treatment. A little bit of revenge going on here?"

"Yeah, Laura. A little bit." He drew a deep breath. "Waiting for your next contact . . . waiting for little pieces of the truth . . . waiting, waiting. Meanwhile, getting continually harassed by the feds. Then forced to get down in the dirt with a mob boss just to make sure you don't get killed. Yeah, maybe it's *your* turn to wonder what the hell is going on." He stiffened, peering at the traffic ahead. "Get out of sight. Now!"

"What?"

"*NOW!*"

She slid down. Seconds later, three black SUVs whipped past, heading north.

"Okay, it's clear."

She sat up and craned to look. "If that's what I think it is . . ."

"It is."

"I'm not really under arrest, am I? What are you really doing, Scott?"

"Sticking my neck out for you! So will you please shut up and let me drive?"

She studied his profile, intent on the road. There was something . . . a dampness at the corner of his eye. She watched him wipe it away with the back of his hand.

"I promise to shut up if you'll answer one more question," she said quietly.

"What is it?"

"When did you decide to cross the line? To help me?"

He glanced at his watch. "Twenty-three hours ago."

Laura stayed quiet for the rest of the trip. She didn't even ask where they were going. By the time they blew past the I-75 ramp that would have taken them west, directly to Naples, she was no longer paying attention.

By then, her mind had drifted back to the monitor.

And the crib.

And the baby she had lost.

# 30

The house stood at the end of a wooded, brick-paved cul-de-sac in the Silver Bluff area of northeast Coconut Grove. As their vehicle entered the driveway, the door to one section of a three-car garage rose. Jardine drove straight in and parked next to a late-model Range Rover. The door descended behind them.

He led Laura through a door and guided her along a hallway of polished wood into a vast living room. It was not just lushly furnished, it was opulent, overloaded with furnishings and artwork to draw the eye and overpower the senses.

Comfortably ensconced on an ornate couch, with her legs neatly tucked up, was Renate Richter.

Laura threw a look at Scott. All she got in response was a clenched jaw. *So that's why you weren't talking.*

Renate gestured at the other end of the couch. Laura sat. Jardine took a chair nearby.

Laura locked cold eyes on Renate. "You told Dominic Lanza where to find me."

"I did. And I also told Detective Jardine. Together, we have just prevented you from getting yourself arrested. Or killed."

After what had just happened, Laura was in no position to argue. She took a deep breath. "I accept that. Thank you. But how did you know? How did you know it wasn't Lanza?"

"After our meeting at Realmonte, after you called to say you would help, I didn't hear from you. You failed to report anything you had learned about the infant trafficking that Gaetano and I had brought to your attention. I didn't know if you had made progress. Then I saw the Interpol Red Notice for Conrad Nelthorp. The metadata referred to smuggling offenses at the Port of Catania, and probable links to the Italian-American Mafia. I had already located your apartment in Catania, so I sent Gaetano to find you. You weren't there. He asked at the port, but got no cooperation. He worried that if he was too persistent with his questions, he might arouse unwelcome suspicions. Then we learned that the American consul in Palermo had died under suspicious circumstances. I eventually tracked you to Florida, but before I could make contact through a secure channel, you disappeared. The next thing I heard, you were a fugitive, wanted for murder.

"Shortly after you disappeared, Gaetano called me. Through the church, he was acquainted with Silvio Lanza, a prominent landowner in central Sicily. Silvio and Dominic Lanza are first cousins. Silvio had heard through his own network of sources that Nelthorp was being sought for two reasons: counterfeit goods smuggling and"—she faltered—"there was an Italian expression he used for it."

"*Traffico di bambini.*"

"That was it. According to Gaetano, when Silvio learned that the Lanza family was suspected of these activities, he was deeply insulted. He called Dominic to ask him about it, and was told what I am sure you were told today. Although Silvio Lanza has not led an exemplary life, he remains a religious man. He was aware that Gaetano was somehow associated with the Vatican, so he invited him to his home for a private discussion. He admitted nothing about the fake goods arrangement, but he insisted that Gaetano assure his superiors in Rome that no member of the Lanza family in Italy or America had ever been involved in human trafficking. Gaetano delivered that message to the Vatican, as requested. He also delivered it to me."

Laura saw where this was heading. "You were going to tell me all this when I hung up on you."

"I was."

"I destroyed the SIM card."

"I guessed that, because I tried to call you back." A pause, then she continued. "The counterfeit goods trade may have been a big part of your mission in Sicily, but you must understand that it barely registers at the U.N. We leave those investigations to international law enforcement and the World Trade Organization. On the other hand, stopping human trafficking of any description is one of our top priorities. After Gaetano told me about his meeting with Silvio, I used our intelligence resources to identify Nelthorp's residence in Trieste and then track the ownership. We established that it is owned by a Swiss company. The Swiss company is owned by a company in the British Virgin Islands, and that company is owned, in turn, by an Italian company registered with the chamber of commerce in Palermo. The sole director and shareholder of that company is a man named Rocco Russo. Mr. Russo happens to be a second-generation *avvocato* to a Cosa Nostra family in Palermo called—"

"Mazzara."

"You know this?"

"Lanza gave us a name. Gustavo Mazzara."

At that moment, a thickset blond man materialized in the doorway.

"Come in, Rolf," Renate said. "Meet our guest. Laura, this is Rolf Karppa. He works with me. He has brought your motorbike."

"It's in the garage," he told Laura. "But I suggest you don't use it unless we can arrange for new number plates."

"You all knew where I was staying in Clewiston!" Laura left her seat, suddenly agitated. Renate and Scott exchanged a glance and stood up. "Why didn't one of you just come to my door? Explain the facts of life? Why the show-and-tell with Dominic Lanza?"

Renate replied, "Because—how do you say it in English?—you needed to hear it from the horse's mouth. We can't afford—*you* can't afford—to waste any more time chasing false leads. After our interrupted telephone call, would you have believed it from me?"

"Probably not. But what if it had all gone wrong? This is the Mafia! Scott and I could have ended up dead!"

"No. You're worth more to Lanza alive. But we were ready for that contingency."

"Ready, how?"

"Rolf and Paolo were monitoring the meeting from unit three."

"Who's Paolo?"

"You'll meet him in a minute. He's making dinner."

Laura stared at Renate Richter. She stared at Rolf Karppa. She stared at Scott Jardine.

*Detective* Scott Jardine.

It was all too surreal.

"The feds on the highway . . ."

"It took your Homeland people a few days, but this morning they told the FBI that you might be using an old alias that had never been retired: Barbara Hyatt. Rolf and I visited Scott and persuaded him to help extract you. I stayed here to monitor the FBI radio traffic. And Rolf stayed behind in Clewiston after you and Scott left to record the event. Show her."

Rolf passed his cell phone to Laura. A video played. There was the sprawling rust-colored motel in Clewiston, the office, the Coke machine, the marquis proclaiming CLEAN ROOMS HBO FREE COFFEE HIGH-SPEED INTERNET. Judging by the angle, the film was shot from the laundromat across the street.

A few seconds passed, and suddenly the lifeless scene erupted with activity. Black SUVs and marked police units pulled into the parking lot. Through the passageway to the alley, she could see other emergency units arriving behind the motel. A team of agents, suited up and armed with assault rifles, closed on Laura's unit. One agent ran to the office and reemerged seconds later. He used a key card to unlock the door to her unit and the cops piled in.

The screen went black.

Laura let out a long breath.

"That video was shot forty minutes after Scott took you away."

"How did my bike get here?"

"We rented a van," Rolf said. "I loaded it as soon as you entered your room."

Laura turned to Scott. She looked up into his troubled face and said, "Thank you."

"You're wel—"

She grabbed his shirt and kissed him on the mouth. He took a step back. His face flushed.

"Am I still in custody?"

"Protective custody," Renate responded, answering for Jardine, who was looking too confused to answer. "And I think you'll find the food's much better than in some federal holding facility."

As she spoke, a handsome young man materialized in the doorway. He was clad in kitchen whites and a chef's hat.

"You have a chef?"

"An *Italian* chef. This is the U.N., remember? This is Rolf's friend, Paolo Nori. He helps us from time to time."

"And not just in the kitchen," Laura suggested, taking in Paolo's body-builder biceps.

"Correct."

Paolo responded with a puckish grin, and disappeared.

# 31

It was a late dinner.

Not by Italian standards, of course, as Laura well knew. Back in Catania, sitting down for a big meal at nine or ten in the evening had been pretty much standard. Those heroic meals had played hell with her sleep pattern, but she'd eventually adapted. Good thing, too, because Paolo didn't start rolling out the courses until after ten.

As soon as they sat down, an eye-popping selection of dishes appeared on the beautifully set table.

"Because it's getting late, Rolf asked Paolo to combine the courses," Renate said. "Try the *pasticcio di pollo*," she urged. "He's made it for us before. He says it's his grandmother's recipe."

Laura helped herself to a wedge of the pistachio-accented chicken pie. Suddenly aware of how hungry she was, she eyed the spread before her and went for a prawn dish she recognized—*gamberi e capperi*.

For a few minutes, everyone ate in silence.

"What is this place?" Laura finally asked, taking in the vaulted ceiling, the massive cypress beams, and the inlaid flooring.

"The house belongs to a Russian oligarch. He thinks he's leased it to a Swiss private bank."

"Why would the U.N. rent a house in Miami?"

"Our unit maintains safe houses in seventeen countries, all leased, all changed frequently. Right now we have three in the U.S."

"How long have you had this one?"

"A week."

Laura got it. "Interesting timing . . ."

"We'd like you to stay."

"I'm not sure that would be wise."

"It is entirely your choice. But you will not last long"—Renate waved her butter knife at a window—"out there."

"Because?" Laura asked, eyeing Paolo, who had now joined them at the table and was at that moment happily digging into some unidentifiable dish consisting of pasta wheels and ground sausage.

"Because you've lost your cover identity, and you are about to lose your cell phone system."

"How do you know that?"

"The FBI is talking to the NSA. They're talking about you."

Renate let that sink in.

"Even if you restrict your phone use to incoming calls, it won't take them long to discover your general location. Then they'll send out a team with a Stingray."

Laura knew about Stingrays. They were surveillance devices originally developed for the military. A Stingray masqueraded as a cell phone tower, sending out signals that tricked cell phones in the area into transmitting their real-time locations and other identifying information. They could also be used to capture phone conversations, and even text messages. The devices were controversial because, while they were tracking a target's phone, they were also soaking up information from all the other cell phones in the area.

"They'd need to know what phone number I'm using—in fact, all three of them—before they could narrow their search."

"No, they'd just need to know what phone Richard Bird is using."

A thick silence fell across the table.

Laura's stomach tightened. "What's happened?"

"Nothing yet."

"But?"

"But . . . if we figured out he's been helping you, so will Homeland. They know he became involved in your famous case, and that he risked his life for you. They will pass that information to the FBI, if they haven't already. It will only be a matter of time before the investigators focus on him. You need to stop him from calling you."

"From what you're saying, I'd be putting him at risk just getting that message to him."

"We can do that for you," Renate said.

Laura scanned the faces at the table—two U.N. spooks, a sheriff's detective, and an Italian-agent-cum-hobby-chef. She was beginning to wonder if she was in some kind of dream.

"Considering what the FBI knows, where is the last place they'd look for you?" Renate asked.

"At a U.N. dinner party, in a Russian kleptocrat's house, sitting across the table from a Collier County cop."

"I suppose that's one way to put it," Jardine muttered.

More silence. More eating.

Finally, Jardine spoke. "I have a question." He was looking at Laura. She waited.

"Let's say we get you out of this. All charges dropped."

"Yes, let's say that."

"What then? Back to Homeland?"

"No. That's behind me. Even if I clear my name, they'll bury me."

"You're an embarrassment."

"That's right. They'll be afraid to fire me, so they'll transfer me into some dead-end office job and cross their fingers I'll resign. When I do, they'll remind me I signed a nondisclosure agreement and they're not waiving it. They'll be afraid I'll go public. They'll want to hide their negligence."

"Or complicity," Renate added.

Laura was tempted to agree, but she kept the thought to herself.

A platter of roasted peppers was being handed around, but she passed on it. Her mind was roiling and her appetite had suddenly evaporated. She pushed back her chair and stood at the window, trying to gather her thoughts.

From behind her, Jardine's voice. "Thanks, Paolo. Great dinner. But what I really need is sleep." A chair scraped. "Laura, your things are still in my car. I'll get them."

She turned. "You're leaving?"

"In the morning. Renate gave me a bed."

"What about work?"

"I'm on at seven tomorrow morning."

"We need to talk."

"Yeah, we do. But I need a clear head. I've had six hours' sleep in two days."

"Your bedroom is also ready, Laura," Renate said.

"My bedroom?"

"It's your choice, but where else can you go?"

# 32

"Why have you done all this? I understand the U.N.'s focus on human trafficking, but why go to so much trouble to protect Dominic Lanza from me, or me from him, or me from getting arrested? What aren't you telling me?"

Laura and Renate were back in the living room, glasses of wine in hand. Jardine, Paolo, and Rolf had all bid them good night.

"It's personal," Renate said.

"What is?"

"Helping you."

"Why?"

"Because of Monte Sole."

It took a few seconds for the words to sink in. "How could you—?"

"My grandfather was a member of the 16th SS-Panzergrenadier Division."

Laura was stunned into silence.

"You want to ask me if my grandfather served in Italy."

"Did he?" But she had already guessed the answer.

"He was transferred from the Russian front. I have dreaded telling you this, Laura, but I must." Renate closed her eyes and took a breath. "He was at Casaglia."

Her words hung like smoke in the air between them.

"He was convicted *in absentia* by an Italian military court and sentenced to life imprisonment. But that was in 2005 and by then he was very old and very sick. He was never extradited. He died four months after the verdict." Renate studied Laura's face. "I can hear you wondering . . . did I know? Not until the trial. He never spoke about the war, at least, not to his grandchildren. All we knew was that our Opa had fought on the Russian front. My brother and I didn't even know he had been in Italy until the trial was about to be reported in the news. Only then did my father call us and ask us to come home. He refused to tell us why. I was in London, and Jürgen was in Stockholm. When we were both there, he took us into his study and told us the truth. It is the only time I have ever seen my father cry." Renate closed her eyes. Shame etched her features. "Laura, I know your grandmother was in the cemetery in that village. I'm sorry. I truly am."

"Telling me this . . . do you also know about—?"

"Your mother and father? *Ja*. I received a complete profile."

Laura blinked.

"I already knew your real name when we met in Sicily. I assumed you were working under a false identity because of that case with the politician."

"But how could you know all that? From what I've heard, the U.N.'s intelligence-gathering ability is pretty substandard."

"It is true that many governments, and the American government in particular, make no secret of their contempt for the secretary general's intelligence unit. But that group is just for show. I don't work for them."

"Then who do you work for?"

"A different unit. We're 'off the books,' as you Americans say."

"How could the U.N. operate anything like that without the U.S. government knowing about it?"

"Because of the know-it-all attitude that you just expressed. Our secretary general is from Finland. The permanent members of the Security Council have always been dismissive of the intelligence-gathering abilities of small countries. When the council members recommended our SG's appointment, they knew he had once served as the director general of the Finnish SIS. But they never really understood how advanced that intelligence service was. After he took up his post, he decided that as long as member states were refusing to share vital intelligence with the U.N., he would just have to help himself. There is very little that the NSA, or the U.K.'s GCHQ, or Russia's SVR, or for that matter any national intelligence service can hide from us. We just let them think they can."

Laura made a connection. "Rolf Karppa . . . His name sounds—"

"Yes. Rolf is a Finn. The SG brought him over from the SIS."

Inside Laura's head, their conversation was only partially registering. Her questions had just been to fill space while her mind struggled to realign itself with yet another perspective of Renate Richter. She found herself examining the facial details of the woman whose grandfather had taken part in the murder of Nonna's aunt, cousins, and countless of her neighbors and friends.

Examining her cornflower-blue eyes—*did she have her grandfather's eyes?*

Studying the curve of her lips—*had that been the shape of a killer's lips?*

Staring at that taut, pale, flawless skin . . .

"What was his name?" she asked, not knowing what else to ask, or to say.

"Erich. Erich Richter." Then, as if a dam had burst, came another flood of words. "He was only sixteen when the war started. He joined the SS in 1941. He was sent to Russia, and then to Italy in 1944. He married my grandmother in 1952. He was eighty-two when the Italian judges finally caught up with him. But he never really answered for his crimes. The court's investigators knew his name, but they didn't know where he was living. They didn't even know if he was still alive. It wasn't even an investigator who found him. It was a journalist from Milan. That's when it became a media story."

"Do you know . . . what part he played?"

"I only know he was at Casaglia. There were other massacres on that mountain during that week, and he was probably involved. My father obtained a German translation of the trial transcript. After he finished reading, he burned it. He has never spoken of his father again."

For long seconds, Laura was silent. Finally, she said, "Renate?"

"Yes?"

"I think I'd like to go to my bedroom now. Would you show me the way?"


The décor and furnishings of her new quarters were carefully understated, but unmistakably top-of-the-line: deep carpet, a vast bed, recessed lighting, and a spotless en suite with a marble bathtub.

Laura barely noticed. She had a quick rinse in the shower and went to bed.

But sleep didn't find her.

Not for hours.

Her mind raced with memories of her grandmother's life.

Silvana Pace had been one of only seven survivors of the massacre in the cemetery. Nearly two hundred others had died, most of them women and children. After escaping over the wall, and spending three days roaming the forested slopes of Monte Sole, hungry, footsore, torn by brambles, and constantly hiding from Nazi patrols, she had finally located the ragtag remnants of Stella Rossa. Her first contact was with a female fighter, a sinewy young woman named Anna Conte. Anna dressed her bleeding lacerations, fed her, and coaxed her back to life. A bond was born between Silvana and Anna that would come to sustain them through the months of savagery to come.

And now it sustained Laura, because Anna Conte's blood ran in her veins.

At first, Silvana was enlisted as a *staffetta,* supporting the fighters by acting as a nurse, a courier, and an armorer, cleaning and loading their weapons. But in a running firefight with a German patrol, she quickly proved her worth, bringing down the Nazi squad leader with a single rifle shot. Soon she was joining Anna and the men on sabotage missions and armed attacks on the hated Fascisti and, whenever the opportunity presented itself, isolated German patrols. Her comrades soon discovered that, even in the heat of battle, this seventeen-year-old girl moved like a gazelle and never lost her nerve. Every fighter was assigned a battle name to protect his or her extended family from fascist reprisals. From the beginning, Silvana's *nome di battaglia* was Piccola Baronessa.

Little Baroness.

Not yet out of her teens, Silvana accepted that any given day might be her last. She was an outlaw, and yet in the Italy of 1944, this made her proud. As young as she was, she had already learned one of life's most bitter and important lessons: that law and justice can be diametrically opposed. Long before she joined the brigade, she had seen her enemy up close. She had seen them for what they were—cruel men claiming "lawful" orders. Monsters who did what they were commanded to do, ruthlessly and meticulously, and took deep satisfaction in their evil. In fighting against men like this, she had chosen justice over law. That was all she needed.

When her band eventually moved north, she marched with them.

She ended her war near Lago d'Iseo, preying on retreating German troops.

In late 1945, although unmarried, she took advantage of the postwar chaos in Italy to adopt Angelo, the seven-month-old son of Anna Conte.

Anna and the infant's father, a fellow fighter, had both been killed in the same operation. Angelo had been one of the dozens of orphans delivered to a convent of nuns and then, due to food shortages, speedily put out for adoption with very little paperwork. Silvana ensured that the boy was given to her.

Two years later, she managed to embed herself and little Angelo in the flood of displaced war victims finding a new life in America, and they had sailed for New York.

But death had never stopped coming.

In 1983, Angelo's wife, Catherine, Laura's mother, went into convulsions and slipped into a coma within minutes of giving birth to Laura. She died of eclampsia on the following day.

Five years later, Laura's father, who had been raising her with the help of his devoted adoptive mother, died in the Pan Am crash at Lockerbie, Scotland. He had been on his way home from a business trip to England and Italy.

It had fallen to Silvana to raise her only grandchild.

Apart from a bitter sense of perpetual loss, Laura's formative years were constantly informed by her grandmother's recounted memories of the war. In Silvana's eyes, Laura was a vulnerable orphan who was maturing, all too quickly, from wide-eyed child, to gawky teenager, to dangerously attractive young woman. She had been determined that Laura would be properly prepared for the harsh realities of life in an unpitying world. Her wartime tales—at first related as watered-down bedtime parables, later decanted with ever more vivid and unblinking detail as Laura matured—were meant as both cautionary tales and lessons for life. Laura had not only absorbed the lessons of her grandmother's life, but in her imagination had lived and breathed every minute, every week, every month of the old woman's violent youthful education.

Laura was self-aware enough to recognize the woman she was—on the inside, inhabiting her own protected, distinctive world; on the outside, sometimes distant, sometimes unforgiving.

Long ago, she had decided she could live with that.

She could live with being the roughly assembled product of Silvana Pace's obsessions.

*Law and justice . . .*

Today, Laura Pace was a fugitive from the law, hunted for crimes she didn't commit.

*Law and justice . . .*

Today, a police officer had broken the law to prevent her from being arrested.

*Law and justice . . .*

Tonight, she was lying in a bed in a safe house run by a secret United Nations intelligence unit whose activities probably violated a score of U.S. federal statutes.

*Nonna would completely understand.*

She fell asleep.

# 33

The safe house was a two-storied, forty-eight-hundred-square-foot residence that, apart from a manicured garden and a few century-old oak trees, looked just like any other home in the area. Inside, as Laura had already discovered, it was another story—every room the embodiment of luxury.

But she wasn't there to luxuriate.

She found Renate and Rolf breakfasting on the terrace under a milky sky.

Laura joined them and poured herself some coffee.

"If you're interested," Renate said, "Paolo's making omelets."

"Coffee's fine for now. I wanted to ask about communications. If you're right, mine aren't secure."

"You were having your calls forwarded through three cell numbers," she replied. She nodded to Rolf, who reached into a pocket, pulled out a phone, and handed it to her. "We use five, and encrypted VOI links."

"Thank you." She examined the phone. "Is it safe for me to call Richard Bird?"

"I wouldn't recommend it. There's no guarantee of security at his end."

Laura glanced at the house. "What time did Scott leave?"

"Six this morning. He didn't want me to wake you."

"Why?"

"I think he's . . . how do you say . . . conflicted."

Laura took a breath. "It's understandable. He just risked his career for me. That must be why he was so quiet last night. He's got to be worrying . . . if I'm caught, even if I'm finally cleared of charges, if I ever let it slip that he helped me, his life will be ruined."

"I don't think that's the only thing he's conflicted about."

"What do you mean?"

"For such a smart woman, you're a bit blind."

Paolo appeared from the house carrying omelet-laden plates.

"Something for you, signorina?" he asked Laura.

She answered him in Italian. "No, thank you, Paolo. Maybe I'll have some toast a bit later."

"*Va bene.*"

She turned back to Renate. "Are you just giving me a hideout here, or do you have something more in mind?"

"We didn't go to all this trouble just to walk away."

"In that case, we need to find Conrad Nelthorp before the feds do. Your people could help."

"We can't involve our full unit directly. That would require too much explaining. Rolf is here as a volunteer. Paolo works for AISE, the Italian intelligence agency. He was posted in the Balkans, but they lent him to us because they owe Rolf a favor."

"So this isn't a U.N. operation at all."

"Let's just say the SG told me he wouldn't stand in our way, but he will deny all knowledge if anything goes wrong."

"What if everything goes right?"

"He'll still deny."

"So where does that leave us?"

"We have certain facilities. We're monitoring Interpol. I've programmed an alarm in my phone that will tell us if Nelthorp is located. But the FBI will be notified at the same time. With our limited manpower, it will be impossible to get out in front unless we can find him before the police do."

"Have there been any leads at all?" Laura asked. "Any alerts? Any tripwires?"

"Nothing."

"He can't be traveling under his own name."

"That's right, and that's a problem."

Laura was thoughtful. "Maybe not."

"What do you mean?"

"Dominic Lanza. You told him where I was staying. You arranged for

Scott to walk me straight into that room. You knew we would be safe. You know more about him than you're letting on."

"You're very perceptive. The U.N. has a file on Mr. Lanza. Twice in the past forty years he has supplied information to the Italian police that helped them break up illegal mining operations that were being run by criminal gangs. Gangs that were using child labor."

"*Rival* criminal gangs? Like the Mazzaras."

"The first time, yes. But not the second time. He'd learned that children were being exploited in an underground mine in the Madonie Mountains and he took the information personally to the commandant of the Carabinieri in Palermo. When I called him a few days ago, he already knew he'd been implicated in a baby-laundering investigation. Remember . . . his cousin had called him in February. I could tell from his reaction that he wouldn't harm you—that he just wanted to set you straight."

"Okay. That all fits. But my point is that he also admitted he was behind the auto parts shipments."

"He did?"

"Yes. And that Nelthorp was his partner in that business. So, now that he knows Nelthorp was also involved in the baby trade—"

"—he might tell us if he had another identity."

"Right."

"Even if he does, it won't help us if Nelthorp's carrying an EU passport and he's still in the Schengen area. That would give him access to twenty-six countries without border inspection."

"He'd still have to produce a passport to rent a room," Rolf pointed out.

"That would take days to check."

"If he has a passport in any name," Laura said, "it will be American."

"Why do you say that?"

"He told me English was all he needed in Europe. I don't think he's fluent in any another language."

"It's worth a try." As if on an unspoken signal, Renate and Rolf both stood up, left their omelets, and went into the house.

Moments later, Paolo joined Laura, carrying his own omelet. He scanned the unfinished food on the table. He looked aggrieved. "No respect for good food," he muttered in Italian.

Laura watched him eat for a few minutes. Then, keeping it going in Italian, she said, "Renate says you're here because your agency owes Rolf a favor."

He shrugged. "Or because he loves Italian cooking." There was a slight edge in his voice.

"What did he do for them?"

Long silence, then: "Them, and me." He took a few more bites of his omelet. "We were security. At the World Figure Skating Championships. I was there with the Italian team; Rolf was in charge of the squad from Finland. One of the Italian skaters was the favorite for the women's singles title. The SIS found out some Russians were planning to attack her. Rolf came to warn me."

"That sounds like—"

"—that thing with those two American skaters, back in the nineties. Yes, but this was worse. There were three Russian agents. They were going to break her legs. Rolf stopped them."

"How?"

"He made them disappear."

"Alone?"

"I went as backup, but he took care of it."

"I've never heard about this."

"Our governments kept it quiet."

He returned to his breakfast.

Soon after, Rolf and Renate were back.

"William Stockton," Renate announced calmly. "We think he's probably in Switzerland. A United States citizen named William John Stockton landed at Charles de Gaulle eight days ago. He arrived on a flight from Tunis and connected for Zurich on the same day."

"Tunis?"

"My guess is he—or, more likely, the Mazzaras—have contacts there. People on the payroll. Immigration officials and police who would protect him. When he disappeared after you were attacked in Catania, he knew the Italian police would be looking for him. He probably drove to Palermo and reported what happened to the Mazzaras, and they put him on a ferry. Two lines run direct sailings from Palermo to Tunis."

"If the Mazzaras let him live," Rolf growled, "it can only mean one thing. They think he's still useful to them."

"Probably to set up a new operation. He's the one with the network of recruiters. The ones who steal the babies from the camps."

"You said Zurich," Laura said. "Is that all we know?"

"I'm running a check on the hotels there. But we're facing the problem I mentioned. Switzerland isn't in the EU but it's part of the Schengen zone. Nelthorp could be in any one of those twenty-six countries by now."

"I don't think he is."

"Explain."

"I think he's in Geneva. The first time I met with him, he talked a lot about Trieste. But at one point he told me how much he loved Geneva. He babbled about it like a tourist. He said there was one place that brews some kind of amazing white chocolate coffee . . . his words. He said it was called Precision."

"What was?" Renate asked. "The place, or the coffee?"

"He didn't say. But it shouldn't take much to find out if there's a restaurant named Precision, or one with a menu that lists white chocolate coffee under that name. Try TripAdvisor."

Renate worked her phone. "It's a restaurant, on Rue David-Dufour."

"Have you got anyone placed near there you can trust?"

"Gaetano's in Rome. It's an hour's flight."

"Not exactly a job for a priest," Paolo said, speaking up for the first time.

"It is for this one."

"He won't be able to sit in the restaurant all day," Laura said. "So he'll need to find somewhere nearby where he can keep watch. If there's no sign of Nelthorp after a few days, it probably means I'm wrong."

"He'll do it."

It took two days.

Two long days for Laura, who was beginning to chafe at the inaction.

Renate had returned to New York. Just before dinner on the second day, she phoned Rolf from her office at the U.N. When the call came in, Paolo was banging around in the kitchen, and Laura and Rolf were playing cards by the pool.

Rolf put her on speaker.

"He's there. Gaetano spotted him at Precision yesterday and followed him back to his room. He's staying at a B&B on Boulevard Carl-Vogt. But there's a problem. He's getting ready to move."

"Do we know where?"

"It looks like Genoa. Gaetano followed him to the Cornavin train station. When he went to a ticket machine, Gaetano took the one next to him and pretended to buy a ticket while he kept an eye on Nelthorp's screen."

"How many trains per day leave that station for Genoa?"

"None. His ticket will take him to Milan. He'll change trains there."

"Do you have a plan?"

"Gaetano is flying from Geneva to Genoa. He'll be waiting when Nelthorp gets off the train."

"How will he know what train he's on?"

"We have . . . certain software. Gaetano gave me the serial number of the machine he used and the time when the ticket was issued. I'm tracking the bar code on Nelthorp's ticket. As soon as he boards his connection in Milan, we will know."

Laura said, "I should be there."

Rolf straightened. "Be where?"

Renate answered for her. "Genoa. She's right, Rolf. Every day increases the risk that Europol will find Nelthorp. We need to move on this. Laura?"

"Yes?"

"I need a head-and-shoulders photograph of you. Passport style, blank backdrop. Digital is fine. Send it to me and I'll get you a U.N. laissez-passer."

"But how can she travel?" Rolf asked. "With the FBI watching every—"

"You'll have to go private. I can arrange a jet out of Kendall Airport. Leave that with me."

"Renate—"

"Just a minute. I'm thinking. We'll need to get the pilot to file a flight plan for Genoa, with a stop at Teterboro, New Jersey. It's the nearest non-commercial airport to my office. I'll meet the plane there with the laissez-passer for Laura. Laura, send me your clothing sizes, including shoes. You'll need a suitable wardrobe."

"Will do."

"No one will question a senior official of the United Nations carrying a red passport, especially when she arrives on a private jet. I'll make sure Gaetano is there to meet the flight."

"You're serious?" Rolf again.

"Yes, I am. Gaetano is willing, but he isn't trained. He'll need Laura."

"Nelthorp knows what she looks like."

"That's not going to matter," Laura said quietly.

Rolf looked into a pair of cold, dark eyes, and he understood. "I'm also trained."

"I was hoping you'd say that," Laura replied.

"Okay. You both go," Renate said.

"What about Paolo?" Rolf asked.

"Close up the house and bring him with you. I'll pick him up at Teterboro. The Italian delegation's security team is short staffed and his supervisor asked to borrow him back. And, Rolf?"

"Yes?"

"Don't brief him on this operation. We don't know how much information he's feeding back to his people."

"You're worried about the SG."

"Yes. We need to protect him, and you know how the politics can be around this place."

Laura interposed: "Renate, this identity you're giving me . . . what's my backstory?"

"You speak fluent Italian, so you'll be Italian. I'll give you a full briefing at Teterboro."

"Okay, but I want her first name to be Anna."

"Why?"

"My biological grandmother's name was Anna. She was killed in 1945."

Renate knew better than to argue. "Agreed. Anything else?"

"Yes. We'll need to make one extra stop. Before Genoa."

# 34

When the Gulfstream G450 made its long banking turn past Etna, the volcano was still spewing sulfur and living up to its reputation as the mountain that never sleeps. They landed just after dawn and taxied to the predesignated spot on the apron. The jet's engines spooled down.

Watching at a window, Laura saw the familiar lights of the main terminal at Fontanarossa Airport. Crawling toward them, almost invisible against that polychromatic backdrop, she could just make out the strobing blue lights of an emergency vehicle. The copilot appeared from the cockpit and opened the main door. The jet's hydraulic steps automatically deployed, reaching the ground just as the vehicle pulled to a stop.

Laura recognized the gray paint with yellow markings. It was one of the Guardia's SUVs.

She was on edge.

She was about to find out if Marco Sinatra was the man she had judged him to be.

When Renate had come aboard at Teterboro, she had recited the instructions she'd given to Laura's unsuspecting friend. "I said he'd be needed for a couple of days, so pack an overnight bag and meet the flight out on the tarmac. I instructed him to tell ATC that high-level U.N. personnel were aboard and would not be disembarking, so they were to designate an isolated parking spot on the apron. I told him to bring a trusted Immigration officer out to the plane to clear the passengers, but that he was to board first so he could be briefed. Only after that was the Immigration officer to board the aircraft."

"How did he react?"

"No problem. The head of our field support office in Vienna is a friend of the Guardia's commanding general. The general had already called Marco, so he was expecting my call."

"But he doesn't know who he's meeting."

"That's right. It's up to you now."

Marco was mounting the steps. He was in full uniform.

*Now or never. . . .*

Laura got up from her seat. She stood nervously in the middle of the aisle, facing the entrance.

Marco removed his hat, shook hands with the copilot, and stepped into the cabin.

Laura watched his eyes as he absorbed the startling sight before him—the young woman he had once known as CBP Agent Sarah Lockhart, now a fugitive from American justice, attired in a designer pant suit, elegant heels, and power makeup.

His eyes filled.

He took three long steps and enveloped her in his arms.

*"Carissima! Carissima Sarah!"*

It was going to be okay.

Rolf appeared from the aft cabin. She made a quick introduction, using Rolf's real name, and then pushed Marco onto a divan. "I need to explain."

"No, you don't. I never believed it. Just tell me what name you're using so I don't make a mistake, and I'll get Ignacio aboard to clear you. You can tell me the rest on the flight." He paused and gave a quizzical look. "By the way, where are we going?"

"Genoa."

"Good. I was based there once. I know the city."

He checked their passports—Laura's red laissez-passer and Rolf's blue one, also in a false name—and memorized the details.

And so it was done. The Immigration officer came aboard and quickly cleared the two United Nations VIPs, Baronessa Anna Alessandra D'Angelo and her bodyguard, Mielo Benedict Jarvi, along with their chartered jet's American flight crew. He disembarked and drove the Guardia patrol vehicle back to the terminal.

After they were in the air, Laura sat with Marco. The first thing she told him was her name.

"Not Sarah? I love that name! Not . . . what was this passport? Anna D'Angelo? Not Sarah, but Anna. Not Anna, but Laura? Laura Pace?" He pronounced her surname the Italian way: "Pah-che? Pah-che means 'peace'! But there is no peace in Sarah's life!"

"And no peace in Laura's."

He hugged her again.

"I have something you should see," he said. "Perhaps a small piece of the puzzle." He fiddled with his phone and then passed it to her. A video was set to play. "That was taken by a CCTV camera just after seven o'clock on the night Consul Nicosia was killed. The camera is mounted on the building across the street from the entrance to the consulate building." On the screen, a van pulled up, obscuring the view of the main door. It looked as if two men exited the van's side door and entered the building. The camera only caught a fleeting shot of them from behind. The van drove away. Then the film appeared to jump. "Now it's 7:26. Watch the door." Two men appeared from inside the building. The van reappeared, but an instant before it blocked the view, the film zoomed in and froze, framing the men's faces. One of them had a wide strip of medical tape across his nose.

"The one with the tape—he's the goon who pulled me into the van."

"That's what Inspector Gallo said—she was the female officer who was facing you when you met with Nelthorp. We think the man on the right was probably the driver."

"Maybe. I only had a glimpse of him when he pulled his gun. But you can close your case on the one with the tape. His name is Danny Quintavalle, and he's dead. The other one is probably dead too, but I couldn't swear to it."

Laura told him everything.

Everything, all the way back to the senator.

She spoke in Italian, so that she could be sure he understood every word.

As the jet descended toward Christopher Columbus Airport, she took him by the hand.

"One more thing." She led him to the front of the cabin. She opened a closet. "These clothes are for you."

Marco Sinatra stared, uncomprehending.

# 35

The ship was moored at Via Giovanni Bettolo. Loading was nearly complete. The captain sent a junior officer to make contact with him at the Trattoria Gazzolo. He had just finished a late dinner when the officer arrived.

The officer handed him a sealed envelope. "Captain say you read first."

The note inside warned him that the man delivering the envelope was not aware of their relationship. The ship would be sailing at 7:00 A.M. on the day after tomorrow. However, there would be too much activity quay-side for him to board close to that time. "If you still wish to sail with us, I will wait for you by the gangway at midnight tomorrow. Do not be late. Give Mr. Andreas your answer."

"Please tell your captain I said yes," he said.

The man left. He paid for his meal, downed the complimentary grappa, and left the restaurant through the kitchen. Outside, a flight of stairs led up to a single door, the entrance to a small apartment he had rented from the restaurant's owner. It wasn't much—water stains on the ceiling, bub-bled wallpaper, filthy curtains—but he'd paid less for a full week than he'd paid for a single night in Geneva.

It had been a long run, and he was weary of it. Three tense days in Pal-ermo, then endless weeks in that dung heap in Tunis. Only the last moves had been tolerable—Zurich, then Geneva—but it couldn't go on. It was only a matter of time before some random street cop who'd seen the Interpol notice would lock eyes on him. The Mazzaras were under pressure from the

Guardia. Pressure they'd brought on themselves—first by botching the grab on that Lockhart bitch, then by their stupid attempts to eliminate witnesses. To top it off, their second attempt to take out Lockhart, this time in Florida, had failed as well. He wondered if the FBI had caught up with her. How much did she know? What was she telling them?

The Palermo crew had limited resources. The family's real money was in New York. They'd been bankrolling him in Tunisia, but he couldn't stay there forever, and he couldn't be effective wandering around Europe, burning up cash and not earning any. He knew how it worked. If he didn't come up with a workable plan, they'd make a decision to cut their losses. That would include making sure he disappeared forever. He'd told them repeatedly that he'd be better off stateside, where it was easier to blend in. Where he could sit down with the *capo bastone* and lay out a new plan.

A plan that would make money for everyone.

It still mystified him. The whole Mazzara structure, with Antonio running everything from a jail in Milan, while his underboss, Gus Mazzara, ran the New York operation from the basement of a warehouse in Brooklyn, and his thickheaded cousin, "Taffi" Tafuro, ran the branch in Palermo. He'd even been told that the don, who was doing a life sentence, spent his ample spare time raising quail on the prison's farm—a farm named after Al Capone.

It was like a bad mob movie.

But finally, a message had come back.

The don had agreed.

The U.S. crew would arrange some plastic surgery for him with one of their on-call doctors, get him a new identity and a passport, and send him back. He'd work out a new transport route, and start up again.

There'd been something else in the message—a garbled warning about watching out for a priest. Some priest from the Vatican who might be tailing him. He half-recalled a thin man wearing a clerical collar buying a ticket from the machine next to his at Cornavin station. But there were no priests on the train to Milan, and none on the train to Genoa. He'd walked every car, twice on each trip, just to be sure.

This time, he decided, he'd run the baby business from Bosnia. His associates there could be trusted to keep him protected. It was in their economic interests.

And he'd be closer to the action.

Twenty years ago, Sarajevo was on the verge of annihilation. Not now.

The shrapnel spalling had been plastered over, the upscale restaurants were proliferating, and the *klepe* dumplings were the best in the Balkans.

That's where he should have set up the first time.

He unlocked the door to his apartment.

When he stepped in, the first thing he saw was a tall man standing by the window. He was wearing black shoes, black trousers, and a gray clerical shirt and collar.

A priest was standing in his apartment.

"What are you doing in here?" Nelthorp's right hand inched toward the Beretta tucked in his waistband. He hesitated, not quite ready to pull a gun on a man wearing that collar.

"He's with me," came a female voice.

Sarah Lockhart stepped out of the bedroom.

She glanced past him. "And so is he."

The blow came from behind.

He was unconscious before he hit the floor.


A face full of cold water brought him around.

He was tied to a chair. He struggled against his bindings, but there was no give.

Sarah Lockhart's face swam in front of him. "Duct tape is so clichéd, don't you think?" she said. "My friend here much prefers electrical cord. And he's very good with knots." He looked up to see the hazy figure of a man standing behind her. "Oh, I'm sorry. Meet Rolf. He came along to help me with the questions. And this gentleman"—she gestured to Nelthorp's left, where the priest was sitting at the kitchenette table holding a small digital device—"is Father Marco. He'll be recording the proceedings."

"What proceedings?" he croaked.

Water was still dripping from his hair and face, and a reddish stain was spreading down his shirt. "Let me help you with that," Laura offered. She pressed a tea towel against his head. "It's okay. The bleeding's almost stopped." She held up her hand. "How many fingers do you see?"

"What proceedings, Sarah?"

"Oh, that's not my name. But don't worry about that. Worry about your knees."

"My knees?"

"Yes. I'll explain in a minute. But first, here's what we know. We know that while you were busy smuggling fake auto parts for Dominic Lanza, you were also smuggling stolen babies for Antonio Mazzara. You told Mazzara about your deal with Lanza, but you didn't tell Lanza about your deal with Mazzara. Big mistake. Then, when the Guardia and I were closing in, you thought it would be a good idea to eliminate me. So you arranged that boneheaded attempt to snatch me off the street in Catania. When that didn't work, you tried again in Florida. What was it, Conrad. Schoolboy petulance? Upset because I wouldn't sleep with you?"

"I had nothing to do with that."

"Which part?"

He stared back at her and said nothing.

"Not talking? That's okay. I'll talk for you. You've been operating a network. You call your people recruiters, but they're just criminals. Fraud artists who go into the refugee camps in Hungary and all across the Balkans, and probably in Turkey as well. They convince desperate mothers that they can offer their babies a better life. But that con doesn't work too often, so for backup you employ crews of kidnappers who get the job done anyway. Of course, your victims are people who have lost everything in the Syrian civil war. In other words, people whose complaints fall on deaf ears. And, of course, there are always a few unaccompanied minors to snatch for sale into the sex trade. But those kids are just a side bonus. For you, the cash cow is the black market baby trade."

"You know so much, what do you need from me?"

"Well, you see, Father Marco has that little state-of-the-art recorder running, but so far the only information on it has come from me. So now it's your turn. You're going to tell us everything we don't know. You're going to give us the names of your recruiters, the names of all those women you've used as nannies, the names of every Ikaria captain who's involved, and the names of every Mazzara family member you've been working with. And you're going to tell us why you just happen to be in Genoa at the same time as the *Olympic Dawn*. We looked it up—it's one of Ikaria's container ships."

"I won't be telling you any of that."

"In that case, let me tell you about your knees."

"What are you talking about?"

"Your knees are the most vulnerable joint in your body. They don't have the protection of a ball and socket, like your hip, but they carry all of your weight and they absorb the impact when you walk, run, or jump. Did you know that sports doctors actually call knee joints the Achilles' heel of professional athletes?"

"Why are you—"

"Have you ever heard of Roland Lewis?"

"No."

"I'm surprised. He was the goon you and your people paid to dissolve my body in acid and flush me into a Florida swamp. But he went back on his word. Kept me alive for a couple of months."

Nelthorp stayed silent.

"Anyway, poor Roland's knee had an unfortunate collision with my foot, and now he'll be on crutches for a very long time. Probably forever, unless he can afford a replacement operation. But today, we have something far more effective than my dainty little foot."

She stepped to one side. Rolf was holding a three-foot-long steel wrecking bar. The hardware store label was still attached.

Nelthorp gaped at the bar, and then looked at the priest. Father Marco was sitting calmly at the table, adjusting a control on the recorder.

"You're not going to torture me in front of a priest."

"Oh?" She turned. "Father? Would you prefer to leave?"

"The Inquisition's methods were brutal," the fake cleric replied in Marco Sinatra's beautifully accented English, "but our Mother Church never shrank from its duty. I will gladly hear Mr. Nelthorp's confession."

"Nice bluff!" Nelthorp growled.

One swing of the wrecking bar and Conrad Nelthorp quickly revised his opinion.

It was after midnight when he finally stopped talking.

# 36

"So you let him go."

Laura, Renate, and Rolf were seated in the cabin of the Gulfstream. They had just taken off from Teterboro on the final leg of their long flight back from Genoa to Florida.

Laura was still feeling the strain from the arrival in New Jersey. United Nations passport or not, there was no way she could have risked an international landing in Florida. Her face was on FBI Wanted notices across the federal system, and slapping on a bit of makeup wasn't going to change her appearance. So they'd flown back to Teterboro, where Renate had been on hand to make sure everything went smoothly for the arrival of the secretary general's "Special Adviser on Syria" and her bodyguard. Renate had been magnificent. She'd accompanied the Immigration officer onto the jet, and immediately engaged Laura in a deep discussion about her just-completed mission to Damascus, letting the officer hear just enough to intrigue him—and distract him—while he processed their arrival. Laura had known exactly what to say because she and Renate had rehearsed the conversation over an encrypted satellite phone connection while the Gulfstream was crossing the Atlantic. By comparison, getting her off the plane at Kendall after a domestic flight would be painless.

"Lanza was telling the truth. This was a Mazzara racket, and Nelthorp never told Lanza about it. He gave us quite a lot on the network contacts at the European end. He knew the names of a few recruiters, but mainly he worked through ethnic gang leaders—Bosnians, Croatians, Albanians. At one time, they were all rivals, but money talks and now they're working together. He said the nannies don't get paid. They do it for a chance to land in the States without a visa. There's no shortage of women in Eastern Europe who would do anything for a chance like that. The problem is, he claimed he doesn't know anything about the network in the U.S. He says he's just the wholesaler, that the Mazzaras run the retail side of the operation. We got everything on tape. Marco kept the original, but he uploaded the interview onto my phone. But it's going to take time to backtrack from what we know to what we don't."

"You're sounding like a cop again. Our first job is to clear you of the charges, remember? And you're saying he didn't give you anything that can help us over here."

"Just one thing. Before we got to him, Nelthorp had already decided to come back to the States to regroup, using help from the New York Mazzaras. He didn't want to risk landing at Logan or JFK. Even with his Stockton passport, some alert Immigration officer might recognize him from the notices, or he could get nailed by facial recognition software. We don't use that software at seaports, so he was coming by freighter."

Renate nodded as she made the connection. "But the ship's not going to Boston or New York. It's heading for Miami—which means he knows it's safe to land there."

"That's right. He knew about Bailey, and he knew he'd been killed, but he said Gus Mazzara told him not to worry, that they had someone else in place. That's why we let him board the ship. To identify the second agent."

"And the broken kneecap? How was he going to explain that?"

"A fall on some stairs. Rolf bought him crutches."

From Rolf, a quiet chuckle.

"Why would he cooperate? As soon as he went aboard, he could have tipped off the captain, and got him to pass a message to the contact in Miami."

"Marco gave him a choice."

"Our cop priest."

"We couldn't ask Father Giardini to sit through a kneecapping. And it was better to have Marco there. A cop we can trust."

"Interesting cop. What was the choice he gave him?"

"Work with us or be arrested. Marco told him he'd be held in Ucciardone Prison in Palermo while the different regional prosecutors argued about who would try him first. He rattled off a bunch of charges in

Italian and I translated. Nelthorp's no fool. He knew he'd last about two days in that prison before the Mazzaras found out he was there and arranged to have him killed."

"But he's on the ship now, and Marco isn't. He's free to tip off the captain."

"We told him if he turned on us, we would know, and Marco would send an audio file of our little interview to the Mazzara boss in Palermo, who would be sure to send it to his *capo bastone* in New York."

"Nice. So, assuming he keeps his word, what happens after he lands?"

"The Mazzaras will send a car for him. It'll be waiting at the Bayside Marketplace. It's right next to the port. We follow them, snatch Nelthorp back, and he tells us who landed him." She glanced at Rolf. "The thing is . . . I'm not sure we have the manpower to pull that off without attracting police attention."

"We don't. And what would we do with Nelthorp once we have him?" She noticed their expressions. "But you have a plan."

"Two plans," Rolf replied. "Plan A . . . since we can only trust Nelthorp up to a point, we try to get separate verification of who clears him. We get eyes on the ship when it arrives."

"How do we do that?"

Laura supplied the answer. "Immigration officers go out on the pilot boats. That way they can clear the crew before the ship ties up. They usually send one of the officers who works the cruise ships on Dodge Island, but there'll be no way to identify who that is until it's too late. We talked about positioning someone with a camera and a long lens to video the officer who disembarks after the ship comes alongside. But then we had a better idea."

"What?"

"Plant someone on the pilot boat. I have a CI at the pilot station on Lummus Island. Javier Espinal. He's a helmsman. I've used him before."

"You can't use him now."

"I think I can. He had a small legal problem—his wife and daughter were illegals. They were about to be deported. I helped him get that fixed."

"You'd have to meet him off-site."

"There's a place we always met. A coffee bar in Little Havana. If we get a message to him, he'll be there."

"He could turn you in. Help the FBI set up a trap."

"He won't. He calls me his *salvadora*."

Renate thought about that. "And plan B?"

"Talk to Lanza. Let his people intercept the Mazzara escort, grab Nelthorp, and get us the Immigration officer's name," Rolf said.

"Lanza would just have Nelthorp killed."

"He might make a deal to let him live."

"Laura, don't you need Nelthorp to help clear your name?"

"Maybe. But if he makes it to New York, we've lost him. Either the Mazzaras find out he ratted and they kill him, or he disappears on his own. At least Dominic Lanza might agree to keep him on ice in return for us exposing the baby-smuggling network and getting a bunch of Mazzaras arrested."

"And if not?"

"That's why we have plan A," Rolf growled.

"And why we can't tell Detective Jardine about plan B," Renate stated flatly.

Silence.

"There's someone more important than Nelthorp," Laura said.

"Who?"

"A baby. A real baby with a fake name. Gisella Pelizon. She's the baby who was never delivered to the Edens. If her birth date on the fake paperwork is close to accurate, she's now about seven months old." Despite her determination to stay calm and focused, Laura couldn't suppress the urgency in her tone. "That little girl is somebody's daughter, and because of me—because I talked Marco into letting her go on that ship—she's lost! We need to track down the Mazzaras' bogus adoption agency. It's called Engender. It's not in any phone book. We need to find their baby salesman, and expose all those so-called *respectable* people who are raising kidnapped babies! But most important, we need to find Gisella. And when this is over—" Her voice caught. "When this—"

*Here comes the rain . . .*

*NO, DAMN IT!*

A tear spilled. She took a deep, shaky breath. "If I live through this, then if I have to walk through every fucking refugee camp from Hungary to the Syrian border carrying that baby's photograph, I'm going to find her parents and deliver their little girl back to them."

Renate looked at Rolf. One of his eyebrows had notched higher. He answered Renate's glance with an imperceptible nod.

"We'll help you do that," Renate said gently, squeezing Laura's hand. "You have our word."

# 37

The shortest sea route from Genoa to Miami is just under fifty-four hundred nautical miles. The normal steaming speed for midsize container vessels was 20–25 knots. Based on that, and on a website that gave distances by sea from any port in the world to any other port, Laura calculated the *Olympic Dawn*'s crossing would take anywhere from 8.9 to 11.2 days.

While her calculations provided a sort of comfort, the waiting seemed like an eternity. She ticked off the days on a calendar in her bedroom as her high-energy personality once again chafed against the barriers of enforced inaction.

Renate and Rolf had both returned to New York—"For appearances," Renate had explained—so her only companion was Paolo, who, after some behind-the-scenes lobbying by Renate, had been released from his U.N. security duties to rejoin them. Although Laura appreciated the company, his relaxed equanimity and foodie obsessions didn't quite fill the void imposed by her idleness. Laura spent most of her time reading or playing solitaire, and occasionally sharing a bottle from Paolo's small cellar of Super Tuscans.

"Unsanctioned operations call for unsanctioned grapes," he told her with a grin. She had to Google "Super Tuscans" before she understood the joke.

The days of waiting were punctuated by a momentarily unsettling occurrence. One evening, after an early supper, Laura was sitting on her bedroom's small balcony. It overlooked one of the rear garden's ancient oaks. From somewhere down below the foliage, she heard Paolo's voice. It sounded like he was speaking on a phone. The odd thing was, he wasn't speaking English. Or Italian. He was speaking some other language.

A language Laura vaguely recognized.

He was speaking Sicilianu.

She listened, fascinated. Much of what he said was incomprehensible. But she recognized some of the words, some of the phrases, and a name.

Over breakfast the next morning, she asked him about it.

At first he blinked, but then he laughed. "Sorry. I was talking too loud. That's our way."

Based on her own experience, it wasn't necessarily the "way" in Sicily to speak loudly, but she let that go.

"It sounded like you were speaking Sicilianu. My Guardia friend's wife spoke it sometimes."

"I was."

"Did you grow up in Sicily?"

"Calabria. But we have our own dialect that is very close to Sicilianu." He hastened to explain. "I was talking to my office. We use Sicilianu whenever we speak on open channels. The dialect is part of our training. Very few people speak it, so we use it. Maybe you've heard about the code talkers."

"World War Two . . . the Navajo soldiers in the Pacific."

"Not just the Navajo. The Americans used six different Native American languages for voice communication with their units. The Japanese thought they were codes and wasted months trying to break them. We work on the same theory. I'm not sure about my cell phone over here, so I spoke to my boss using the dialect."

"Your boss in Italy?"

"Yeah."

"Does he know where you are?"

"No. I didn't want to tell him I was standing beside a swimming pool in Florida."

"Or hiding a wanted killer from the FBI."

He grinned. "That too."

After breakfast, Laura called Renate, as she did every day after logging in on an open-source ship tracker website. Each time a chart of the Atlantic

206 / DOUGLAS SCHOFIELD

Ocean materialized on her screen, showing the *Olympic Dawn*'s latest position.

This time, she went for a walk in the garden while she made her call.

Then she waited some more.

On the morning of the seventh day, the usual legend appeared next to the freighter's position in the western Atlantic, showing speed, heading, and time since last position report:

OLYMPIC DAWN *[GR] 23.4 KNOTS/260°*
*POSITION RECEIVED 1 HOUR, 25 MINUTES AGO*
*DESTINATION: MIAMI*

It was getting close. She calculated it would arrive at Miami within forty-eight hours. Knowing her access to the Customs database had been terminated when she became a murder suspect, she used the arrivals table on the Port of Miami's own website to find the *Olympic Dawn*'s calculated ETA. Then she called Javier to make sure he was assigned to the right pilot boat.

Then she called Renate.

Then she paced some more.

Nine days and twenty-one hours after the ship left Genoa, Laura sat with the whole team. Renate and Rolf had arrived the night before, and Paolo had managed to drag himself out of the kitchen. Javier Espinal was sending a streaming video in real time directly to Renate's phone. He was filming surreptitiously from the wheelhouse of a harbor pilot's boat, and they were watching the unfolding action on a big plasma screen mounted on the living-room wall. The boat had just been made fast against the hull of *Olympic Dawn*, but that hadn't done much to improve the quality of the picture. Luckily, despite the lurching, rolling view, they were still able to make out what was happening. A few minutes earlier, they had watched a flexible ladder being lowered from the deck of the freighter.

Sitting there, Laura was recalling a conversation she'd had with Marco during their flight from Catania to Genoa.

"Did an ICE agent ever call you? A man named David Kemp?"

"No." A pause. "Well, maybe."

"What does that mean?"

"There were two calls. The first one was from your boss. Corbin. She said an investigation team had been assigned, and they'd be sending an officer over for a full briefing."

"When was that?"

"February. Not long after you went home."

"Did they send anyone over?"

"No. Then, maybe a week or so later, I got another call. The man said he was with ICE. I don't remember his name. It might have been this Kemp. He talked very fast. He said his superiors were reviewing the file. He used the words, 'because of recent developments.' He wouldn't tell me what developments. I didn't like the sound of that."

*Neither do I,* Laura had thought.

"I did some searching on the internet. I didn't find anything until I searched your name—I mean, your Sarah name—and found out you were wanted for murder."

On the screen, three figures clad in identical high-visibility buoyancy jackets had congregated at the bottom of the ladder. One of them was obviously a deckhand. He held the ladder while the person next to him started the climb.

Seconds later, the pilot started to climb.

But, by then, Laura had stopped paying attention.

She'd stopped paying attention because she'd recognized the first person on the ladder.

Phyllis Corbin.

*CORBIN?*

Had Laura's own supervisor conspired with the Mazzara crime family to sell kidnapped babies, preying on wealthy couples who would not otherwise qualify to adopt?

Was there any other explanation for her being there?

Was there any other explanation for the CBP's Miami area director conducting an everyday clearance for the Lummus Island container port? Any other explanation for just happening to be the Department of Homeland Security official to clear Conrad Nelthorp, aka William Stockton, an international fugitive from justice, to enter the United States?

*Unless . . .* the corrupt officer the Mazzaras were paying off had been unexpectedly sidelined. Sidelined, and now in custody, because Corbin was on to him, and had replaced him on the pilot boat for all the right reasons.

If Conrad Nelthorp left the Port of Miami locked in the back of an ICE cruiser, Laura's worst fears about Phyllis were wrong.

But if he hobbled out on his crutches and climbed into a waiting car, they were justified.

They would know in a few hours.



Renate took the call on her cell.

"Yes?"

For three minutes, she listened without speaking.

"Thank you. We'll wait for your call." She disconnected.

"Lanza's men found the Mazzara car. It wasn't difficult—two men sitting in a full-size Lincoln with the engine running. About thirty minutes ago, a car showed up at the main entrance to the shopping mall. A man with crutches got out. He had one small suitcase. The car that delivered him drove away. The Lincoln picked him up. It is now heading north on Highway 1. They're following it."

"Lanza?" Paolo interjected. "I thought he was out of this."

"He agreed to help out, since we're short of manpower," Rolf replied evenly.

Paolo looked faintly miffed that he'd been left out of the loop.

Laura asked, "Did they see who was driving the car that dropped him off?"

"Only that it was a dark-blue SUV."

"Corbin drives a dark-blue Santa Fe."

"Then it looks like you have your answer," Rolf said.

"Using her own car?"

"She's comfortable. Which means Nelthorp stayed on script."

Laura didn't reply. She was reexamining the last year of her life. Reexamining all her interactions with the woman. All the meetings before she left for Italy.

*Phyllis Corbin . . .*

*What did I miss?*

*And why did I miss it?*

Corbin . . . trafficking babies?

Corbin . . . setting up Bailey's murder? Sacrificing a confederate, along with two unsuspecting ICE officers, just to save her own ass?

Just to shield the Mazzaras?

It beggared belief.

Or, maybe it didn't . . .

*"Never forget the treachery of human beings," Nonna had warned. "Always keep the knife in your hand. The danger of your enemies will never equal the danger of false friends. People talk about the differences between men and women, but they are the same. Both are capable of great acts of courage. But never forget that a woman, as much as a man, is capable of deadly acts of betrayal. In my war, some of our best men died because of those women. When they were caught, Anna and I were chosen to execute them. We did our duty.*

*In your life, a terrible day may come when you will face such a choice. If that happens, you must do your duty as well."*

Renate received another call.

The Lincoln had joined Interstate 95, continued north, and then left the highway.

"They took an exit called Glades Road."

"That's at Boca Raton," Laura said.

"They stopped at a house on Northwest 35th Street. They all went inside."

"That's not far from the Boca airport," Laura said. "They're not going to risk a two-day drive with Nelthorp in the car. It would only take one nosy cop at a traffic stop and they'd be in trouble. They're going to fly him to New York, probably on a private plane. They're staying out of sight until it arrives."

"Which means," Rolf added, "if Lanza's men are going to make a move, it will be now."

Nobody spoke.

When her phone rang again, ninety minutes later, Paolo and Rolf were in the kitchen and Renate and Laura were alone.

The caller was Carlo Barbieri. His report was brief and to the point: Nelthorp's escorts had been "taken care of," Nelthorp was unharmed, and he had "agreed to cooperate" with Dominic Lanza.

"He says the Immigration officer was a woman," Barbieri told her. "She didn't tell him her name." The description he recited fit Phyllis Corbin. Not that they really needed it now that they had her immortalized on video, boarding the ship.

"Something else the boss wants you to know. One of the Mazzaras was carrying a burner. Our men took it when they left. A while later, the phone got a text message. It said: 'You're being tailed. Get out of there.' Boss said to tell you . . . don't call him again."

He hung up.

Renate looked pale. "So . . . we have another player in our little game."

Laura grabbed her arm.

"What?"

"We need Dickie."

# 38

Scott Jardine felt like his brain would explode.

First, there was the guilt.

By coordinating Laura Pace's meeting with a crime boss, and then pulling her out of that motel before the FBI could arrest her, he had acted against every legal and professional principle he had sworn to uphold. He had breached his oath. He had obstructed justice in more ways than he could count. His father was a retired Highway Patrol trooper, living in Tampa. If he ever learned what his only son had just done, he'd disown him.

And probably turn him in.

So, *guilt* . . . yes. No escaping it.

But then there was something else.

Something that kept undermining and eroding that guilt.

The deep attraction he felt for the woman with the searchlight eyes. The woman whose grace captivated him, whose predicament terrified him, and whose very existence kept him awake at night.

The attraction he felt for this astonishing woman challenged his guilt, defied his guilt, dared his guilt to bury it.

And then . . . there was the contempt.

He should be directing that contempt at himself, and in his unrelenting cycle of self-doubt, he did. But his deepest well of scorn was reserved for Special Agent Alan Turnbull.

The man defined *contemptible*.

He kept showing up at the Everglades substation, where Scott was now spending most of his time. In fact, almost all of his time . . . because Turnbull had turned up the heat on the sheriff, who had told Jardine his presence was required at the district 7 office to assist the feds in any way they requested. "You're needed there because of your rapport with the fugitive," the sheriff had told him bluntly. His laughable mispronunciation of "rapport" revealed that he was merely parroting a line from a confidential memo, and the expression on his face conveyed the additional message that Scott's job might be on the line because of the FBI's behind-the-scenes defamations.

Turnbull was obviously keeping track of his shifts because he kept appearing at the substation at odd hours when Scott was working at his desk. He never missed an opportunity to ask him if his "girlfriend" had called. The question was invariably accompanied by an insinuating look. Scott figured it was only a matter of time before Turnbull persuaded some compliant judge to authorize an intercept order on his private phone.

On that score, he wasn't too worried. He was a few burners ahead of Alan Turnbull.

*Listen to yourself, Jardine! Remember "guilt?"*

Lately, since the failed raid at the motel in Clewiston, the insinuations had become more worrisome. More laden with suspicion.

"That woman's prints were all over the room! Who knew about the raid? Who knew about the timing? How is it that she disappeared that same day?"

"How do you know she disappeared that same day?"

"Desk clerk says she bought a paper. Said she was carrying takeout. We checked around. A Mexican place on the highway sold her a takeout dinner just after six. And all of a sudden, she's gone? Left the dinner, and gone. Someone tipped her. Who in this office knew about that motel? Just you!"

Scott had had it with this guy, and he knew how to deflect with the best of them.

"The lieutenant knew!" he fumed. "And Belrose. But the only thing we knew was the name of the town—*not* the name of motel, *not* your plans, and *not* your timing. Maybe you should take a good look at the security in your own office, Turnbull!"

All he got in reply was a disbelieving sneer.

So, yes . . . Turnbull was contemptible. And, not just because he viewed Laura Pace as nothing more than a beast of prey. Not just because he didn't seem to have the imagination to even wonder in passing what really lay behind the bizarre crimes alleged against her.

But because, yesterday, Scott had overheard him laughing in the station coffee room.

Laughing about a search warrant in an unrelated case.

Laughing about a warrant he and his agents had executed at four o'clock in the morning.

Laughing about exploding into the slumber of an entire family, about the shouts of fear, about the cries of the children, and about a trembling, terrified grandmother.

Laughing about his bullying questioning of an agitated, half-naked nineteen-year-old girlfriend of a vanished bank robbery suspect.

Laughing at conduct that should have filled him with shame.

Listening to that, Scott Jardine, who *did* have an imagination, began to wonder how Laura Pace would be treated if Alan Turnbull ever got his hands on her.

Yesterday was also noteworthy for another incident. It happened late in the day, long after Turnbull and his agents had returned to Miami. Scott had been in the file storage room, hunting for an archived investigation file, when he heard someone talking.

Someone repeating his own words.

This morning, after setting out some bait, he had watched and waited.

And it happened again.

He was debating with himself about what to do when he got a ping on his burner. It was from a New York area number.

The message said:

*PLS CALL*
*R.R.*

# 39

The call from the U.N. woman couldn't have come at a better time. Richard Bird's tiny office at the State Department was stacked with printouts, and the workload had become more and more oppressive.

*Paper! Who the hell uses paper anymore?*

It was annual report time and suddenly it was all about graphs and tables and pontificating assessments. Compute the crime rate in country A. Are the statistics honestly presented or deceptive? What should we tell American tourists considering a visit there? Review the capital-friendliness markers for country B. Should our multinational corporations risk investment there? The U.S. ranked fifteenth on the U.N.'s latest World Happiness Report. Why? What are those other fourteen countries doing that our government isn't? Should the secretary congratulate their leaders or keep his embarrassed mouth shut?

In other words, it was the kind of work that would make any sane analyst pray for the weekend.

So the call from Renate Richter with a message from Laura, asking him to take two weeks' leave, pack a bag, and be at a small airport in Virginia by seven tomorrow night came as a welcome piece of excitement.

"This is the endgame, Mr. Bird."

"I'll bring my gear."

"I'll put something on the plane that might help."

"I have a pretty good suite."

"Do you have a Lac 9352?"

"*A Lacaille!* I thought they were just a myth!"

"Just because it can't be seen with the naked eye doesn't mean it's not there. It will allow you and me to interface wherever we are. And I think you'll like the software." A pause. "But, Richard, a small caution . . ."

"What?"

"It's a loan, not a present."

That little exchange had upped the excitement tenfold for Richard. Lacaille laptops were the stuff of fable on the darknet, a hacker's ultimate wet dream. Named after a red dwarf star in the constellation Piscis Austinus, they were supposedly created in some secret lab in South Africa and sold for a small fortune on a website Richard had never been able to find. Even at the annual Defcon conference in Las Vegas—an annual gathering for digital scofflaws that Richard had attended a few times under an assumed name—the topic had only come up late at night after too many drinks. And even then, it came up very rarely. There was almost a superstition about it. Defcon panelists always underscored the fact that people are the weakest link in cybersecurity, so it was understandable that no one wanted to acknowledge, publicly or privately, a software ground assault unit that didn't require a human weakness to exploit.

It was a system reputedly stolen from Tailored Access Operations, the NSA's premier hacking unit.

Stolen . . . and improved.

Manassas Regional Airport was an hour's drive from his house. The Gulfstream was waiting on the apron when he arrived. As he sauntered toward the terminal, a uniformed copilot emerged through the main doors to greet him. He was quickly escorted through security and out to the plane.

"Is this a U.N. jet?" Dickie asked, a bit awestruck as he stepped into a forty-foot-long hushed world of woven carpet and upholstered divans.

The pilot notched an eyebrow. "Sometimes." He gestured. "Galley's here. There's beer in the fridge. Help yourself and grab a seat. We're leaving right away."

"How long's the flight?"

"Two hours." He started for the cockpit, then turned back. "Oh, by the way"—he pointed at a built-in credenza sitting midcabin—"there's a package for you in the left side drawer."

Left alone in the spacious cabin, with wide comfortable seats, LED lighting, and a wireless broadband multilink system, Dickie spent those two hours in the thrall of a brand-new Lacaille. Renate Richter had been right. There was nothing in his own computer that wasn't already loaded on the Lacaille. And so much more.

Treasures beyond compare.

He was still picking his way through the software when the captain announced they were turning on final.

The next hour was a little more unsettling. Even though he knew that Laura had vanished into the protection of some nameless United Nations unit, it was still a bit unnerving to be met by a hard-looking man with a tattoo on his neck and a ring in his ear holding an Android tablet with a lit-up screen that read: R.B.

"I'm Rolf," the man said, as he took Richard's bag and led him straight out the nearest set of doors to a Range Rover with smoked-out windows. Two things struck Richard immediately. First, that the vehicle was parked at the curb right outside the door in a clearly marked No Stopping zone. Second, that the vehicle had diplomatic license plates.

Rolf opened the curbside rear door and gestured that he should get in. He complied.

As they pulled away, his escort said, "Lie down and stay out of sight." He complied.

They drove for fifteen minutes, then turned sharply. The light dimmed. Richard looked up and saw concrete. They were in a parkade. Rolf got out. Almost immediately, the silence of the garage was punctured by the whine of an electric drill motor. From the direction of the sound, and the vibration of the vehicle, he could tell it was applied first to the front, then to the rear.

*He's switching license plates. . . .*

Rolf got back behind the wheel. They drove off. When they hit the street, Rolf leaned back.

"Do you understand what just happened?"

*Do I play dumb?*

*Laura will laugh.*

"Yes, sir."

"Welcome to our world, Mr. Bird."

# 40

Laura was under no illusions about Conrad Nelthorp's future prospects. She guessed that when his usefulness ran out, he'd probably end up in a landfill somewhere. Lanza had promised Renate that he would be "circumspect"—his word—in his treatment of the man, depending on how much information he provided on the Mazzaras, and how much could be salvaged from the auto parts business. But it didn't take much insight to realize that, deal or no deal, from Lanza'a point of view, Nelthorp knew too much. If he ended up in federal custody, he'd try to trade Gustavo Mazzara's involvement in the baby-smuggling ring for immunity. But if the U.S. attorney balked at the offer, Laura had no doubt that Nelthorp would throw in Lanza as a sweetener.

Lanza couldn't take that risk, and Laura knew that.

The fact remained that Laura had left law-abiding scruples in her rear view the moment she'd awakened from her amnesiac dreamland and discovered she'd been framed for murder. She'd already made the choice to use Nelthorp—an unrepentant trafficker in children who had attempted to have her abducted and killed back in Catania—and then leave him to whatever fate Lanza had in store for him.

She had made that choice, and a few others she wasn't proud of, and she and the rest of the team had agreed on those choices.

They'd also agreed that there was no reason for Dickie or Scott to know about them.

Laura was waiting in the foyer when Rolf showed up with Dickie. In his polo shirt, chinos, and scruffy sneakers, her old friend was as charmingly unkempt as ever, although a good bit more wide-eyed than usual. Fortunately he didn't try to collect on the promised kiss right in front of Rolf, so after a deeply felt hug, she led him into the living room.

Watching Dickie's expression as he entered the room to face this enigmatic crew of Euro-spooks, she had to suppress a smile. She made the introductions.

They all sat.

Dickie didn't waste time. He addressed Renate. "When you called, you said Laura needed my help. But you weren't really clear about the exact assignment."

Laura supplied the answer. "I'm a fugitive from justice. Wanted for murder—"

"Like I didn't know that."

"—and you're going to help me get caught."

"What?"

"I'll explain later. First, are you hungry? Have you eaten?"

"A few snacks on the plane."

"No problem. I'm sure our chef can whip something up." Dickie looked puzzled. Laura smiled. "Our friend Paolo's not just an ass-kicking agent, he's a fantastic cook."

Grinning, Paolo rose from his seat and took a bow. He headed for the kitchen.

"You'll need a place to work," Renate said. "We'll get you set up in the bedroom next to Laura's. Did you bring the—?"

"Are you kidding? My laptop's got intense software, but nothing like the one you left on the plane." His bag was next to his chair. He unzipped an outer pocket, pulled out a thin, black laptop, and passed it to Laura. It bore a deep carmine-colored circular symbol above an engraved alphanumeric: LACAILLE 9352

"Lacaille? Never heard of it."

"It's a black market design."

"Interception capability?"

"Email, phone, text, in-house apps—private, corporate, government. Anything you want. It's totally, totally badass."

"How fitting. Try not to brag about it too much tomorrow night. We don't want our guest to feel any more uncomfortable than he already does."

"What guest?"

"Rolf didn't tell you? Detective Jardine will be joining us for dinner."

While Dickie gaped, Renate interposed. "Richard, why don't you go with Laura and she'll show you to your room. She'll help you get set up and explain the operation."

If Richard Bird's heart jumped at the idea of being alone in a bedroom with Laura, it was soon disappointed. Laura had a lot to tell him, and it was nonstop until Renate interrupted to announce that Chef Paolo had come through again.

On the following evening, Scott Jardine arrived just before eight. By then the conversation had loosened up over a few glasses of Paolo's unsanctioned Super Tuscan.

As soon as Dickie and Scott had been properly introduced—they'd only spoken for about five seconds when Dickie had cold-called him days before and told him to check his emails—they all sat down for another one of Paolo's extravaganzas.

Laura was feeling deeply ashamed. It was one thing to ask Dickie to join them—he'd known Laura for years, he trusted her, he'd been helping from the start, and . . . well, yeah . . . he always carried a torch for her. But it was a huge imposition to ask Scott to step in again. He'd arranged her meeting with a Mafia don, and he'd saved her from being arrested by the FBI, but he was a police officer, sworn to uphold the law. He must be agonizing over what he'd done—and over the risk to both his career and his freedom if word of it ever came out.

And yet here he was again, dining with Laura's gang of conspirators.

Over the meal, Renate brought Scott up to date, so far as was necessary, and then Laura explained the next step in the plan. It didn't escape her that, during the ensuing discussion, Scott and Dickie carefully avoided asking the obvious question:

*What happened to Nelthorp after he landed?*

She was grateful for their constraint because one thing was certain—if one of them had asked, she wasn't going to lie.

"So, let me get this straight," Jardine said finally. "Three U.N. spooks, working illegally on U.S. soil, and an IT hacker from the State Department, all harboring a fugitive who's wanted for murder and kidnapping. That's the team."

"Right," Laura replied.

"And this team is planning to commit various acts in breach of U.S. law."

"Correct."

"And you want me, a sixteen-year police detective with a clean record, to *once again* break the law by joining this conspiracy?"

"Also correct."

Jardine folded his napkin and dropped it next to his plate. "Well—"

Everyone stiffened in their chairs.

"—when do we start?"

The atmospherics around the table instantly changed.

"We start now," Laura said, "and with you. *Why* are you willing to help?"

"From the beginning?"

"Yes."

"All right. Laura, I wanted to say this after I pulled you out of that motel, but I was . . ." He took a deep breath. "Look, the first twenty-four hours after you escaped from that hospital were pretty miserable. Yeah, you steered us straight to the *pozole* man bust. It turned out that creep Lewis had dissolved at least nine corpses. He's being held without bail. So, I guess I should thank you for that, since no one else ever will. But the FBI were all over me about those two calls I took from you. Their lead agent, Alan Turnbull—" He stopped. "Did you tell them?"

"They know about him and Corbin."

"Okay. So this guy's been leaning hard. He listened to the other deputies' accounts about you. He dismissed the amnesia thing right away. He grilled my partner Eric until he was ready to take it outside. He accused me of being too sympathetic, that there was something I wasn't telling them, that you and I had reached a private understanding, that I'd 'fallen for the Laura Pace legend,' as he put it. It didn't help that you phoned the second time while he was standing at my desk. I tried to give you that message."

"I got it."

"It made it worse that he only heard one side of the conversation. He kept saying—pardon the language—'What's so important about a fucking baby cam?' I told him I didn't know. And back then I didn't. I told him I thought it must be important, that he should have his team check to see if the Edens had purchased a baby monitor. If so, why was it missing? What was on it? He wasn't interested. He only cared that you were calling me." He paused. "There's been some other stuff—bad-mouthing me to the sheriff behind my back. I won't get into that now, but something you all need to know is that Turnbull's got an informant in the substation."

The table went quiet. Even Paolo, who had been enjoying his own cooking and saying little, stopped eating.

"It's the lieutenant's secretary. Her name's Bernice Castellano."

Dickie straightened in his chair. He was about to say something, but Laura shot him a look and he stayed quiet.

"She used to work at Homeland," Jardine continued. "She was a secretary with Customs, back before 9/11. She stayed on after the reorganization. Bounced around some of the Florida offices—Jacksonville, Tampa, Miami. The story is she left the department to get married. The marriage didn't last, but Homeland wouldn't take her back. Someone in HR looked up her old annual assessments and wasn't impressed. She's pushing fifty, so age probably had something to do with it, not that anyone would ever admit it. So she got the job with us a few years ago and moved to Everglades City."

Laura: "And you think—"

"I know. Our facility for handicapped folks is separate from the male and female restrooms. She goes in there to make calls on her cell. She doesn't know that the a/c duct for that bathroom also supplies our file room. Twice now I've overheard her on the phone, repeating comments I've made about your case. The second time, I deliberately said something to the lieutenant when she was in his office. A few minutes later, I saw her enter the handicapped bathroom, so I ducked into the file room. I heard her repeating what I said, word for word. It has to be Turnbull she's calling. She probably figures he'll help her get back into a federal job. It's no secret around our office that he thinks I'm compromised." He smiled weakly. "But then . . . I guess I am."

Laura looked at Dickie. "Go ahead. Tell him."

"Castellano's not calling Turnbull," Dickie said.

# 41

Phyllis Corbin's home on East 18th in Hialeah was a small and very ordinary cinderblock bungalow. It sat in the middle of the block on a street of scuffed driveways, abandoned kids' toys, overflowing trash cans, and nineteen other ordinary bungalows in varying states of disrepair.

All of which had been Corbin's deliberate choice when she bought it with the assistance of a federal employees home mortgage program.

If she'd learned anything in her years with Customs it was to keep your private life private, and your net worth to yourself. Especially when it topped $1.4 million.

But this morning, sitting in her modest kitchen, her knuckles white on her coffee mug, she was thumbing back and forth through the disturbing images on her phone. She had the crawling sensation that her net worth was about to be put at risk.

Not to mention her life.

She'd already known trouble was coming when Nelthorp didn't meet the plane at Boca Raton. After waiting for two hours, the pilot had grabbed a taxi and checked the safe house. The driveway was empty and so was the house. He'd returned to the plane and called New York. Mazzara had told him to fly back right away.

The photographs had arrived twenty minutes ago, accompanied by a message: *call*.

Sarah Lockhart had worked for Corbin, so when the Edens were shot and the ballistics came back with a match to her service weapon, she was one of the first to be interviewed. Alan Turnbull had called to warn her that two FBI agents and a Palm Beach detective were on their way to her office. Alan said it was his investigation, but he was staying out of her interview so there would never be a chance of their relationship coming back on them and tainting her evidence.

She knew what he really meant was coming back on him and besmirching his glorious career, but she kept that thought to herself.

She'd been happy to provide the investigators with a full statement, only leaving out the matter of their quarry's true identity. She told them how Lockhart had been on a dual mission in Sicily, deployed on orders from Washington but under her command. She'd been sent there to enhance the CBP's overseas response to the counterfeit goods trade, and to help the Italians screen the flood of refugees from the conflict in Syria. She explained how her agent had become involved in a separate investigation; how she'd been told to leave that one to ICE; how she'd ignored that order and become so obsessed with the case that she'd burglarized the records office of an orphanage. She related how Lockhart had not only disobeyed a direct order by pursuing the case in Italy, but also returned to Florida midassignment without prior permission. Washington had reacted to all this by arranging for her to be reassigned. She'd ordered Lockhart to brief ICE and then go home and stay there until her transfer became official.

"There was a lot of insubordination going on here. Why no discipline?" she'd been asked.

"It wasn't my call."

"Explain something," one of the FBI agents demanded. "Lockhart isn't even on file. She's nowhere in the system."

"She is if you know where to look. Your SAC will need clearance."

They'd received their clearance a few days later. She'd known exactly when it came through because Alan had called her, all energized by the revelation that he was hunting "a legend," even though the public was not being told her true name. "They're afraid some people might help her just because of who she is," he'd explained.

Since then, Alan had been keeping Corbin up to date. Not officially, of course, but informally. Acting on reasoning she'd already planted in his head, he'd rationalized his leaks on the basis that Corbin herself could be viewed as a victim. After all, this rogue agent they were hunting, who'd murdered the Edens and probably stolen their baby, had been working for Phyllis. It was only right, he said, to keep her in the loop.

Not that Alan's boss, the special agent in charge at the FBI's Miami field office, had given him permission to brief any outside agency on day-to-day progress, or at all.

But then, Turnbull had always been easy to manipulate. Almost too easy. At one point, he asked her about the investigation that had distracted Pace from her work.

"That baby-smuggling thing," he'd called it. "The case you told her to brief ICE on."

She told him baby-smuggling had become Pace's obsession. She'd stumbled on some evidence in Sicily and wouldn't let it go. He needed to understand that the woman had had a weird upbringing. "There's material in her recruitment file about her mother dying after giving birth to her, and her father being a war orphan, and him dying in the Lockerbie crash when Pace was still very young, and her being raised by a bitter old grandmother who wasn't even her natural grandmother. She definitely has a psychological thing going on. That might explain the missing baby."

He had listened to it all, nodded, and suggested they go to bed.

Long ago, Corbin had figured out that Turnbull had a mother-goddess complex. At least he seemed to fit most of the so-called diagnostic indicators that she'd been able to track down on the internet. So she had played into it. Just as his now-deceased mother must have done, she pampered him with praise, fed his neurotic vanity and grandiosity . . . and screwed his brains out with "come-to-Momma" sex whenever he asked.

She'd taken him to bed right after that conversation and he'd never mentioned ICE again. There was no way Alan Turnbull was going to let his quarry's psychological issues get in the way of his own.

Two months had passed since Corbin's witness interview, and now Laura Pace, who should have been dead, was very much alive. And the little bitch hadn't lost her touch. She had Alan and his team chasing their tails.

Two weeks ago, Alan told her he'd been present when Laura phoned Scott Jardine, the Collier County detective who'd originally taken her into custody, only to lose her again. She'd been asking Jardine about the baby cam at the Edens. The Mazzara thugs who'd grabbed her were dead, but before the collision they'd told Corbin the camera was at the bottom of Lake Worth Lagoon, but it sounded like Pace might be thinking there was some way to find archived footage.

Alan was raging after they'd tracked her through an unretired false identity to a motel in Clewiston, but got there too late. There was no doubt Pace had been staying there, but the motel staff had no idea when she'd left.

Alan had told her more than once that he suspected Jardine was communicating with the fugitive behind his back, but he didn't have enough to get a warrant for the detective's phones. So, just in case Jardine *was* in touch with Pace, Corbin had recruited one of her former employees from the old days in Jacksonville to keep her advised on anything Jardine had to say about the case. All it took was the promise of another shot at a job at Homeland to persuade Bernice Castellano to keep her ears open. The woman's brass hair and heavy makeup probably hadn't worked very well for her at her last set of interviews, but this was the federal bureaucracy, where anything could be fixed. One quick lunch at Wajiro's in Tamiami had been enough to convince Bernice that a bit of undercover work for Homeland would look good on her CV, and was probably all it would take to reverse the HR department's attitude. "Anything those detectives over there are holding back—anything you pick up, no matter how trivial it might sound—could be just what we need to track down this rogue agent," she'd told her. "The one to really watch is Detective Jardine."

And now this.

High-res photographs of two very dead Mazzara heavies, bullet holes in their skulls, right there on her cell phone.

When it suddenly rang in her hand, she nearly dropped it in her coffee. "Yes?"

"You alone? Boss wants to talk."

She recognized the raspy voice of Vincent Basso, the Mazzaras' lawyer. "Yes, I'm alone."

Gus Mazzara came on the line.

"Why didn't you call?" He sounded concerned, but she knew what lay beneath.

"I was in the shower," she lied. "Just saw the pictures."

"Lanza's behind it. He sent those photos to a burner we were using to talk to Nelthorp when he was in Italy, so he's got him and he's talked. I need you to move those files."

"Don't you mean, burn them?"

"No. It's gonna take cash to set up a new supply chain, so we'll use that paperwork to shake down our old customers. Those people won't want the world to know they paid for a kidnapped kid. We'll get an extra hundred per."

"That's risky!"

"You'll get your cut. Now listen . . . Vincent rented a new storage locker near the airport. He'll give you the details. Move the files and then stay low. If Lanza's got Nelthorp, he probably knows who you are."

"How? I didn't tell him my name."

"Lanza has connections. Assume he knows. But I doubt he'll touch you. For one thing, you're a fed, and for another, he can't use you to get to me, and he'll know that."

"Very comforting!"

"I think of it this way, Corbin. I'm not only protected by your uniform, but also by how little I care for you."

*And by the knowledge that if I'm ever arrested, I'll be dead before I can testify.*

Struggling to quell the sick feeling in her stomach, she changed the subject. "What about Riley?"

"I'm pulling him out. He's moving to Philly."

"What's there?"

"A branch office. Too much heat in Florida right now. He's gonna be running the shakedown from there. He knows the customers, so he knows the pressure points."

"There's still that nanny and the kid he's working on. They're sitting in that—"

"Forget them! Go to your job, keep your head down, and leave the cleanup to us. The main problem right now is Lockhart . . . Pace . . . whatever her name is. Why didn't you give us a heads up on the raid at that motel?"

"Alan didn't say anything to me until after."

"Losing your touch? Don't worry. We're ahead of your clown-boy boyfriend now." .

"What do you mean?"

"We're way ahead. We'll get her. Now, here's Vincent. Get those files moved today!"

"Wait a minute . . . what about that Lewis guy? He's sitting on remand over at Immokalee. How much does he know about us?"

"Nothing."

"You're sure?"

"Yeah. He's the Cubans' problem, and they're fixing it."

It was the third story on the 10:00 A.M. news.

Roland Lewis, a man who was being held at the Immokalee Jail Center on multiple counts of accessory to murder, had been found dead in his cell. The cause of death was still being investigated but, as the news anchor was quick to add: *"Lewis was also rumored to be involved in the short-lived apprehension of fugitive Sarah Lockhart earlier this month. Lockhart is wanted in connection with a double murder in Palm Beach. She is once again at large after escaping from a hospital in Naples within hours of being taken into custody. Authorities have refused to comment on her alleged connection to Lewis."*

It didn't take long for Corbin to find the new storage locker behind the tire shop on NW 32nd, but it took a bit longer to locate the wrecked '97 Saturn at the auto wrecker's next door so she could retrieve the magnetic box under the left rear fender that contained the key to its padlock. Corbin didn't know who to curse the most: Vincent Basso, or the family's local associate who'd wasted her time with a scavenger hunt.

She'd just finished unloading the files into the unit when her phone pinged.

A text message from Bernice: *Got something.*

Corbin called her.

"Jardine got a call on his cell. As soon as he saw the number, he went into the lieutenant's office. Powell's not here today. The door didn't close all the way and I could hear him talking about that prisoner Roland Lewis, the one who was found dead in his cell. He said it was murder. Some kind of drug, injected in his neck."

Corbin played along. "Okay, how does that—?"

"The thing is, whoever he was talking to, he was angry. Here . . . I wrote down what he said: *'I told you I wouldn't cross that line. Yeah, well obviously somebody helping you did, so you're on your own. Where? Not smart. Someone might decide to search that place again. Goodbye, and don't call me again.'* And then he hung up."

"Was that it?"

"Yeah. He left the office right after that looking totally pissed off. Any idea what all that meant?"

"Maybe. I'll have to think about it. Thanks, Bernice."

The moment she disconnected, Corbin locked up the storage unit and got in her car. Her service pistol was in the gun safe at home, which was fine. It would be useless to her anyway. She lifted the armrest between the front seats and removed the custom insert she'd had fabricated by an independent body shop right after she bought the vehicle. Inside was a Heckler & Koch P2000SK—a subcompact version of her CBP-issued weapon. The SK was small, lightweight, and accurate.

But its main virtue was that it was unregistered.

She checked the magazine. Full load.

As her Santa Fe rolled up the westbound ramp to the Dolphin Expressway, she checked the GPS. Fifty-two miles. The Dolphin was a toll road, but it was Sunday, she was off-duty, and no one was looking for Phyllis Corbin's car. She knew she could be tracked for the ten miles from the airport until the turn south on Route 825, but that meant nothing. For the rest of the trip, the cameras thinned down to zero.

*"Where? Not smart. Someone might decide to search that place again."*

Right before Jardine said that, he'd been talking about Roland Lewis's murder. So, *what place* would be searched again?

Roland Lewis's cabin.

Which was exactly where Laura Pace would think no one would look for her—hiding out in the shack where Lewis had kept her prisoner.

Back at the storage unit, Corbin had debated calling Gus Mazzara.

Debated for about five seconds.

Mazzara and his crew were in New York, their only two assets in Florida had been eliminated by Lanza's people, and by the time he lined up some help from the Cubans, Pace could be gone.

She'd take care of this herself.

It was early afternoon when she slowed her vehicle near the big bend on Loop Road and started looking for the gate into Lewis's property. She'd only been here once before. She'd driven by, following directions sent by Mazzara, who asked her to check the place out and take a couple of photos.

"Don't let the mug see you. Just make sure you get a good one of the turnoff . . . the gate or whatever, so the boys don't miss it."

And suddenly, there it was, the metal gate, the misspelled warning sign, the rutted driveway through the trees.

The gate was closed, but not chained as it had been before.

She rolled past, upping her speed, looking for a place to ditch her vehicle. A few hundred yards along, she found a pullout next to an alligator hole. She parked, got out, and tucked her pistol into the waistband of her jeans. She walked back and slipped through the gate. A length of chain glinted in the weeds next to one of the gateposts. She kneeled to check it. It had been cut with bolt cutters—either by the police, or by Laura Pace.

Just in case the police were on the scene, she edged up the driveway, keeping to one side, ready to duck into the brush. She came to the cabin—a sagging clapboard eyesore sitting on the edge of an algae-choked channel of swamp water. There were no vehicles in sight. She stepped into the trees and circled. Eventually, the other side of the cabin came into view.

No cars . . . but one motorcycle, parked next to the building.

Bingo.

The bike's tag number matched the one that came up when she'd run Pace's grandmother on DAVID. A registration that had somehow been miraculously renewed after the date on the old woman's death certificate.

Just another little nugget she hadn't bothered to share with Alan.

She focused on the cabin's windows, looking for signs of movement inside.

There!

She circulated back until she reached a point of concealment closest to the building.

She pulled out her gun and racked a round into the chamber. The sound was louder than she'd remembered. She'd forgotten how strong the recoil spring was on this little gun.

She waited, watching for any change in the pattern of movement inside the cabin.

Nothing happened.

She moved.

# 42

Laura was standing at Roland's beat-up kitchen table, stuffing clothes into her knapsack, when the door banged open behind her. She wheeled to find herself staring straight into the muzzle of a pistol.

A pistol held by Phyllis Corbin.

"Well, look at this!" Corbin said.

Laura was calm. "I could say the same thing."

"Turn around. On your knees! Hands on your head!"

Laura's eyes turned to stone. She didn't move.

*"NOW!"*

Slowly, she turned.

"On your knees!"

When Laura complied, Corbin shoved her violently to the floor, kneeled on the small of her back, and snapped handcuffs on her wrists. Then, slowly and carefully, she frisked her.

Laura could smell the woman's sweat.

*She's afraid.*

"Stay down!" Corbin barked. She quickly searched the cabin. As Laura knew, there wasn't much to see: a combination kitchen-dining-sitting room, one small bedroom, and a closed door with a hasp, but no padlock. Corbin opened that door carefully and stepped in, gun up. Laura already knew the safe room's Spartan furnishings were unchanged since her imprisonment: a cot, a lamp, a chair, and a bucket.

"So that's where the little worm was keeping you."

She concluded her search by checking the pot Laura had left on the stove. Its bottom was lined with the burnt remains from a tin of baked beans.

"Did you really think you could hide out here forever?"

"Where's the rest of your team, Phyllis? Where's the FBI?"

"On their way."

"No, they're not. They don't even know you're here."

"You know nothing."

"Nothing? I know all about you and Gus Mazzara and your sick little baby-selling racket. I know exactly how many babies you've smuggled into the country. Forty-two. I know exactly how many you've sold. Forty-one. I know you've been using a shell company in Delaware to salt away your take, using it to buy rental properties. I know you helped frame me for the Edens' murders, and then tried to make me disappear. Oh, and, I know that Mazzara is now planning to blackmail all your former customers and you're more than happy to take your cut of the proceeds."

Corbin jammed her pistol against the back of Laura's head. *"How the fuck could you know all that?"*

"Doing your own hits now, Corbin? I thought you left that to Mazzara's thugs."

*BOOM!*

The door flew open with a force that nearly tore it from its hinges. Corbin stumbled backward as her gun swung up.

A powerful-looking man with a tattooed neck was standing in the doorway.

He advanced toward her.

He was unarmed.

Corbin pulled the trigger.

*Click.*

She fired again.

*Click.*

In three strides, Rolf was on her. He ripped the gun out of her hand and drove his fist into her stomach.

She dropped to the floor.

He searched her, took her keys, and unlocked Laura's handcuffs. He helped her to her feet.

"You okay?"

"Yeah. Go ahead. I'll finish up here."

Rolf returned to Corbin's panting form. He cuffed her and yanked a black cloth bag over her head. He lifted her off the floor, tossed her across his shoulder like a sack of grain, and headed out the door.

Minutes later, Laura exited the cabin carrying her knapsack. She set off down the trail toward the shed by the river.

Inside the shed, two chairs had been set facing each other. By the time Laura entered, Corbin was already tied hand and foot to one of them. Her mouth was an intermittent outline in the cloth bag as her breath came in short gasps.

Laura dropped her knapsack beside the empty chair and sat down. She nodded to Rolf. He pulled the bag off. Phyllis Corbin's head whipped around, her eyes sweeping her surroundings. They settled on the vat in the corner, lingered there, and then cut back to her captors.

Laura took the cloth bag from Rolf's hand and used it to wipe a dribble of saliva from the stunned woman's chin. "You know, Phyllis," she said, "I once admired you. Tough, decisive. A credit to women in law enforcement. I don't know what happened to turn you into a monster, and I don't care. You tried to have me killed. That's all I need to know. You aced the audition, and now you've got the part."

"What?"

"Welcome to my personal revenge movie."

Corbin said nothing. Her eyes flicked about above Laura's head, as if she was looking for a camera. They finally settled on Rolf, who stood, expressionless and menacing, at the side of the former Customs agent Corbin had once privately scorned as overrated.

Laura held up her right hand.

Rolf handed her Corbin's gun.

Laura jammed the muzzle between Corbin's breasts.

"*NO!*"

Laura pulled the trigger.

*Click.*

She drew back the weapon and released the magazine. She held it in front of Corbin's shocked face.

"We found your throw-down piece in that little hidey-hole in your car. We reloaded it with rounds filled with rock salt. There's this great thing about rock salt, Phyllis—it weighs the same as gunpowder. Even a gun fanatic can't tell the difference just by picking up a loaded gun. It just . . . feels right." She tossed the gun and magazine aside. "We reloaded your service weapon as well, just in case you were stupid enough to bring it along. Your gun safe is a joke, by the way. You should look into that. But, then again, you're not going to get the chance."

"What do you want?" Corbin rasped. "Money? I can—"

She was cut short by a hard slap in the face.

"Want to try again?" Laura hissed.

Rolf dropped a warning hand on Laura's shoulder. She glanced up at him. "You're right. Let her hear it."

He reached inside his jacket and brought out a cell phone.

"Yes, it looks like an ordinary cell phone," Laura said. "And that's because it is."

Rolf thumbed in a code.

*"Why didn't you call?"*

*"I was in the shower. Just saw the pictures."*

*"Lanza's behind it. He sent those photos to a burner we were using to talk to Nelthorp when he was in Italy, so he's got him and he's talked. I need you to move those files."*

*"Don't you mean, burn them?"*

*"No. It's gonna take cash to set up a new supply chain, so we'll use that paperwork to shake down our old customers. Those people won't want the world to know they paid for a kidnapped kid. We'll get an extra hundred per."*

The audio went silent.

Laura leaned toward Corbin. "There's lots more."

"How? How did you—?"

Laura ignored the question. "We have audio on every call you've made or received in the last five days. On both your phones. Oh, and we also have all your texts since the last time you wiped them, which was about the time I got back from Sicily."

Corbin stared. "How?"

"That's not your concern. What *is* your concern is what we discovered. That your boyfriend, Alan Turnbull, was keeping you up to date on the search for me. That you've been playing him. We could see that, so we have to wonder why he didn't. Eventually, that will have to be looked into. What else did we find? That you've got an informant at the Collier Sheriff's Department. Someone your FBI lover boy doesn't know about, a woman named Bernice Castellano who's been feeding you information, mainly about a detective named Jardine."

Laura let that sink in.

"We have something else . . ."

*". . . I know you helped frame me for the Edens' murders, and then tried*

*to make me disappear. Oh, and, I know that Mazzara is now planning to blackmail all your former customers and you're more than happy to take your cut of the proceeds."*

"How the fuck could you know all that?"

*"Doing your own hits now, Corbin? I thought you left that to Mazzara's thugs."*

"You bugged the cabin?"

Laura touched an earring—one of the ceramic bead studs Marco had given her in Catania and hadn't taken back. Dickie had isolated the frequency, figured out how to recharge them, and put them back in service. "You look, but you do not see. Women on the run from the law don't usually stop to put on their earrings." She changed subjects. "How long has he had his hooks in you?"

"Who?"

"Mazzara! How long?"

A second passed.

"Since Jacksonville. It's a long story."

"You can keep your long story. Here's what's going to happen: You're going to tell us everything you know about the baby-smuggling operation. You're going to give us the names of everyone who has even been marginally involved. You're going to tell us where you moved the files on those forty-one adoptions. And, you're going to tell me what happened to baby number forty-two, the one with the fake name Gisella Pelizon."

"If I do that, I'll be dead in a week."

"If you don't, you'll be dead in ten minutes."

"You won't kill me! I'm your only chance to clear your name."

"That's just it. That recording of you and Mazzara is all I need. No U.S. attorney will worry about little niceties like unlawful interception once he's heard it. He'll be only too happy to launch a full investigation into human trafficking by corrupt CBP officers working in league with the Mafia. He'll be hugging himself, knowing how well that will play for him later, during his campaign for Congress." Laura stabbed a finger at the vat. "Phyllis Corbin can disappear forever, and it won't make a shred of difference. The FBI will waste years of money and manpower looking for you while Laura Pace lives comfortably on book and movie deals, and a fat financial settlement from Homeland."

"The Collier cops drained that vat!"

"That's right. In fact, they took the whole thing away. This is a nice new one." Corbin's throat tightened, and Laura went in for the kill. "I read all the news stories. The sheriff's public statement talked about Lewis dissolving corpses in acid. Actually, he was boiling them in potassium hydroxide, which isn't even an acid; it's a base. The problem for him was that it doesn't dissolve teeth. Obviously, you need to disappear completely. We considered fluoroantimonic acid because it will dissolve a human body in an hour. But that stuff is so powerful, it can only be stored in a vessel lined with Teflon. It also reacts violently with water, and we need to be able to flush you into the swamp without attracting attention. So we settled on sulfuric acid. It will take a day or two, but we can wait." She paused. "This is what you planned for me, Phyllis. There's just one little difference."

"What?"

"You'll be going into that vat alive."

Corbin took the bait. "You're bluffing! If there was acid in there, we'd smell it."

"Sulfuric acid is odorless unless it's heated. Or . . . unless it's dissolving something."

Laura unzipped her knapsack and extracted a pair of black, neoprene gloves. She handed them to Rolf, who pulled them on. Next she handed him a plastic bag. He stepped over to the vat, opened the bag, and pulled out a dead rat. Holding it by the tail, he lowered it. From their seated positions, his gloved hand disappeared from view.

There was a crackling sound, and smoky fumes rose. In seconds, the shed was filled with the smell of rotten eggs.

Rolf raised his arm. The rat's tail was attached to a pulpy, dripping, yellowish red mass. He dropped it in a bucket.

Corbin's face was ashen. "I know you, Pace! You wouldn't do this!"

"You're right. I wouldn't. But I won't be here. It'll just be you and my associate."

Now Corbin's eyes were bulging. "Don't you see? Even if I tell you everything and you don't kill me, even if I end up in prison, even if I cut a deal in return for my testimony, it won't matter! *This is the Mafia!* I'll never make it to a witness stand alive. Why should I tell you anything if I'm going to die anyway?"

Laura picked up her knapsack. "I see I haven't done a very good job explaining your new reality." She rose to her feet. "My friend will take it from here."

*"Okay, okay! You win!"*

*/ / /*

Forty minutes later, Laura stepped out of the shed. First she called Renate, then she called Scott.

"You heard?" she asked.

"Dickie looped me in."

"Renate is using the tape to bait the hook."

"Good. What about Corbin?"

"We'll lock her in the safe room."

"Okay. Leave the key on the table. And, Laura . . ."

"What?"

"This could still go bad."

"I know."

"Be careful. Please!"

# 43

They found Frank Riley at the airport in Boca Raton.

Waiting for a plane that would arrive too late.

Laura had to hand it to Renate. When fast action was needed, her people delivered. Working from information supplied by Dickie, they discovered that a privately owned Learjet 36 was being readied for a flight out of Long Island's Republic Airport. The flight plan recorded its destination as KBCT.

Boca Raton Airport.

The jet was registered to a holding company belonging to Gus Mazzara's attorney, Vincent Basso. From there, it had been a short step to ensure that its departure from Republic would be delayed for several hours by an unforeseen mechanical problem.

So now it was just a matter of flushing Riley out of the Boca terminal.

The private terminal was well appointed, but it wasn't elaborate. There were no facilities for arriving international flights, all of which had to clear customs at another airport before proceeding to this upscale enclave on the coast. That deficiency had kept things simple. There was only one obvious exit into the parking lot.

Rolf waited there while Laura walked in.

It didn't take long to spot him. He was sitting on a stool at a small coffee bar, back to the wall, with a takeaway cup in front of him and a laptop case sitting next to it.

That suited Laura perfectly. She didn't need to approach the man. All she had to do was let him see her. She walked slowly past his position, her eyes scanning, pretending she was searching for someone among the surges of arriving and departing humanity, embracing couples, and car service chauffeurs holding up signs.

Of course, her circuit through the terminal was all an act. She knew Riley would recognize her. And she knew that when he did, he'd scuttle for the exit.

Which was exactly what he did.

He didn't struggle when Rolf strong-armed him into the backseat of their waiting car. That might have been because of the gun stuck into the small of his back. Laura exited the building a few seconds behind Riley, strode to the car, and slid behind the wheel.

She checked the rear view as they wheeled out of the lot. What she saw was the trembling jowls of a terrified con man with the muzzle of a pistol pressed against his throat.

"So, we meet again, Mr. Riley. Or is it Agent Kemp? But then, you're not really an ICE agent, are you? You're just a dirtbag who sells children."

She swung the vehicle off Airport Road, drove across a parking lot, and parked in a dark service bay behind a movie theater. She swung in her seat and pointed Corbin's unregistered SK with its dud rounds directly at Riley's head. Rolf tucked his own weapon away and then shoved the man's torso forward, facedown on his knees. As Laura pressed the muzzle of her pistol against Riley's skull, she had the satisfaction of hearing his muffled whimper, *"Please! I'll do anything!"* while Rolf zip-tied his wrists behind his back.

Rolf yanked the man upright. Riley's face was contorted with fear and uncertainty.

"We have Corbin," Laura said. "And we have all the files. Paperwork on forty-one kids. You're finished, Riley. And after everything you've done to destroy all those families and"—she raised her voice—"*ruin my life,* there's really only one reason why you're still alive."

"The last kid," Riley croaked.

"Where's her file?"

"In my bag."

"Good start. One other thing . . ."

"You want to find her."

"We know where she is. Corbin drew us a map."

"Then what—?"

"Your boss gave you a little job to do before you head north."

Frank Riley sat very still, silent and sweating. He looked more afraid than ever.

"There are six car rental companies in Boca. Which one is it, and what name did you use?"

# 44

Early the next morning, Laura stood at the opening of a rutted dirt track than ran into the bush off a gravel road. To her right was the bed of an old irrigation canal, puddled here and there with murky water. To her left, dense growths of acacia, slash pine, and myrtle.

The steamy hiss of the bush brought back memories. Memories of another gravel road, surrounded by another bush. Memories of being confused and alone.

Memories of being afraid.

*About a mile off the main road,* Corbin had told them. *On the left.*

She was five miles south of LaBelle, Florida.

Thirty-five miles from Clewiston.

*I was this close and never knew.*

They were about to visit a migrant camp—the home of undocumented immigrants from Mexico and Central America who had come to pick oranges and tomatoes. They lived in these scattered ghettos all across the state, miles from the closest towns, their lives controlled by ruthless labor contractors who kept them in poverty with loans for food and rent they could never repay. Their overseers were usually armed, and always dangerous. With good reason, these workers lived in mortal fear of these bosses.

A hundred and fifty years after the Civil War, slavery lived on in the dark corners of America.

All of this Laura knew from her training, but she had never worked with the Border Patrol and ICE teams who had sporadically, and mostly ineffectively, raided these camps.

She got back in the car. "Let's go."

Rolf was at the wheel, with Paolo next to him, and Renate and Laura in the back.

Minutes later, the Range Rover rolled into a clearing in the bush. What met the team's eyes was a jumble of rusting trailers and sagging plywood shacks squatting at the edge of a swamp.

They got out and stood looking around. There wasn't a soul in sight. The air was thick, the atmosphere brooding.

Laura swatted at a mosquito. "This is no place for a baby."

"This is no place for anyone," Rolf replied. "How can your country allow it?" She looked at him. Once in a while, the hard man surprised her.

"Let's get started," Renate said, taking the lead. She pointed. "Paolo, you and Laura start at that end, and we'll start here."

Paolo nodded and headed across the compound. He and Laura went from shack to shack, trailer to trailer, opening unlocked doors, forcing those that weren't, searching every room, every cupboard. Every shelter was the same: stained mattresses, stinking sleeping bags, blackened camp stoves, grimy shelves of canned food . . . and no human beings, living or dead.

"Where is everyone?" Laura muttered to Paolo.

"Probably in the fields."

They came to a rotting 1960s-era travel trailer. It had been backed into the trees, its tail end suspended above a froth-covered cesspool of camp effluent. There were no steps in front of the door. Laura went in first. As she pulled herself up, the trailer leaned slightly under her weight. Obviously its suspension was shot.

Then she heard it.

A weak cry.

Laura peered into the trailer's interior. A woman was standing in the archway leading to the rear compartment. She was holding a baby.

It took a few seconds for Laura to realize she was the same young woman she had watched carry baby Gisella onto the *Atromos III*. Yes, it was definitely her, but she was almost unrecognizable—thinner, hollow-eyed, her face and arms blotched with mosquito bites, and trembling with fear.

From outside came the sound of a shout. It was Renate.

*"ROLF!"*

The rattle of an automatic weapon split the air. One burst . . . two . . .

Laura spun around . . . and found herself facing Paolo.

He was holding an automatic pistol, and it was pointed at her chest.

"It's loaded . . . and not with salt," he said in Italian.

From behind Laura, stumbling steps and the baby's startled whimper marked the nanny's panicked retreat to the rear of the trailer.

Laura answered Paolo in English. "How do you know? How do you know we didn't suspect you? With all that time you've been spending in the kitchen, how do you know we didn't switch your ammo?"

"Why don't we find out?" The impish chef's grin was gone, replaced by a malevolent smile.

"Yes. Why don't we?" She took a step toward him.

Her unruffled response startled him. He stepped back.

"Your phone conversation," she continued, trying to fill the space between them with words. "That night . . . under the tree. When I asked you about it the next morning, you forgot to mention a few things."

He stared, uncertain. "What things."

"You weren't talking to your boss at AISE. You were talking to your other boss—Taffi Tafuro, the Palermo thug who helped Nelthorp escape to Tunisia. You've been feeding Tafuro information about us." She saw from his expression that her words had hit home.

"How do you know that?"

"Because of the thing *I* didn't tell you that morning."

"What?"

"I understand Sicilianu . . . enough to get by."

"You can practice on Gus Mazzara before he kills you." The malevolent smile was back. "He'll be here in a minute."

"Not likely. He was arrested four hours ago."

At that instant, Rolf exploded through the doorway of the trailer. His sudden appearance was all the distraction Laura needed to rip the weapon from Paolo's grip and break his wrist in the process. Rolf seized the Italian by the throat and dragged him outside. It was only Jardine's timely appearance, accompanied by four uniformed officers, that prevented Rolf from snapping Paolo's neck right there.

The trap Gus Mazzara and Paolo Nori had planned for Laura, Renate, and Rolf had been doomed from the start. After Highway Patrol intercepted a pair of rented SUVs as they drove out of the Hertz lot and arrested Mazzara and his mixed crew of Italian and Cuban gun thugs, Scott Jardine and a squad of state troopers took up positions in the bush surrounding the migrant compound. They were already in place when Laura's party arrived. Unknown to Paolo, everyone was wired up, and the cops were listening to his conversation with Laura in real time. They were closing in on the trailer when Rolf's rage at his former friend's betrayal boiled over.

It would be months before Paolo heard the whole story:

That Laura had been alerted to listen to his backyard conversation after hearing him repeat Nelthorp's name, and soon deduced that he wasn't just reporting to his AISE supervisor, as Renate had first suspected.

That, with Dickie's assistance, they had intercepted a later call and Laura had pieced together enough of the Sicilianu chatter to realize that Paolo was on Taffi Tafuro's payroll.

That, shortly after they locked Corbin in the safe room, Dickie recorded a direct conversation in English between Paolo and Gus Mazzara. Paolo warned Mazzara that the team had Corbin in custody, that she'd revealed the location of the migrant camp where Riley had stashed the nanny and baby, and that they were planning to rescue them the next morning.

That, minutes later, Mazzara had called back to outline his plan to eliminate the entire team and make their bodies disappear, ending the call with a boast that he would lead the attack himself.

And that Renate's shouted warning and the automatic weapons fire had been carefully staged for his benefit.

All of this Paolo Nori would learn at his extradition hearing after the Italian courts issued a warrant for his arrest for multiple offenses against that country's *Codice Penale* and *Codice Unico Anti-Mafia*.

Not that the Italians would get their hands on him anytime soon. The American justice system took a dim view of conspiracy to commit murder.

# 45

Laura went to the young woman with the baby. She was cowering against the rear wall of the trailer, child in her arms and weak with fear.

"*Lei parla Italiano?*" she asked her.

The woman shook her head.

"English?"

"A little." Her voice trembled.

The trailer swayed, and the woman's eyes widened with fresh apprehension, as Jardine and a burly trooper entered. Jardine advanced straight to Laura.

"You gave us a scare," he said.

"Sorry." She shot him a warning look and turned her attention back to the woman. "My name is Laura. I'm a Customs officer. This is Scott. He's with the police. We both understand your situation. Please tell us your name?"

"Lavinia . . . Lavinia Dalca."

"Where are you from, Lavinia?"

"Romania."

"I've seen you before. In Sicily. I watched you board a freighter with this baby. I know you must be very frightened, especially after what just happened. I want you to know that we'll take care of you and you will be well treated. You have our word."

Lavinia burst into tears.

Laura held out her arms and Lavinia gave up the child.

"Is there a bottle for her? Some milk?"

Lavinia pointed to a shelf. Scott retrieved a half-full baby bottle. Laura sat on a discolored couch, with the baby on her lap. She held out her hand, palm up.

"I need a sample."

Scott squirted a sample liquid onto her hand.

She smelled it, and then tasted it. "It's okay."

She started to feed Gisella.


*She hadn't felt well.*

*A pinching sensation. Barely noticeable, but enough to intrude into her few moments of quietude.*

*She hadn't noticed that she'd missed her period, but when she did, she put it out of her mind. She was only a week late. It had happened before.*

*But then it was two weeks.*

*She knew before the test.*

*She knew . . . because she felt different.*

*She knew because her favorite Primitivo smelled like vinegar.*

*But, when she finally knew, her reaction was exactly the opposite of what she'd always thought it would be.*

*She felt complete.*

*She felt . . . perfect.*

*The father was a boyfriend of a few months. Not even a boyfriend. A college liaison. A man-child wrapped in his own dreams. Predictably, he freaked. He freaked, and then he disappeared.*

*But his selfishness, his cowardice, didn't bother her.*

*She felt complete, and that was all that mattered. She still had that little white spot in the ultrasound image. That little white spot that was her baby.*

*Her child . . . growing.*

*Growing for four and a half magnificent, soul-soothing months.*

*Growing until she wasn't.*

*"There is no easy way to say this," the doctor said, taking her hand. "Your daughter has no heartbeat. She has died."*

*She refused to believe him.*

*It was pouring rain when she drove home from the doctor's office. An oldies station was playing Annie Lennox, and Annie was singing about the rain.*

*Four days later, she drove back to the doctor's office. It was still raining, and Annie Lennox was still singing about the rain.*

*Four days of rain. Four days of hell. . . .*

*Four days to finally run out of ways to deny the truth.*

*She hadn't told her grandmother. Nonna had raised her to be tough, and she was.*

*But being pregnant, and then not pregnant, made her understand something her Nonna had never taught her. When it came to losing a child, Laura Pace was just like everyone else.*

*It had almost destroyed her.*


Laura started to feed Gisella, and for a few fleeting seconds, she left the rain behind.

Gisella had taken the nipple, but she wasn't drinking. She wasn't sucking, and she wasn't swallowing. She just lay there in Laura's arms, staring up at her.

Staring, but not focused.

Silent.

Too silent.

Laura felt her forehead. "Scott, I think she needs a doctor!"

"I keep telling them!" Lavinia sobbed. Fresh tears flowed.

Scott turned to the trooper. "Blake, call an ambulance!"

"No." Laura lurched to her feet. "Get us into a unit, light it up, and take us to the nearest clinic. There must be one in LaBelle. Lavinia, come with us!"

Later, while the doctor gently questioned Lavinia and examined Gisella, Jardine stepped outside to take a call on his cell. When he returned, he pulled Laura out into the reception area. He looked upset.

"What was that ammo talk? That gun was loaded with live rounds!"

"He was speaking Italian. I answered in English to get the message across to you. So you'd know he had a gun on me."

"I got that, but you took a huge risk, taunting him like that! We could've arrested him anytime. We had the evidence from Dickie's interceptions."

"*Illegal* interceptions! Scott, we talked about this. We agreed to flush him out. Now we've got him on tape in a one-party-consent intercept. Why all the second-guessing?"

"Because . . . hell! Don't you get it, woman?" He let out a rattling breath, dropped onto a chair, and grabbed a magazine.

Laura took the seat next to him. He ignored her. She glanced at the article he was pretending to read.

CHRISTMAS DECORATING IDEAS

She leaned close. "By the way, I knew it was live ammo. But Rolf removed the firing pin from Paolo's gun two nights ago, when he was cooking dinner."

"Renate told me."

"You know? Then why all the fuss?"

He turned, his face inches from hers, his eyes wet with relief. "Because that was Rolf on the phone. He says Paolo brought a different gun."

For the first time since he'd met Laura Pace, Scott Jardine saw uncertainty flash through those searchlight eyes.

She leaned against him.

He held her tight.

# 46

*The rain came, soaking the battlefield.*

*It soaked the living. And it soaked the dead.*

*The operation had gone well. Their brigade had grown to over two hundred strong, and a quarter of the fighters were women. Anna Conte led an all-female squad, with Silvana as her next-in-command. Together with three squads of men, they had switched from the usual tactic of taking on the last few trucks in a German column, striking hard, and then melting away. This time, they had engaged an entire twenty-vehicle column of transports, stopping it in its tracks and wiping it out.*

*They had carried the day because of Anna's courage and imagination.*

*Wearing a brightly colored dress, and with her thick black hair falling across her shoulders, she had stumbled out into the roadway ahead of the convoy, startling the lead vehicle's driver with the spectacle of a pretty, well-dressed woman in apparent distress. He hit the brakes, forcing the entire column behind him to halt. Instantly, both his truck and the rearmost vehicle were destroyed by antitank weapons, blocking the road in each direction and boxing in the column. Withering rifle and machine gunfire from the forest on both sides of the narrow mountain road had completed the job.*

*Yes, the action had been a success. Scores of German soldiers were dead, and the brigade had sustained only nine casualties—but one of them was Anna Conte.*

*Silvana Pace sat in the downpour, holding Anna's head on her lap, watching her beloved friend's life drain away into the mud.*

*She held her, and she listened, and she wept.*

*She wept for a beautiful, courageous woman . . . and for the death of hope.*

*Even if this war was won—and at last it looked as if it would be—for Silvana Pace, in that time, and in that place, all hope was lost in a wasteland of brutality.*

*"Giovanni!" Anna gasped.*

*Anna's lover was among the dead. Silvana knew it, but she couldn't find the words. It didn't matter. Even through dying eyes, Anna Conte had read her face. She accepted the news with an unearthly sigh.*

*"Angelo," she whispered. "He's with the nuns."*

*Their son had been born in the home of Giovanni's sister. Giovanni had been with Anna for the birth but, hunted by the secret police and threatened by a tightening ring of betrayal, they'd been forced to leave the baby with the sister and return to the brigade.*

*A month ago, news had reached them that Giovanni's sister had died in an air raid and Angelo had been left with a convent.*

*"Find him, Silvana! Tell him our stories. Give him your love." Blood welled from her throat as she gasped her last words. "Give him hope."*

*"I promise," Silvana whispered.*

*To Silvana Pace, those words had seemed a hopeless promise, made out of loyalty and compassion to ease her beloved friend's passing.*

*But not long after that blood-soaked day, the war had ended, and cautious, watchful hope had returned from the wasteland.*

*She had found Angelo. She had told him the stories. She had given him love. And she had given him hope.*

*When that hope died in a fireball over Scotland, she began again.*

*Telling her granddaughter the stories.*

*Giving her love.*

*And teaching her cautious, watchful hope.*

# 47

The black Ford Expedition came off Route 41 in a squealing controlled slide that swiveled heads in the parking lot at the Everglades Chamber of Commerce Information Center. But the incensed driver wasn't on a quest for tourist brochures. He was heading for the Collier County sheriff's district 7 substation right next door.

A dozen people were gathered near the steps leading to the station's front door.

Behind the crowd was a mobile TV van.

That tableau just further enraged the driver.

FBI Special Agent Alan Turnbull slammed on the brakes six feet from the crowd, causing a few of the nearest members to blurt obscenities. He bailed out, leaving his door open as he mounted the steps at double time, brushed past a wooden podium, and barreled for the station entrance. He didn't notice the two shoulder-mounted cameras that had just documented his reckless driving and were now recording his frenzied rush for the door.

Don Henderson, one of the two agents who exited the vehicle behind Turnbull, had noticed. He reached in, shut off the engine, retrieved the keys, and carefully closed the driver's door. Both he and his companion, Special Agent Ed Schenk, were pretty sure that Turnbull would come to regret that little performance, but each man kept that thought to himself. They followed their boss into the building at a deliberately unhurried pace, but with bemused looks on their faces that—unforeseen by them—would play again and again, nationwide, on news segments to come.

They entered the building in time to hear Turnbull shouting.

*"You catch my fugitive and don't even give me a heads up? And what's with all the fucking reporters outside? Grandstanding on my case? I'll have your badge, you asshole!"*

A calm male voice replied. "No, you won't. But I'll have yours."

The two agents exchanged glances and quickened their pace. They entered the substation's mishmash of desks and cubicles in time to see their boss face to face with Detective Jardine. A burly deputy was striding toward them, hand on his cuffs. Henderson and Schenk rushed to intervene.

Breathing hard, Turnbull backed off. "Where's the prisoner?"

A question, but delivered as a demand.

"Deputy Newman will show you to the cell. Take all the time you want. I'll be in the lieutenant's office."

As Scott Jardine strode through the room toward Lieutenant Powell's office, a dozen faces followed his progress. Every face wore a smile. At the doorway, he turned.

A dozen pairs of hands applauded.


It took four minutes.

Turnbull stormed into the lieutenant's office without knocking. It was touch and go. To the observers in the room behind him, it looked as if Special Agent Schenk's hand on Turnbull's jacket was all that prevented him from assaulting Jardine.

In fact, it was the scene confronting Turnbull that had stayed the enraged agent's hand. Lieutenant Powell was sitting at his desk. Scott Jardine was standing at his side. And Laura Pace was sitting comfortably in a visitor chair, bottle-feeding a baby.

Next to her chair was a neat pile of banker boxes.

"Sit down, Mr. Turnbull," the lieutenant said quietly. He shot a look at Schenk and Henderson, standing in the doorway. "You two should hear this."

When everyone was in place, the lieutenant said, "Go ahead, Scott."

Jardine looked directly at Turnbull. "You'd like to know why your girlfriend is in custody."

Turnbull didn't say anything. He just gave an abrupt nod. It was obvious that trouble was coming, and that it was coming for him.

Jardine addressed Henderson and Schenk. "For your information, gentlemen, the prisoner in our holding cell is CBP's Miami port director, Phyllis Corbin. A U.S. Marshals transport is on its way here now. Corbin will be moved to the federal detention center in Miami. She'll sit there while the state attorneys for four different Florida counties and the United States attorney decide on the charges she'll face. I've been told that those charges will include"—he read from his notebook—"murder, attempted murder, kidnapping, money laundering, conspiracy to commit visa fraud, and a very long list of immigration offenses. Also facing some or all of those charges are Gustavo Mazzara and Francis Riley. Mazzara is a known organized crime boss from New York. Both men are already lodged in cells at the detention center, along with several of Mazzara's associates who are being held on various parole violations and firearms charges. We are also processing an Italian national named Paolo Nori." He turned his gaze back to Turnbull. "The problem for you, Agent Turnbull, is that Phyllis Corbin is your longtime girlfriend, and during your team's hunt for Customs agent Laura Pace, you have been feeding Corbin information about the operation. The additional problem for you is that Corbin and her Mafia accomplices—" He stopped as all three FBI agents stiffened in their seats. "Yes, gentlemen, I said Mafia. Your own field office in New York confirms that Mazzara is old-school Mafia. As I was saying . . . they framed Agent Pace for the murder of Kenneth and Darlene Eden. Corbin was passing all the information you gave her directly to her accomplices, and she was doing everything she could to get to Agent Pace before you did. Not to apprehend her. To kill her."

He let that sink in, then continued. "Lieutenant Powell has been advised that the director of the Bureau's Inspection Division is on her way here. She wants to hear the recordings we have. I assume that she will then decide whether to recommend your suspension from duty."

The fight had gone out of Turnbull. He sat there, shrunken in his chair.

"Along with what I've just said, Agent Turnbull, there's something else you will need to explain."

"What?"

"I knew your office wouldn't cooperate, so I asked the Palm Beach detective who was present during Phyllis Corbin's witness interview to send me a copy of her statement. At one point Corbin said"—again, he read from his notebook—"'I ordered Lockhart to brief ICE and then go home and stay there until her transfer became official.'"

"What about it?"

"Would you like to explain why you never sent anyone to find out if Agent Lockhart—whom you now know is Laura Pace, this lady sitting here—had ever briefed anyone at ICE about a baby-smuggling investigation, and if so, who?"

Turnbull was silent.

Although they were sitting near Turnbull, Jardine could see by their expressions and body language that Henderson and Schenk were already distancing themselves from their boss.

Schenk broke the silence. "You said something about recordings."

Jardine pulled an electronic device out of his pocket.

# 48

Lieutenant Powell and Detective Jardine exited the station through the front doors. The scrum of reporters was still waiting, augmented by a growing number of curious locals and tourists who had drifted over from the information center next door.

A microphone had been set up on the podium. Lieutenant Powell spoke first:

"Some of what you will hear today will not be easy to listen to. Some of what you hear will not make you proud to be an American. I could stand up here and say pretty words about justice coming through in the end. It has, but as you are about to learn, for many lives justice has come too late. Now I'm going to turn this microphone over to Detective Scott Jardine, who will explain why we asked you to join us today."

He stepped away and Jardine took his place.

"Thank you, Lieutenant Powell. And thank you all for coming today. By the time you return to your vehicles, I think you will agree that your attendance was worth the long wait. We have today taken into custody a senior Customs agent whom we suspect on very strong evidence to have been responsible for a long series of criminal acts that will be revealed to you in the coming days and weeks. But that is not the real story today. There is someone here we want you to meet. A courageous young woman who has spent the last two months as a fugitive from federal, state, and local law enforcement. A hunted woman who also happened to be a highly decorated

Customs agent herself. A woman who was on the run from the law because she was wanted for a double murder in Palm Beach, Florida." He paused. "Yes, I can hear you asking: Why are you, a police officer, standing before us and praising this dangerous woman? Because we now know that she was deliberately framed for those crimes. And, because she is not only responsible for the apprehension of one of the key members of the conspiracy to have her falsely accused—the person I mentioned that we now have in custody—but because she is single-handedly responsible for exposing a criminal organization that has been trafficking in kidnapped children."

He let the audience marinate in that sick concept for a few seconds, and then continued.

"I said children, but let me be more specific. I'm talking about *babies*. At this moment in the investigation, we have evidence of forty-two infants who were stolen from their parents in the refugee camps of Eastern Europe, the Balkans, and probably Turkey, only to be smuggled into America for sale to high-end bidders in the black market adoption industry. The dauntless woman who exposed this barbaric trade conducted much of her investigation while she was herself a fugitive. That is why I describe her as courageous, and that is why I believe it is time for the world to meet her."

Jardine turned to face the door. It swung open, and Laura emerged, carrying Gisella in her arms. As she walked toward the podium, Jardine turned back to the reporters.

"And one more thing, ladies and gentlemen of the press . . . many of you standing here are already familiar with this woman's name. Please meet Special Agent Laura Pace."

Scattered murmuring quickly morphed into claps and whistles. There was a ripple of movement as the entire crowd pressed closer.

Laura gently delivered the baby into Jardine's arms.

She stepped to the microphone.

The parking lot went silent.

"The little girl Detective Jardine is holding has a name. But we don't know what it is. All we know is that she is number forty-two. When we found her two days ago, she was severely dehydrated. That was because, unlike forty-one other babies who are being raised in homes across the United States, she had not yet been adopted. But she has one thing in common with the other forty-one children: All of them were stolen from their parents."

*/ / /*

At Dominic Lanza's house in Florham Park, New Jersey, he and Carlo Barbieri sat in matching chairs. A big-screen television was on, and Laura Pace's voice was filling the room.

*"The story I'm about to tell you began two years ago, and what I say will probably become very controversial. I am unable to give you all the details; much of this story will have to await an eventual trial, or, more likely, a series of trials both in this country and across the Atlantic. What I can say to you now is that extremely serious criminal charges will be sought against certain American citizens and against the citizens of at least ten European countries. These charges arise, as Detective Jardine has told you, from a vast conspiracy to traffic in infant children."*

"She might let something slip. About us. About the auto parts."

"She won't."

Carlo's phone rang. He answered. He listened. He disconnected.

"It's done."

"Italy?"

"Clean sweep."

"Nelthorp?"

"Bottom of Providence Channel."

Dominic nodded and went back to watching the TV.

"Miss Pace and that U.N. woman. They will guess. About Nelthorp. They won't be happy."

"I made no promises. They understood that."

*"I'm speaking here of the kidnapping and sale of babies, some of whom were as young as three months when they were taken. They were stolen from their helpless parents in those refugee camps for the sole purpose of selling them to wealthy, childless couples in the United States. They were stolen, and in rare cases purchased, from parents who have lost everything. People with no voice and no influence. People whose complaints fall on deaf ears. These babies are now being raised by people who probably tell themselves every night when they put that child to bed that they are doing a good thing. That they have saved a child from a life without hope."* She paused. *"That will be for them to explain when they are located. And locating them will not be difficult. We have recovered the fake adoption files relating to each and every one of the forty-one children who preceded this little girl into this country."*

In his D.C. apartment, Richard Bird polished off a second glass of champagne as he stared at his television, riveted by the girl he had adored since high school. Riveted by seeing her do exactly what she had sworn to him she would do—"blow this thing wide open."

*"Without the assistance of Detective Jardine, one of the ringleaders of this despicable baby laundering network would never have been arrested. And who is that person? She—and yes, I said 'she'—is a senior official at Customs and Border Protection. Detective Jardine was careful not to name her, and so I will not, but I have no problem in telling you that for the past eighteen months, this woman was my own direct supervisor."*

In her spotless office at the U.N., Renate Richter sat at her desk, watching Laura's face above the shimmering BREAKING NEWS crawler at the bottom of the screen.

*"Apart from a long list of other crimes, she participated in a conspiracy to have me falsely accused of murder, and then to have me killed. She is also someone, I make clear, who was involved in a sexual relationship with the FBI special agent who was in charge of hunting me down for crimes I did not commit. That agent will have much to answer for as this investigation proceeds."*

There was a knock. The door opened and the secretary general entered. He carefully shut the door behind him. He pulled up a chair.

*"I will, of course, cooperate in every way I can with federal and state law enforcement authorities. However, in view of my recent experiences, I will not speak with any of them unless I am accompanied by a criminal law attorney of my choice and by Detective Scott Jardine. Detective Jardine is the only law enforcement officer in this country who believed I was innocent when no one else would, and right now, he is the only one I completely trust."*

"I thought you'd want to see this," the SG said. He laid a newspaper in front of Renate. His index finger tapped a headline:

FOUR UNDERWORLD FIGURES DIE IN PALERMO, SICILY
ITALIAN POLICE DESCRIBE 'MAFIA-STYLE HITS'

He pointed to another headline farther down the page:

MAFIA 'PADRINO' ANTONIO MAZZARA DEAD IN ITALIAN PRISON

"Collateral damage," Renate said.

"A success, then?" the SG asked. It wasn't really a question.

*"Ja."*

On the screen, Laura was wrapping up.

*"Sometimes we Americans tend to be smug about corruption. We like to think the worst corruption is somewhere else . . . 'over there' . . . in those other countries we call the Third World. Since 2001, we have spent a trillion dollars creating a gigantic, secretive security bureaucracy. But we forgot something. We forgot human nature. We forgot to keep a close eye on the people who are supposed to be keeping us safe. We were asking for corruption, and that's what we got.*

*"I don't know if this conspiracy goes higher in the department. That will be for other investigators to determine. Effective immediately, I am resigning from my position with the Department of Homeland Security. The paperwork shouldn't be difficult, since I've been under suspension without pay since I was framed for murder by one of the department's own officials. In that respect, the director may expect to hear from my attorney.*

*"This is the only time I will appear before the media to discuss this case. I am very grateful to all of you for taking the time to come here today. Thank you."*

The scene erupted in a clamor of waving arms and shouted questions.

*"I'm sorry, but I won't be taking any questions."*

Laura Pace turned away. She took Gisella back from Jardine. Holding the little girl close, she walked toward the door. Lieutenant Powell held it open for her. The image on the screen blurred, then resolved, as the camera zoomed in. It followed her until she disappeared from view.

"Are we seeing recruitment possibilities here?"

"Yes, sir," Renate replied. "I'm planning on it."


Lieutenant Powell escorted Laura back to his office. Scott Jardine followed a few minutes later.

"It's crazy out there!" he blurted as he shut the door. "They were begging me to get you back."

"We agreed," Laura stated flatly. "No questions."

"I know."

"Are they still out there?" the lieutenant asked.

"Most of them. Talking a mile a minute on their cell phones."

"I'm going back," Powell said. "I have an announcement to make."

"What announcement?" Jardine asked.

"While Laura was making her statement, I took a call from the U.S.

attorney in Miami. All federal charges have been dismissed. Guess you could say I shamed him into it."

Laura was engrossed in rocking Gisella. To her relief, the child was happily cooing in response. She glanced up.

"Shamed?"

"I called him this morning," Powell replied, with a twisted smile. "Told him the state attorney in Palm Beach had already dismissed your murder charges. I asked about the federal indictment, and he mumbled some shit about his people 'reviewing the situation.' So I pointed out that the connection between Corbin and the FBI's lead agent in the hunt for you was about to become very public, very fast, and if he kept dragging his feet, I'd be naming names on the evening news."

"So, not so much shaming him as blackmailing him," Laura ventured, with a note of admiration in her voice.

Gisella started giggling, as if she'd understood every word.

The lieutenant grinned. "Smart girl."

During this discussion, every extension on Powell's desk phone had been flashing. Ignoring the distraction, he pushed back his chair and stood up. Before he could take a step, the door opened and Eric Belrose stepped in, accompanied by the sound of stridently ringing telephones.

"Phones are ringing off the hook! Networks . . . major papers . . . everybody wants a piece of this story." He peered across the room. "Two calls holding for you, Laura. Won't take no for an answer."

"Laura's not taking calls," Jardine said. "You know that."

"Yeah, but one's the U.N. secretary general. He's on line three."

"And the other one?"

Belrose chewed on his lip before he answered. "Says he's Dominic Lanza."

A second passed.

"What line is he on?" Laura asked quietly.